The Lonely Monarch

Poet, novelist, playwright and children's writer, SUNIL GANGOPADHYAY (1934–2012) was an eminent and prolific literary figure. His literary career began in 1953 with the publication of the first issue of *Krittibas*, a poetry magazine of which he was founder editor. Although a popular writer in different genres, he considered poetry to be his first love. He is the author of the Sahitya Akademi Award-winning magnum opus *Sei Samay* (Those Days). *Pratham Alo* (First Light) and *Purbo–Paschim* (East–West) are his other well-known novels. He has been awarded the Bankim Puraskar, Ananda Puraskar and Saraswati Samman besides other awards for his literary contributions.

*

SWAPNA DUTTA has been writing, mostly for children, for the last four decades and has more than forty titles to her credit, including translations. She was awarded a fellowship from the Ministry of Culture, Government of India, for translating a selection of poems by twenty contemporary Bengali poets into English. Her translations of works by Rabindranath Tagore, Premchand, Parashuram, Sunil Gangopadhyay, Ashapurna Debi, Lila Majumdar, Samaresh Basu, Samar Sen, Shankha Ghosh, Shrikant Varma and others have been published in literary magazines and by English-language publishers.

The Lonely Monarch

Sunil Gangopadhyay

Translated from the Bengali original by
Swapna Dutta

First published in Bengali as *Nihsanga Samrat* by Ananda Publishers in 2005

This translation first published in 2013 by Hachette India
(Registered name: Hachette Book Publishing India Pvt. Ltd)
An Hachette UK company
www.hachetteindia.com

1

Copyright © 2005 Sunil Gangopadhyay
This English translation © 2013 Swapna Dutta

Sunil Gangopadhyay and Swapna Dutta assert the moral right to be identified
respectively as the author and the translator of this work

ISBN 978-93-5009-628-4

Hachette Book Publishing India Pvt. Ltd
4th & 5th Floors, Corporate Centre
Plot No. 94, Sector 44, Gurgaon 122003, India

Typeset in ITC Legacy Serif Std 10.5/13.7
by Eleven Arts, New Delhi

Printed and bound in India
by Manipal Technologies Limited, Manipal

Translator's Note

I met Sunil Gangopadhyay for the first time in 1982, just over thirty years ago.

I was at Ananda Bazar Patrika's office in Calcutta to meet Nirendranath Chakrabarty, then editor of *Anandamela*, a popular children's magazine. Nirendranath Chakrabarty was busy in a meeting so I asked quite casually if I could see Sunil Gangopadhyay instead. Those were the days when anyone could walk into a newspaper office and meet whoever they wanted provided he/she was available at the time. One of the clerks pointed out Sunil-da's room and I walked in. Sunil-da, who was busy writing, looked up with a frown but asked me to take a seat as soon as he heard that I was a writer – albeit a writer of children's books – based in Delhi.

Although I had enjoyed Sunil-da's *Sei Samay* (for which he was to receive the Sahitya Akademi Award four years later), I was not particularly fond of his other novels. I preferred his poems and short stories, many of which I thought brilliant.

And of course I had enjoyed his *Sabuj Dwiper Raja* (both the novel and its film version) and his stories for children. As we got talking I blurted out the names of some of his novels which I had not liked and told him as much. Instead of taking offence he merely smiled and said that *he* did not like everything he wrote and didn't expect his readers to either! I asked him if I could translate some of his poems and short stories. 'Of course,' he said.

My translations of a few of his poems appeared in *Indian Literature* and *Heritage* magazines a few months later and he asked me if I would translate one of his articles on Tagore. It was the beginning of a spontaneous, meaningful bond, kept alive through occasional letters and phone calls, and meetings at functions whenever he came to Delhi. I translated many more of his poems and some short stories over the years, which were published in various magazines and anthologies.

Yet, I never felt like translating any of his novels as I did not feel close enough or interested enough in them – until I came across *Nihsanga Samrat*, which I had picked up casually, not really knowing what to expect. I knew very little about the theatre scene in Bengal and even less about the people involved in it. Sisir Bhaduri was no more than a name to me; I merely knew that he had been an actor of repute. But once I started reading the book I was fascinated, enthralled and unable to put it down. Even though the novel did not have the wide canvas of *Sei Samay*, *Nihsanga Samrat* brought to life another era, as it did the celebrities who had been mere names before, and Sisirkumar Bhaduri, the 'lonely monarch', seemed more real than anyone I had met in person. Sunil-da's writing breathed life into every scene, every sequence, and I loved the crisp dialogues that rang true and sounded so convincing.

I collaborated closely with Sunil-da on all my translations of his work and normally called him up if I needed any clarification. *Nihsanga Samrat* has many quotations from poems and as I have always been rather finicky when it comes to translating verse (feeling strongly that the feel and music of the original should be retained even in translation), I told him that it was beyond me to do justice to some of the poems by Tagore. He said, 'Translate as much as you are comfortable doing. It need not be the whole extract, just enough so people understand which poem we are talking about.' I had asked him if he liked the lines I had translated. 'Yes,' he had said, and had concluded his reply (dated 8 December 2011) with the words, 'Kaajtake egiye niye jao' (proceed with the project).

That was his last letter to me. I really wish he had lived to see the work completed.

Swapna Dutta
December 2012, Bangalore

Postscript: Normally a translator's note should not require a postscript. But as *Nihsanga Samrat* is the chronicle of an important era and mentions several celebrities whom people outside Bengal might not know, I felt I should include here a few words about some of the important personalities and the time when these celebrities were around in relation to the protagonist of the book, Sisirkumar Bhaduri (1889–1959).

Michael Madhusudan Dutt (1824–1873), a famous poet and dramatist especially remembered for his blank verse.

Dwijendra Lal Roy (1863–1913), poet and playwright.

Gaganendranath Tagore (1867–1938), a self-taught artist who founded the Indian Society of Oriental Art with his brother Abanindranath Tagore in 1907. He was Rabindranath Tagore's nephew.

Chittaranjan Das (1870–1925), a revolutionary freedom fighter, affectionately called 'Deshbandhu' (friend of the nation).

Abanindranath Tagore (1871–1951), artist and writer; also the principal founder of the Indian Society of Oriental Art. The younger brother of Gaganendranath, he too was a nephew of Rabindranath Tagore.

Saratchandra Chattopadhyay (1876–1938), one of the most popular and widely read Bengali novelists.

Satyendranath Datta (1882–1922), poet, often described as 'the wizard of rhymes'.

Rakhaldas Bandopadhyay (1885–1930), a historian of repute.

Jamini Roy (1887–1972), one of the first 'modern' artists.

Manilal Gangopadhyay (1888–1929), writer and editor.

Narendra Deb (1888–1971), poet and playwright.

Hemendra Kumar Roy (1888–1963), editor and writer, who later became famous for his adventure and fantasy stories for children.

Kalidas Roy (1889–1975), poet.

Sunitikumar Chattopadhyay (1890–1977), linguist, educationist and litterateur.

Srikumar Bandopadhyay (1892–1970), scholar and writer

Dilip Kumar Roy (1897–1980), musician, musicologist and writer.

Kazi Nazrul Islam (1899–1976), the 'rebel poet' of Bengal.

Achintyakumar Sengupta (1903–1976), writer, part of the literary movement known as *Kallol*.

Premendra Mitra (1904–1988), writer and poet, who also belonged to the *Kallol* group.

Budhhadeb Bose (1908–1974), writer, poet and playwright, also part of the *Kallol* group.

1

Dol Purnima, 21 March 1924

Manilal alighted from a horse-drawn carriage in front of a double-storeyed house near Maniktala. A man of refined taste, just past his prime, he was dressed in a yellow silk panjabi, an exquisitely pleated dhoti from Shantipur and a stole slung over his shoulder. On his nose was a pince-nez and his hair was carefully styled in the latest fashion. A steady drizzle since the morning had made the roads somewhat slushy. As Manilal headed towards the door, carefully holding up the ends of his dhoti, his smart Moroccan leather sandals were splattered with mud.

After a few knocks a servant opened the door. Recognizing Manilal he said, 'Please come in, sir.'

'Where's your Baro Babu?' asked Manilal, stepping into the drawing room. 'Has he gone out?'

'Oh no. No sir. He's fast asleep,' replied the servant.

Manilal whisked out his round gold watch from the tiny

breast pocket of his panjabi and looked at the time. It was nearly half past ten.

His eyebrows shot up. 'Still asleep?' he asked, surprised. 'Where's Ma?'

'She's inside, slicing betel nuts. Would you like to see her? She's done with her morning pujas.'

The small central courtyard inside had a tap that carried water from the Ganga. It was used for washing dirty dishes. From the enormous pile of unwashed utensils it was easy to guess that the family was a large one. A maid sat scrubbing the utensils with tamarind and ashes.

Across the courtyard, in her room, Kamalekamini sat on her four-poster bed. She had lost her husband about a decade ago. Although she was dressed in white and had gained some weight she still looked extraordinarily beautiful and regal. Her sons called her 'Queen Victoria' behind her back. Her fair complexion was indeed something to write home about. Of late her rheumatism had made her somewhat immobile so she seldom stepped out, reigning over her large domain from her room. But she remained well-versed with all that happened within the house down to the minutest detail. Even now, everyone in the household had to take her permission at every step, even while choosing ingredients for a vegetable curry. Kamalekamini sat slicing betel nuts with a deft hand and placing them on the newspaper spread before her. A gleaming container of betel leaves stood beside it. Manilal realized that whenever he had seen her earlier he had found her similarly occupied. Obviously, the household required an enormous quantity of betel nuts!

Manilal removed his sandals and stepped into the room. He bent down and touched her feet, which were the colour of sandalwood paste. 'May you live to be a hundred,' said Kamalekamini, blessing him in a muffled voice.

She looked at him and asked, 'How did you manage to come? It's Dol today! Didn't the boys dunk you in colour?'

'I came in a horse-drawn carriage. The revellers aren't out in the streets yet. Besides, it's raining.'

'Take a seat, dear. How's Aban Babu?'

'He's fine, as always. Hale and hearty,' replied Manilal, still standing. 'I was told Sisir is fast asleep although it's so late. He isn't ill, is he?'

'Oh no, he isn't,' said Kamalekamini, 'but you know how he is. There are times when he doesn't sleep at night and goes to bed at dawn. I wonder what happened last night. I heard him roaring like a lion and muttering poetry to himself as he paced up and down. I can hear him quite clearly down here, especially when he recites miles of poetry and strides along the balcony upstairs. But I couldn't make out what he was saying as it was all in English. When I woke up last night, at around half past three, I could still hear him pacing up and down, mumbling verses. I have no idea when he finally went to bed.'

'But I need him to come with me right away,' said Manilal. 'Can't somebody call him?'

Kamalekamini opened her large eyes wide. 'Goodness! Don't you know what his temper is like? Who's going to risk confronting him, knowing full well that he's likely to get his head bitten off or a tight slap across his cheek?' she asked.

'May I give it a try, Ma?' asked Manilal.

Kamalekamini burst out laughing. 'Yes, please do,' she said, 'you could give it right back if he tries to shout at you.'

Manilal touched her feet once again and walked out of the room. Looking around, he spotted a servant nearby and called him. 'What does your Baro Babu have in the morning when he wakes up? Tea or coffee?'

The servant stood quietly for a moment and sheepishly said. 'He isn't likely to wake up now.'

'I'm asking you whether he drinks tea or coffee,' said Manilal in a stern voice.

'Sometimes he asks for a glass of bel juice. But mostly he has coffee.'

'Very well then. Make two cups of coffee and bring them upstairs. Quick!'

As Manilal climbed the stairs he met Bishwanath, a slim man, dressed in a dhoti and vest. He joined his palms to greet Manilal and said, 'Dada isn't up yet. He went to bed well after dawn so he isn't likely to wake up before mid-day.'

'I'll deal with him,' said Manilal, 'but please make sure you're there on time. In fact, you'd better go with a little time to spare – definitely before four o' clock. Who is going to fetch Deshbandhu? I hope that has been arranged.'

'Oh yes,' said Bishwanath. 'Tara will be going. Deshbandhu has said that he does not require a car. He will come in his own. But someone should accompany him.'

Manilal went up the stairs. A long veranda had a row of rooms on one side. On the other side, above the railing, hung a few bird cages. Faint sounds of voices came from inside the rooms. The door to the room at the end of the veranda stood ajar. A short flight of steps led to a smaller balcony below. A mango tree grew right next to it, its branches so close that in season, one could pick the mangoes from the balcony itself.

Once, someone in the family had died in his sleep and his body had to be removed after breaking the door open. Ever since, no one bolted their doors at night and they remained loosely shut. The door to Sisirkumar's room swung open as soon as Manilal tapped on it. The bed, evidently meant for a single man, was not an elaborate four-poster. Thirty-five-year-old Sisirkumar, Kamalekamini's eldest son, lay on his back, fast asleep. He had inherited his mother's complexion but not her perfect features. He had a strongly built body and was wearing a silk lungi with a silk vest. A muga coverlet lay beside him as the nights were still a little chilly. But the sleeping man had either not bothered or not felt the need to use it.

Manilal stood still for a few minutes in the room. There were books everywhere, spilling out from all sides. The racks on the walls were full of them. There were books on the floor, books under the bed and books scattered on it as well. A few books had their pages open. Manilal knew that here was a man who could not live without books, not for a single moment. Although he enjoyed speaking to people, there were times when he felt lonely; only poetry and literature were his companions then. One glimpse at the room was enough to make an onlooker realize that it had not received a woman's caring touch. The servants were not allowed to touch his books either. Manilal wondered for a moment whether he had been right in dragging this man from the world of letters into the world of theatre. But it was far too late now. An arrow once released could only charge ahead whether it managed to hit the target or not.

Manilal did not need to call. Sisirkumar's eyes fluttered open, and he shouted groggily, 'What is it, stupid? Who asked you to come in here? And how dare you wake me up?'

'No one asked me,' Manilal replied in a firm voice. 'I came on my own. Besides, it's unhealthy to keep awake all night and sleep during the day. Get up at once.'

Sisirkumar crinkled his eyes and looked pointedly at the speaker's face. He sat up with a jerk. 'Mani! Why are you here so early in the morning? What's wrong? Is anyone dead?'

'No one's dead and it's not early morning,' replied Manilal. 'It's a quarter to eleven. Get ready, quick. We must leave right away.'

'Where do we have to go?' asked Sisirkumar, sounding bewildered.

'I heard you were up all night,' said Manilal. 'How many bottles did you finish?'

'Not one, believe me,' said Sisirkumar rubbing his eyes. 'I didn't drink a drop last night.'

'Sounds too good to be true,' said Manilal. 'Bravo, if you really mean it. Excellent! I'm aware of your will power, Sisir. Now get ready quickly. We have no time to lose.'

'But where are we going?' asked Sisirkumar again.

'Really, Sisir, don't you remember what day it is? We have to go and check if everything has been arranged properly. They are supposed to supply the new lights around noon.'

Sisirkumar stretched and yawned, and got off the bed looking vexed. He rubbed his chin and realized he hadn't shaved for two days. Looking towards the wall he said, 'Just stop it!'

'Stop what?' asked Manilal, astonished.

'We are not having the opening ceremony tonight. Cancel everything. Arrange to refund all the tickets.' Then he lit a cheroot without even washing his face.

Manilal slumped into a chair. 'What are you saying, Sisir? Have you gone crazy? Everything has been finalized already. The entire city is plastered with posters and I doubt if there's an empty wall anywhere. It's the first show of your own group! Deshbandhu Chittaranjan is going to light the ceremonial lamp and the hall will be chock-full of distinguished guests.'

'And what, I ask you, are they going to see? Do you think I am going to make a fool of myself?' shouted Sisirkumar.

'Don't worry, it's going to be a hit,' said Manilal. 'We've invited Krishnachandra Dey to sing. And we've asked Nazrul Islam, who's quite a name these days, to recite some of his poems.'

'Rubbish!' said Sisirkumar. 'The audience will expect to see Sisir Bhaduri act. When they realize that I'm nowhere in the picture and there's not going to be a play at all, won't they be furious? They will throw stones. They will break chairs! Did I join the theatre for this? To present a bunch of sentimental songs, irrelevant dancing and nonsensical weeping and wailing? This is cheating, pure and simple, I refuse to be party to it! I shall *not* be there tonight. To hell with the show! You'd better stick a notice on the door of the theatre announcing that the show has been cancelled.'

2

Flashback

Sisirkumar Bhaduri, scion of a declining zamindar family, had been a hero to his friends from his early years. Bright, handsome and sharp-witted, he was a brilliant student though not an attentive one. He read far more than the others but was not particularly keen to be among the toppers. He took up teaching at the Metropolitan College after completing his Masters in English and was very popular with his students. They would listen to him spellbound when he recited from Shakespeare. He was equally adept at reciting in Bengali.

Sisirkumar loved acting right from his student days. He would often participate in amateur plays put up at the University Institute, in English as well as Bengali. Once, Rabindranath Tagore himself came to see *Baikunther Khata* (Baikuntha's Diary), one of his own plays, being performed. That was before he received the Nobel Prize. After the performance he had asked one of his companions, 'Who is that lad who played Kedar?

Watching him on stage made me envious. It's a role I was once famous for.'

Sisirkumar had played the lead in a number of plays during the six years he had taught in the college. Then he gave up teaching and joined the theatre as a professional. Until then no other man as highly educated and well bred as him had become a professional actor. This was partly because of the notoriety connected to the world of theatre. The actresses were from the red light area. The actors were mostly uneducated and given to various vices. In fact, one of the prime reasons for Sisirkumar joining this sordid world was his ardent desire to cleanse the stage of its stigma and make it integral to the nation's culture. He wanted theatre to be instrumental in shaping and redefining popular taste as had happened in many other countries.

Girishchandra, the undisputed king of Bengali theatre, had passed away in 1912, leaving the stage virtually bereft of talent. Now, in the handful of theatres that remained, the footlights flickered dimly. There were hardly any plays or actors left who could attract audiences. Dani Babu, Girishchandra's son, was the sole star of the day. Dani Babu was neither as educated as his father, nor did he have the same command over literature or culture. But he had a marvellous voice, deep and rich with feeling. His success as an actor came from inherited talent rather than careful training.

Sisirkumar had taken many risks when he opted to leave the classroom for the stage. He was not bothered by the disrepute associated with the stage. His anxiety was about his friends with whom he spent a considerable amount of time. They belonged to well-bred, highly educated families and had impeccable taste. Would they cut him out now that he belonged to a different world? Some of his classmates – Sunitikumar Chattopadhyay,

Srikumar Bandopadhyay, Kalidas Ray included – had supported him. Saratchandra, the famous novelist, had encouraged him too. And, most importantly, his mother, although reluctant at first, had finally consented to his joining the stage. Had she been unwilling it would not have been possible for Sisirkumar to pursue his dream.

Sisirkumar's first stage appearance had been in the role of Alamgir on the Cornwallis Stage at Madan Theatre. He had earned quite a name for himself during his days as an amateur. His portrayal of Alamgir was absolutely breathtaking, almost supernatural in its perfection. The entire city was spellbound. The general view was that no one had seen such a brilliant performance before. It was in a different league from Girishchandra's kind of acting.

After witnessing the first show, Achintyakumar Sengupta, a young writer, had told his friends, 'See, I have witnessed three remarkable moments in my life. The first was a raging storm. The winds were so strong and the rain so heavy that night that it seemed as though Doomsday had arrived. Many of us were too frightened to sleep. But when I opened the window the next morning I found the rain had stopped, leaving behind a world that was clean and pure. A gentle breeze blew while the sun rose in the eastern sky. I had never witnessed such a magnificent sunrise before. The second was when I visited Jorasanko early one morning. I was waiting when Rabindranath, freshly bathed, appeared at the door. I was spellbound by the sight of his radiant figure. He looked almost ethereal. The third and last one was when I saw Sisirkumar on stage playing Alamgir. My heart missed a beat. He was brilliance personified. What a broad forehead and amazingly confident voice! I have heard a great deal about Girish Babu's and his contemporaries' brilliance. But this time I heard some of the older members of the audience remark that Girish Babu could never sweep the audience off their feet the way Sisirkumar could with his presence.'

Calcutta wore two different faces on the night *Alamgir* was performed for the first time. One glittered with lights and the other was in total darkness. The Prince of Wales was visiting India and the rulers and their sycophants were in the mood for celebration, while those steeped in nationalistic fervour were in the mood for resistance. Most houses of north Calcutta were in darkness. No vehicles plied on the streets. Many of the roads had been blocked using dustbins as barriers. The performance of *Alamgir* had not been stopped because it had been widely advertised. Besides, theatre was a significant part of the nation's culture. Many spectators arrived in the auditorium well in advance and waited in front of the building since early evening. As a result, the hall was packed to capacity. The audience included luminaries like Gaganendranath Tagore, Abanindranath Tagore, Dilip Kumar Roy and Satyendranath Dutta.

Although subsequent plays staged at Madan Theatre were popular and successful, Sisirkumar began to face opposition from its managers. Sisirkumar was finicky about all aspects of a play's performance, from stage design and lighting to the seating arrangement in the theatre. He disapproved of crudely painted backdrops and believed they should be replaced by realistic and historically relevant ones. For instance, Bhuiyan Raja in *Alamgir* was supposed to be a poor man, a farmer despite being a raja, so his palace too should be portrayed as a humble one befitting his situation. Hence the set, on Sisirkumar's insistence, resembled a delapidated. One day Rustomjee Dhotiwal, J.F. Madan's son-in-law, visited the sets and was livid when he saw the unusually simple backdrop. 'Rubbish! Are people going to be shown this rustic set-up when I have spent lakhs to keep this theatre going?' he said. He sent for Hussain Baig, the painter, and shouted at him. 'Change all of this right away and make it bright and gleaming, with a touch of gold,' he ordered.

Another day, when Sisirkumar was rehearsing a new play with a few others, he heard Rustomjee telling someone, 'These Bengalis are perpetual liars. One can never depend on them.'

The remark enraged Sisirkumar. He confronted Rustomjee immediately and asked, 'What is it that you just said about Bengalis? How dare you?'

Rustomjee's demeanour changed at once and he said, 'I didn't mean *you*, Bhaduri-ji. You are an asset to Bengalis.'

'You have insulted our race,' roared Sisirkumar. 'You've been bleeding Bengalis dry in your drive to make money and yet have the audacity to criticize them! I shall not continue here even for a day. Goodbye.' He dashed out of the premises with Rustomjee following close behind, rubbing his hands nervously. His profits had touched the sky ever since Sisirkumar had joined his theatre. He had no intention of losing his golden goose. 'Listen to me, Bhaduri-ji, just listen to me please,' he pleaded. 'I apologize for what I said.' But Sisirkumar did not stop. He quit his job without a second thought.

There followed a phase of unemployment. He could not go back to teaching either. He regretfully told his friends that he could not possibly continue to act in Bengali plays by catering to the whims of non-Bengali businessmen. How can one pursue an art without freedom?

A few days later he received an offer from a film company. The film was based on Saratchandra's *Andhare Alo* (Light in Darkness). Sisirkumar had acted in films earlier but was not particularly comfortable with the medium. He found the process too mechanical, with far too many interruptions. There was no scope for acting at a stretch or *feeling* the role. But Sisirkumar agreed to play the lead and also directed the film along with his childhood friend Naresh Mitra. But his heart belonged to the theatre. Yet, who would give him the opportunity? He had realized by now that it would not be possible for him to work under anyone else. It would hurt his ego too much. But that's the kind of man he was!

He sought refuge in books.

Literature soothed his heart and obliviated his resentment and frustration if only for a short while. Sometimes, he did not even need books. He knew a great deal of poetry by heart, especially the poems of Michael Madhusudan Dutt and Rabindranath Tagore, Shakespeare and Shelley. He could also reel off pages from the plays of George Bernard Shaw. Sisirkumar's colleagues in college often remarked that although he came to college dressed like an Englishman he was a true Bengali at heart. He taught English literature but his soul revelled in the poetry of Rabindranath.

Sometimes Sisirkumar went to watch plays by others – *Chandragupta* at Minerva Theatre, *Karnarjun* at Star Theatre, and so on. He watched actors like Ahindra Choudhuri, Durgadas Bandopadhyay, Naresh Mitra and others ride the crest of popularity. He saw Dani Babu play the role of Alexander in Manomohan Theatre. Deprived of the arclights, he merely sat amidst the audience now.

One day he heard that *Bisarjan* (The Immersion) was to be performed at First Empire, directed and performed by Rabindranath himself. Sisirkumar immediately bought tickets and went to see the play with his friend Aleek.

Bisarjan was totally different from a professional stage play. The actors and actresses came from well-to-do families. The audience, too, was entirely different. There was no racket, no pandemonium, and the stage design was simple and tasteful. Rabindranath, at sixty-two, played the role of the hero Jay Singh and swept the audience off its feet. Besides his acting, which was breathtaking, the production of the play was superb.

The role of Aparna was played by a lovely young girl who was as beautiful as a fairy. It was not just her looks that made such an impact. Her accent and delivery were as flawless as her graceful movements. Sisirkumar learnt that she was Ranu, the daughter of a scholar from Kashi, whom the poet held in great affection.

As he watched the play Sisirkumar said to his friend, 'If only we could have a heroine like this girl and I could have a theatre group of my own . . .'

When the play was over Aleek said, 'Come, let's go and meet the poet and touch his feet.'

But Sisirkumar refused. 'No, I can't,' he said. 'Who am I? I'm a nobody now.'

After a year of waiting Sisirkumar had his next chance, not on the stage but in an open-air arena.

Christmas was round the corner. A grand fair-cum-exhibition was being planned at the Eden Gardens. The organizers felt that it would be great if there could be a play as well. A Bengali ICS officer was the chairman of the entertainment committee and he was reluctant to have a professional group performing. He knew Sisirkumar well from his days as a lecturer and invited him to take charge instead. It was decided that for a satisfactory remuneration Sisirkumar would not only select the play and the actors but also take charge of the entire production.

Sisirkumar now formed his own theatre group. He decided to take a handful of inexperienced but promising youngsters – including Manoranjan Bhattacharya, Jogesh Chandra Choudhury, Rabi Ray, Jiban Ganguly, plus his two younger brothers, Bishwanath and Tarakumar – and train them himself. It was not possible to get any actresses from good families so he had to recruit professional actresses like Prabha, Nirada and Shefalika. The play selected was *Sita* by Dwijendralal Roy.

Once again, like a magician, Sisirkumar cast a spell on his audience from the very first show. Thousands of people flocked to see the play, ignoring the other attractions of the fair. A makeshift stage was set in the middle of the field but that didn't deter anyone. Rather, they came to watch again and again! Many felt that here was a true hero come at last to enrich the world of Bengali theatre. Sisirkumar in the role of Ram did not appear to be a superman or a demigod. On the contrary, he depicted Ram as an ordinary man devastated by the grief of losing his wife and unborn children. The agony and anguish in his voice echoed in the hearts of the viewers long after the play was over.

The play was originally scheduled to be performed for three nights, but on public demand it continued for twelve nights although the fair had already concluded.

Sisirkumar's friends now advised him to rent a hall and continue to perform independently. Obviously, he was not cut out to knuckle under anyone. He had made some money during the show in Eden Gardens. Some of his friends also came to his aid. He discovered that Alfred Theatre on College Street was lying empty. He took it on lease and named it Natya Mandir, thereby starting a new practice of giving theatres Indian names. Until then it had been the custom to name theatre halls in English. National, Great National, Bengal, Royal Bengal, Star, Emerald, Minerva, Classic and so on. In keeping with the Indian name the rows of seats at Natya Mandir were also numbered in Bengali letters – ka, kha, ga, gha – instead of A, B, C, D.

Since *Sita* had been a success they decided to inaugurate the new theatre with the same play. Sisirkumar edited the play a little and rehearsals began once again. Everyone worked feverishly as the inauguration date had been announced already. Then disaster struck. A formal permission had to be sought from the copyright holder of a play and the fee for the permission paid before it was performed professionally on stage. D.L. Roy, the author of *Sita*, was no more, and Dilip, his only son and the current copyright holder, was away touring Europe. Dilip was a close friend of Sisirkumar. He was sure getting permission from Dilip would not be a problem. But the proprietors of Star Theatre chose to play dirty. It was well known by now that Sisirkumar was about to launch his own troupe. His popularity was already sky-high. The other groups were madly jealous of him and were determined to stop him at any cost.

Dilip Roy returned to India from France by ship and took a train to Calcutta. The proprietors of Star had already found out about the day of his return and were at Howrah Station to receive him. They garlanded him as soon as he got off the train. Then their leader said, 'We would like to perform *Sita* at our theatre. Everything is ready. All we need is your permission. If you kindly sign the contract we can have our first show this Saturday.'

Dilip Roy was astonished. 'But what about Sisir? I was told that he had performed *Sita* magnificently at Eden Gardens. Doesn't he want to stage it anymore?'

'Oh no, he doesn't. We've heard that he's currently busy with another play. He was supposed to perform at Eden Gardens for just three nights, but he carried on for twelve without even taking your permission. But he isn't interested any longer. It's a shame to leave such a brilliant play unperformed. We are determined to take it on and raise it to the top slot without making any compromise on expenditure,' the man said.

Dilip Roy glanced at the group and saw his cousin Nirmalendu Lahiri among them. He was an amateur actor and performed occasionally.

Dilip Roy looked at him and asked, 'Are you a part of this group?'

Nirmalendu nodded.

Someone among them said, 'He is our top star right now and will be playing the lead.'

They whisked Dilip Roy home in their car. The contract was ready. Before Dilip Roy could give it a second thought after his long journey they got him to sign on the dotted line, giving them permission to stage *Sita* for the next one year and promptly paid him a royalty of four hundred and fifty rupees.

Sita was really and truly 'abducted'!

Sisirkumar went to see Dilip Roy the very next morning. 'How could you do such a thing, Dilip? My group is a brand new one and *Sita* was to be the first play to be staged in my new theatre. How could you give Star the rights without once asking me?'

Dilip Roy was astounded. 'How could this be? They told me categorically that you were no longer interested in performing *Sita*; that *they* were absolutely ready with it and wanted to launch it this week itself.'

Sisirkumar took out a handbill from his pocket and handed it to Dilip. It said:

NATYA MANDIR
(Old Alfred Theatre)
(Phone No. 1731 Burrabazar)
Proprietor: Sisirkumar Bhaduri

Our opening show will be inaugurated by the honourable Deshbandhu Chittaranjan Das. Natya Mandir has been newly renovated in keeping with the high standards of contemporary performing arts. Infused with fresh ideas and concepts and a pool of fresh acting talent, we present theatre enriched with music and dance. We cordially invite you all, patrons of art and culture in Bengal.

Opening night
21 March 1924, the evening of Dol purnima
Our first offering to the people of our country

SITA
Ram will be played by Sisirkumar Bhaduri

Dilip Roy turned pale as he read the handbill. 'Twenty-first March! That's just five days away. What a shame!'

Then he turned to Sisirkumar and said, 'They have lied to me, you see. It is a betrayal of faith. How could anyone be so selfish? Or stoop so low? Sisir, this is going to mean a huge loss for you.'

Sisirkumar's fair face had turned red with anger. He could not bring himself to speak and clutched a paperweight tightly in his hand as though he would crush it.

Dilip Roy, deeply overwhelmed with shame, spoke in a shaky voice. 'Believe me, my friend, I didn't have the faintest clue. I have returned home after such a long time. I was not aware of what has been happening. They expressed such a sense of urgency . . . They had brought along my cousin Nirmalendu with them so I did not think they would lie so blatantly. If you feel that I did it for the sake of money, come with me to Star at once and I shall cancel the agreement. Let's go right away.'

Prabodhchandra Guha, the manager of Star, was chatting with Apareshchandra, the acting coach, and some others in his room. They were still elated by the success of their trick and were discussing Sisirkumar. If he didn't manage to stage *Sita* after incurring so much expense, he would be totally ruined! Besides, people would slander him ruthlessly for his failure. However, despite their claim the previous day, Star was not yet ready to put up *Sita*.

They had never imagined Sisirkumar would come there himself and were completely taken by surprise.

On the way to Star Sisirkumar had warned Dilip Roy not to get into an argument. He should just find out if anything could be done or not. And Sisirkumar had no intention of losing his temper.

He refused to sit down despite being asked to, and stood behind the chair that Dilip Roy had taken.

'What you told me yesterday was untrue,' said Dilip Roy. 'It was Sisir who performed *Sita* at the Eden Gardens. So the right to stage it again should belong to him before anyone else. In fact, you never told me that Sisir had already finalized his plans to inaugurate his theatre with *Sita*. You haven't even begun your rehearsals yet. Then why did you make me sign the contract so hurriedly?'

The manager tried to make light of it. 'Such things happen often in all professional groups,' he said. 'Haven't there been countless tussles in the past with Girish Babu's plays? In fact, many times Girish Babu has penned plays for one group while he worked with another. Why make an issue of what happens in our world all the time?'

'Those were different times,' said Dilip Roy. 'Theatrepersons are artists. Why should they stoop so low? Please return my contract. I shall tear it up.'

'But the contract is already with our attorney,' said the manager at once. 'There is no question of cancelling it now.'

'I have brought your signing amount with me. Please take it back,' said Dilip Roy firmly.

Prabodhchandra was an extremely shrewd man and a smart talker. He laughed and said, 'Dilip Babu, I know that theatre folks often delay in paying dues and sometimes they don't pay it at all. But they never take back what they have already paid for. We are very honest in this matter.'

Sisirkumar tapped on Dilip Roy's shoulder impatiently and asked, 'Is it a yes or no?'

'No,' said Prabodhchandra. 'Dilip Babu is legally bound to obey the contract he signed with us.'

Now Sisirkumar threw Star a challenge. He looked at Apareshchandra and said, 'Very well. Put up your version of *Sita* by all means. So shall we. Let both plays run simultaneously. Let there be a decent and fair competition and we shall see which one the audience likes better.'

Before Apareshchandra could say a word, the manager said, 'That wouldn't be fair competition at all. You have already rehearsed the play and are ahead of us. We shall take some time to catch up. By then you'll manage to sway the audience in your direction.'

'Tell me once and for all, is it a final "No"?' asked Sisirkumar.

'Yes it is. *No*, emphatically *no!*' replied Prabodhchandra.

'Dilip, I better leave in that case,' said Sisirkumar.

'Forgive me, Sisir,' said Dilip Roy in a remorseful voice. 'I have harmed you unknowingly. More than money, it is your reputation that will be at stake.'

Sisirkumar walked towards the door.

'Don't make the fatal mistake of staging *Sita* after this,' said Prabodhchandra raising his voice. 'I shall take you to court if you do. I shall force you to close shop on the very first night. That will merely add to your losses.'

Sisirkumar turned around. A bitter smile lurked about his lips. 'I belong to a family of zamindars,' he said with pride. 'I may not have the resources any longer but the blood still runs in my veins. Do not try to scare me with the mention of court and injunction. I'd sooner burn up everything than go through a long-drawn court battle. But don't worry, I shall not set your Star Theatre alight. I am not that petty. I would rather set alight my own Natya Mandir. That would take care of your impediment.'

His brain seemed to be on fire. At that moment his anger knew no bounds. He was raging within. He had no idea how to calm himself. He knew that drinking would intensify the flame further. His inebriation might lead him to act in a way he would surely regret later. Natya Mandir did not belong to him alone. Many lives were involved in it. And it was downright impossible to prepare a new play in a matter of just four or five days.

Where could he go? With whom could he discuss the situation? There seemed to be no one with whom he could share his agony. There was not even a woman in his world!

He walked the streets like a madman. Perhaps his head would feel lighter when he was totally exhausted.

On he walked, aimlessly, seething with rage. Some people recognized him but he was oblivious to them.

'Oh villainy! Ho! Let the door be locked: Treachery! Seek it out,' he muttered to himself.

All of a sudden someone stood before him, tapped him on his chest and called out, 'Sisir!'

Startled, Sisirkumar opened his eyes wide to see his friend Hemendrakumar Roy.

'What's up?' asked Hemendrakumar. 'Where are you headed like a lost soul? We've been calling you for a long time but you didn't seem to hear us.'

A few others stood behind Hemendrakumar. They were Narendra Deb, Premankur Atarthi, Sourindramohan Mukhopadhyay and Manilal Gangopadhyay. All of them contributed to *Bharati*, a popular magazine, and were friends of Sisirkumar. He would often drop in for a chat with them at the *Bharati* office.

'What is it, Sisir?' asked Narendra Deb. 'Your face looks like a dry leaf!'

Sisirkumar abhorred asking for sympathy or expressing personal grief.

'Nothing,' he replied casually. 'I was probably too absent-minded to notice you.'

'The opening ceremony of your Natya Mandir is on Dol purnima. But you haven't given us passes for the show as yet.'

'There will be no opening ceremony,' said Sisirkumar in a bleak voice. 'It has been postponed for the time being.'

Everyone was astonished at his words. 'No inauguration?' asked Manilal. 'But why?'

Finally Sisirkumar was forced to tell them the story of how *Sita* had been wrenched away from him through a lowdown trick by Star Theatre.

'What a shame!' cried Hemendrakumar. 'When will our theatres be free of such shocking meanness? What is the way out now?'

'There's nothing to be done,' said Sisirkumar dismally.

'There *must* be a way!' said Manilal. 'Why should you acknowledge defeat to those rogues? I know it is not possible to put a play together so quickly. But people would surely enjoy a musical soiree on an occasion like Dol. Perhaps we could string together some songs suitable for an opera instead. That shouldn't be too difficult. And your Natya Mandir shall be inaugurated on the scheduled date, as planned.'

'Say we begin the programme with Rabindranath Tagore's popular song, *Ore bhai, Phagun legechhe bone bone* (Oh my friends, spring has arrived in the woods), and follow it up with other songs of spring,' said Hemendrakumar. 'The poet has composed so many beautiful songs on the season. If we fall short we shall all pitch in with some new ones, written by us.'

'Let's find a place where we can discuss this,' suggested Manilal. 'Let's first select the songs from the existing lot. We can fill up the gaps by composing a few new ones. How about naming the show Basanta Leela (Springtime Revelry)?'

Their combined efforts and enthusiasm forced Sisirkumar to agree to their proposal. But frustration raged within him. He would have no role to play in this revelry since he could not sing at all.

Basanta Leela was composed but Sisirkumar refused to take part. They could have the opening ceremony if they wanted to but *he* would not be there. He wouldn't be able to bear it if the audience felt cheated and booed him.

3

Dol Purnima, 21 March 1924, evening

Manilal virtually dragged Sisirkumar to Natya Mandir.

Everyone was busy decorating the building, both the interior and the outside. Two beautifully hand-painted earthen pitchers, with green coconuts on top of them, had been placed on either side of the gate. Tender banana saplings entwined with garlands stood beside them. People stood by, ready to sprinkle rose water on the arriving guests. The walls had been freshly painted. Everything shone and glittered.

Deshbandhu Chittaranjan Das arrived in his Rover at exactly half past six. Revered by the people of Bengal as their honoured and respected leader, he played a significant role in national politics. He was particularly close to Motilal Nehru of the Congress Party and had voiced various demands for his countrymen in consultation with Nehru. They founded the Swaraj Party and had been branded the 'pro-changers', while the conservative group in favour of Gandhiji was called the 'no-changers'. Chittaranjan had given up his lucrative practice as a barrister, a profession that had once earned him lakhs of rupees. He had gifted away most of his assets and had now offered himself totally to the service of his motherland.

There was a time when his suits were laundered in France. But he now wore a simple cotton dhoti and panjabi, with a scarf slung over his shoulder, and round nickel-framed glasses. Sisirkumar and some of his friends were waiting to welcome him.

Deshbandhu alighted from his car, smiled at them and said, 'I couldn't keep my word the last time but I have been punctual this time.'

By 'last time' he meant the opening show of Sisirkumar's *Alamgir* at Madan Theatre. Chittaranjan was supposed to have inaugurated that function. But since he had been organizing a protest against the arrival of the Prince of Wales the following day, he had been imprisoned the night before. So how could he have been there?

It was customary to begin stage performances with English concert music, but Sisirkumar had arranged for an Indian orchestra. The shehnai and the mridangam began as soon as Deshbandhu Chittaranjan took his seat.

Chittaranjan spoke briefly, conveying his blessings and best wishes. The young poet, Kazi Nazrul Islam, started the evening with a recital of 'Bidrohi' (The Rebel), one of his longer poems. Each line of the poem struck listeners like a bolt of lightning.

Krishnachandra Dey, the blind singer, was the next performer. He sang several songs in his melodious voice.

Sisirkumar had never felt nervous or excited during his own performances. But that evening he sat in the wings feeling taut and tense. The audience had not expressed any disapproval so far. In fact, they had shouted 'Encore! Encore!' after a few of the songs. When the function was about halfway through someone shouted, 'Where is Sisir Babu?'

Immediately, Manilal pushed Sisirkumar on to the stage.

They had earlier requested him to appear on the stage a few times although he was not participating in the evening's programme. But Sisirkumar had not agreed. It would look dumb for him to appear when he was not doing anything. He refused to be party to such a farce.

The audience broke into applause as soon as he appeared. They had realized by now that this was to be a musical evening. There would be no play. It was enough for them to get a glimpse of their hero.

The evening passed smoothly.

Before leaving Deshbandhu said, 'Sisir, I have heard you have made a great name as an actor. I couldn't see you act tonight but do call me when you perform the next time.'

'We shall soon be performing *Sita* at Natya Mandir, sir,' said Manilal. 'Please grace the function when we do.'

'What have you done, Mani?' asked Sisirkumar after Deshbandhu left. 'Why have you put me in such a false position? We do not own the rights to *Sita* and there's no chance of our getting it before the year is out. Don't you know that?'

'So what if we don't have the rights?' argued Manilal. 'Didn't Ram have an image of Sita made of gold and kept before him after he sent her on exile? We too shall have a golden Sita!'

Hemendrakumar burst out laughing and said, 'We are quite determined to perform *Sita* at Natya Mandir. And it will be a show that will put Star to shame.'

4

Sunday, 17 August 1924

Sisirkumar had taken to spending his nights in a small room at the back of the theatre. It was sparsely furnished, with just a simple cot, a couple of tin chairs and a wooden cupboard. No one – man or woman – kept him company at night. A full-time servant, Bhikha, had been appointed to run his errands. Bhikha spent almost all day with his master, and so was at the receiving end of his master's ire as well as lavish tips. In the afternoon Bhikha bought Sisirkumar lunch from the 'pice' hotel nearby. Sisirkumar would have a bite when he felt like it, or he would ask Bhikha to have it all. He hardly ever ate anything at night.

Sisirkumar had kept provisions for making tea or coffee in his room. That morning he had already consumed three cups of coffee. The crisp kachoris and mohan-bhog that Bhikha had bought for his breakfast lay untouched, wrapped in sal-leaf, on the table.

August was the month of the rains. It had been raining hard since the morning and that was a good sign. Even if it rained through the day it was likely to clear up by the evening, making it possible for people to venture out on to the streets once again.

Sisirkumar was still in bed, reciting poems out loud. It was not English poetry that he declaimed that morning but lines from Rabindranath Tagore, who reigned over his heart:

> 'Naba naba khela khele adrishta . . .
> New, ever new games played by Fate
> Some oblique, some fine and straight
> Some bitter and some sweet
>   Whate'er it throws my side –
> In this whirl of joy and pain
> I'll lose myself in verse and then –
> Attempt prose, accepting Fortune's
>   Roller-coaster ride.'

He stopped all of a sudden and called for Bhikha.

Bhikha usually remained out of sight but had the strange ability to appear instantly at his master's call, like the djinn of the *Arabian Nights*. He was thin and dark, with closely cropped hair, and it was difficult to guess his age from his appearance.

He stood at the door, his palms joined like an ardent devotee.

'Take the bottle and tumbler out of the cupboard. Give me some water,' ordered Sisirkumar. Bhikha glanced at the wall clock. It was already a quarter to twelve; time for his bath, followed by lunch. But he did not have the courage to voice his protest.

He opened the cupboard to find the bottle of Scotch absolutely empty. Not even a drop was left in it.

Bhikha was not given to talking much. He simply held the empty bottle before Sisirkumar, saying, 'Master.'

'Good heavens! When did I manage to empty it?' said Sisirkumar, and then burst out laughing as he recited:

'Khali botoler pane . . .
At the empty flask I gaze –
'Nothing lasts,' my reason says,
If only wishes and their pull
Could make this empty bottle full
I would succeed at the feat
Of writing prose and verses sweet.'

He fished out a handful of cash from beneath his pillow and handed it to Bhikha without counting it. 'Go and get another one,' he said. 'Run there and head back as soon as you can.'

Sisirkumar lit his cheroot and turned the pages of Tagore's *Chitra*, reading aloud one of the poems:

'Chandra jakhan austey namilo . . .
The moon was just about to set; the night was still not done,
The eastern sky, a-blush with listless glimpse of rising sun –

The horse stopped by the ocean shore and not a soul was there
Just a mountain black that had a gaping cavern bare

The sea was still; the birds of morning were all silent, too,
No draught of fragrant morning breeze from the forest blew

The maid alighted from her steed and, albeit, so did I,
And fell in step behind her to the darkling cavern high.

A lofty castle loomed inside with pillars for decor
Swathed in chains of gold that cradled golden lamps galore.'

He had a habit of reciting poems on days when he was scheduled to perform. Not just because he loved poetry, but also because elocution helped him perfect his accent and voice modulation. Besides, the sound of poetry directed his mind towards the arts.

It was the fifth night of his performance of *Sita*. The venue was a different theatre.

The process of creating a new *Sita* had begun the day after the inauguration of Natya Mandir. The new version had been created at the insistence of Manilal and his other friends. So what if the original play created by Dwijendra Lal Roy was out of his reach? A new *Sita* must be written afresh just for Sisirkumar.

But who would write it?

Hemendrakumar was the first name that came to everyone's mind. But he was busy launching *Nachghar*, a new magazine, and wouldn't be able to spare time to write a play. And they could not afford to wait. As Manilal had often said, strike while the iron is hot and in utmost secrecy. If the news leaked out it would soon be all over the city.

Sisirkumar had said, 'How about an experiment? Some of us can decide on the exact theme and structure of the play and someone absolutely new can write the script based on our ideas. We have an actor in our group called Jogesh Choudhury who used to be a schoolteacher. I have heard him speak during the rehearsals and I have a feeling he has some knowledge of poetry. Let's give him a try.'

Hemendrakumar, Manilal and Sisirkumar arranged a daily session with Jogesh in a place no one was likely to suspect. They chose Manilal's in-laws' house. Abanindranath Tagore was currently not residing there and the house had a few rooms lying empty.

It was decided that the play would begin with Sita's exile. Dwijendra Lal Roy's play had a preface that created a setting for the play but Jogeshchandra was asked to get to the main theme without any preamble. The play proceeded smoothly. Dwijendra Lal Roy had once written a play named *Ananda Biday*, which attacked Rabindranath Tagore unfairly in a rather coarse and indecent manner that many Indians had found unpalatable. When the play was halfway through, Manilal said, 'It's good that we were denied the rights of Dwiju Babu's play. Our new play about Ram and Sita could well be better than his *Sita*.'

The new play was completed in a month's time. It was further modified by Sisirkumar. And then began the rehearsals. But this was going to be a far tougher job since they would have to erase the lines of the original play completely from their minds and learn the new ones by heart. Sisirkumar himself got muddled several times. Dwijendra Lal Roy's play started with Ram addressing his three brothers:

'I was sent on exile at a tender age,
Making the forest my home . . .
I knew not how to rule a kingdom,
Learnt no politics or religion.
My days were spent in hunting
My nights in slumber deep
In my lowly cottage
Deep within the forest.'

In Jogesh's play Ram was made to speak to Durmukh, the messenger who brought ill tidings, while Sita lay fast asleep by his side:

'Do not mind the lady –
Nothing about Ayodhya, our kingdom
Is unknown to her, or a secret.
But Janaki is lost in slumber . . .'

Sisirkumar was particularly careful about his lines and warned the others not to mix up theirs with the other version of the play. 'Don't repeat a single line from the other *Sita* or else the owners of Star Theatre will come after us,' he told them.

At this time Sisirkumar had to change theatres yet again.

The new *Sita* was not ready yet. So he had been performing other plays to keep things going and meet the running expenses of Natya Mandir. But none of them quite worked. The real 'theatre zone' lay between Beadon Street and Shyambazaar and the audience was not willing to come all the way to College Street after sundown to see a play.

Meanwhile, all was not well with Manomohan Theatre on Beadon Street. Dani Babu's dated style of acting no longer attracted an audience. Manomohan Pandey, the owner of the hall, decided to break up his group and hire out his hall rather than face continued losses.

As soon as the news reached Sisirkumar he took it on hire, giving up Alfred Theatre. 'Manomohan' was a well-known name so he merely changed the name to Manomohan Natya Mandir.

The theatre took on a completely new look under the direction of Sisirkumar and the workmanship of Charu Roy, a well-known artist. Every scene, backdrop, costume and piece of music was finalized after proper research on the period depicted in the play. Previously, no one had paid such attention to detail. But now people like Rakhaldas Bandopadhyay, Sunitikumar, Jamini Roy, Kazi Nazrul Islam, Narendra Deb, Srikumar Bandopadhyay and Nolinikanta Sarkar, among others, came forward to help with the production of *Sita*. And of course there were the writers from *Bharati*. Many of them were either friends or ex-classmates of Sisirkumar. But friendship was not the prime force that had brought them here. They came because they were keen on the all-round development and enrichment of Bengali theatre, so it could hold its own when compared to English theatre. The English were so proud of their actors like Irving Garrick and others. They had to be shown that Sisirkumar's talent was no less than theirs. Sisirkumar and his friends wanted the Bengali stage to become an intrinsic part of the culture, at par with literature and art, and they wanted Bengali theatre to awaken a national consciousness in people.

In keeping with the new set-up, the seating arrangements had been changed too. This included better seats for the ladies. Previously they sat in a dark and stuffy corner on the second floor. Those who preferred that kind of privacy could still sit there, but now decent seating arrangements were made for ladies on the ground floor too.

Sisirkumar also got rid of footlights because he felt that they did not do full justice to the facial expressions of the actors. He now introduced top lights and mood lights that were focused from the sides. His intention was to impress the audience by focusing equally on all the actors in the play and not just on the main protagonist. He still had to depend on women from the red light area for the female roles but he did not spare them when they mispronounced words during the rehearsals and did not hesitate to smack them if necessary. At the same time he could not help being impressed by some of them when they learnt things double quick. Among them was a girl who had been sold at birth by her family for three cowries, a common practice in those days, and later shot to fame as Teenkowri Dasi. Prabha, another girl in his group, was also beginning to show unmistakable signs of talent.

Most importantly, what became evident was the gradual shift in the taste of the audience. Producing a play was a tough

job. It was impossible for an outsider to realize how much it
hurt when the pent-up emotions of an actor playing a particular
role were suddenly thwarted. There were always a few people
among the audience who talked loudly amongst themselves
during a performance, or stood up suddenly to crack a dirty
joke in an attempt to make people laugh. Being aware of this,
Sisirkumar had placed four guards along the wall who would
keep a keen eye on the people and promptly throw out anyone
who tried to create a disturbance.

Just before the final rehearsal Manilal said, 'Come on, Sisir,
let's play a practical joke on Star's Art Theatre.'

When Sisirkumar heard the plan he burst out laughing and
agreed to it. Before long newspapers flashed an announcement
stating that *Sita*, directed by Sisir Bhaduri, would soon be
launched at the Manomohan Natya Mandir. The director
himself would play the lead and Srimati Prabha would
play Sita.

The playwright's name was not mentioned.

As expected, the announcement shook up Art Theatre.
Although they had managed to grab the rights of Dwijendra
Lal Roy's *Sita*, they had no plans of launching it immediately.
They were still reaping the profits of their latest production
Karnarjun with Ahindra Choudhuri and Naresh Mitra in the
lead roles. But they were delighted to see that Sisirkumar had
haughtily walked straight into a legal trap. They would now
be able to sue him.

They consulted their attorney, and within two days Sisirkumar
received a legal notice. Sisirkumar read the letter aloud to his
friends and they roared with laughter. Then he tore the notice
to shreds.

Within a couple of days newspapers carried a detailed
advertisement announcing their play. There were posters on the

city's walls too. Both mentioned the name of Jogesh Choudhury as the writer of the play.

Copyright laws did not cover mythological subjects and there was no legal problem with two plays of the same name and subject being launched simultaneously if they were adapted from epics, as long as the language and treatment of the themes were different. The owners of Star Theatre were quite disheartened at first. Then they began to hope that Sisirkumar would land in a mess with an inexperienced playwright's debut attempt. Convinced of this, some of them turned up uninvited for the first show of *Sita* and sat among the audience.

The play was launched . . . and the rest is history!

There was just one subject of discussion on every lip in the city the following day. Many felt that the new version of *Sita* far surpassed the earlier one performed at the Eden Gardens. Sisirkumar was at his very best; Prabha was superb; even the actors who played insignificant roles were perfect. Manoranjan Bhattacharya was so convincing in his role as the sage Valmiki that he was promptly nicknamed 'Maharshi', the Great Sage.

Deshbandhu Chittaranjan had come to inaugurate the opening show as promised. He looked pale; he had not been keeping well. But he sat for four-and-a-half hours and watched the entire play.

'I had never seen your acting earlier, Sisir. I couldn't have believed it had I not seen your performance with my own eyes. You really are a legend,' he told Sisirkumar after the show. 'You have ushered in a new era on the Indian stage. As for the last scene . . . why, you succeeded in bringing tears even to the eyes of a tough man like me!'

'Who says you are a tough man, sir?' asked Sisirkumar.

'You are a poet at heart. But I *was* told that it would be a real challenge to satisfy you.'

'I wasn't just satisfied, I was absolutely overwhelmed! That's what real art does to a person. It charms as well as overwhelms,' said Deshbandhu. 'You have the rare ability to raise the art of performing to great heights. Tell me, have you been facing any difficulties since you joined the theatre?'

'Since you have asked me directly, I feel tempted to tell you one or two things,' said Sisirkumar, 'but it is quite late already and you will get unduly delayed if I speak now.'

Deshbandhu laid a hand on Sisirkumar's shoulder and said in a tired voice, 'No, no. It doesn't matter if I get a little late. Please tell me everything quite frankly. Can we help you in any way?'

'The main reason I gave up teaching and joined the theatre is because I love plays and acting. I had high hopes of presenting really good plays to the viewers of our country,' said Sisirkumar. 'I wanted to modernize everything, from sets to performance. Do you know why I am facing these big hurdles at every step? It's because the professional stage also means business, about which I know nothing. And yet one needs a lot of money to run a show successfully. That is why one has to fall back on commercial gimmicks such as dance and songs, slapstick comedy and tear-jerking devices.'

'You are a true artist. So it's quite natural that you may know nothing at all about the commercial side of theatre,' said Deshbandhu.

'I had joined the Madans at first,' said Sisirkumar, 'but I soon realized that they had no other consideration than making a fast buck, even if it meant ruining a play in the process. That's why I couldn't stick it out with them. Then I performed with my group in a tent in Eden Gardens. And I've had to change halls twice since then. I still seem to be roaming from tent to tent.'

Deshbandhu laughed at his words and said, 'Like a gypsy theatre party, eh? But why do you need to change theatre halls?'

'Because, apart from other problems, the rents are too high,' said Sisirkumar. 'That's why I've been thinking hard. We may not be an independent country but can we not build a national theatre where young boys and girls can learn the art of performing and playwrights create good plays without losing sleep over profit and loss? That's the only way we can change and uplift the taste of the viewers.'

'You're right,' said Deshbhandhu. 'Rabi Babu had also said something similar once. We are a captive nation fighting for our freedom. But, no matter how much Gandhiji hesitates, we will have what is rightfully ours someday soon. I want to see my country free of shackles before I die. And why need we wait that long to build a national theatre? Don't we have the means to do it? Tell me, how much exactly will you need to make a start?'

'I have given it a great deal of thought,' said Sisirkumar. 'We could do it if we had a double-storeyed house and around four lakh rupees.'

Deshbandu laughed and said, 'Had you told me this a few years ago, I could have given you the money myself. Ever since I chose to step out of my barrister's outfit, I no longer have a source of income. I have even donated my house to my party. I am just their tenant now. However, I don't think it should be difficult for me to raise that amount for a good cause. Listen, Sisir, I have to travel out of Calcutta for a few days on a special task. Once I am back, I shall certainly find the means of building your national theatre where you will be able to work in peace.'

Deshbandhu's words held a lot of value, and so Sisirkumar started nurturing his cherished dream once again.

It was the fifth night of *Sita* being staged. Although the play had received immense applause and appreciation from the audience from the very first performance, it almost seemed like this performance was to be an ordeal by fire for, tonight, Rabindranath was coming to see the play.

Sisirkumar believed him to be the best living playwright in Bengali. He was numero uno in everything – direction, production, sets, as well as stage design. Besides, he was a great actor himself. Others might consider Sisirkumar to be fabulous but would he pass with flying colours before the great Tagore? Sisirkumar felt too nervous to whip up his self-confidence.

Perhaps he needed a little something . . .

Bhikha had just arrived with a bottle wrapped in newspaper.

'Why so late, you scoundrel?' cried Sisirkumar.

'Two bulls had locked horns near Hedo,' said Bhikha. 'The traffic had come to a total standstill. It was impossible for even a cat to get through.'

'Well, even if a cat couldn't, I'm sure a rat *could*!' muttered Sisirkumar angrily. 'You're nothing but a rat yourself! Come on, pour it.'

Bhikha took a tumbler out of the cupboard, uncorked the bottle and was about to pour a drink when Sisirkumar stopped him. 'Let it be. Put the bottle away. I shall go for my bath now.'

But he didn't get up. He remained in his bed.

A framed photograph of Sri Ramakrishna hung on the wall beside him along with a poem, hand-written in large letters and with creepers painted on one side.

Ever since Girishchandra had become a devotee of Sri

Ramakrishna, the Paramhansa was looked upon as the guardian angel of the entire theatre community, including theatre owners, actors and actresses. Every theatre would have his photograph. Everyone bowed before it in reverence before going onto the stage. The photo had been in this room even before Sisirkumar started using it. He had not asked anyone to remove it although he didn't believe in this sort of devotion. In fact, he didn't bother about religion or god and made fun of those who did, branding them 'bhagabatia'. He now began reading the framed poem to himself.

Most of the contemporary writers of Bengal were Sisirkumar's friends. The writers of *Bharati* were mostly his friends too. They had recently started a magazine named *Kallol* for the youth. He quite liked it, although it sounded a bit too brash at times.

After the second night's performance of *Sita* Dineshranjan Das, the editor of *Kallol*, had come to the green room with a young poet in tow. He was called Achintyakumar Sengupta. He had said, 'I have seen all your plays, including *Alamgir*, your very first play. But when I saw *Sita* for the first time I felt that there was no need to see any other play; that I should just keep seeing *Sita* over and over again.'

Dineshranjan said, 'He has written a poem about you. He is too shy to tell you about it. Well, Achintya, why don't you recite it?'

Sisirkumar was busy removing the grease paint from his face. He said, 'Yes, please do.'

Achintyakumar had an impressive baritone and read out the lines he had composed:

'He opened wide both arms and cried, "Sita, Sita, Sita"
In a voice full of grief
Calling to his departing love, daughter of the earth,

A pilgrim in the shadow of pain, lost in silent darkness
Now beyond his reach.

Ah creator, seer and poet –
You have lent your voice
To the boundless tears wept by Yaksha
On the banks of rivers – Shipra, Reva and Betravati
And all the lonely, thirsty souls who seek in vain
The lost loves of their lives;
Your profound tears express
The agony of the entire creation –
Timeless and eternal;

Call her, please do call
My love who frees herself from the eager embrace
Of her lover and runs with eager steps beyond his reach
In every age and time;
You have built afresh
A heaven made of anguish, tears and pain,
As sacred as the chanting of the Veda
A world eternal, unbound by chains of time;
You are a poet, a creator in actor's garb
A prophet, a seer, wreathed in greatness true!'

Sisirkumar was moved by the eulogy, as most artists are especially when youngsters pay rich tributes because they are the harbingers of the future. 'Please write it down properly and give it to me,' he told Achintyakumar. 'I shall have it framed and hang it in my room.'

Dineshranjan had the poem bound in a golden frame and presented it to Sisirkumar the very next day.

Sisirkumar read the poem, though distractedly, Rabindranath Tagore's face floating before his eyes every few minutes. His situation was like that of a schoolboy. Would the great poet 'pass' his performance tonight?

No! He simply had to have a few drops to pep himself up.

He took out the bottle and tumbler from the cupboard instead of asking Bhikha to do so.

The door opened before he could pour himself a drink. He saw Golapbala standing outside the threshold. Her actual name was Annakali. But Jogeshchandra had given his protégée this new stage name when he had brought her to Natya Mandir. However, she was known to everyone as 'Jhinge'.

No actor or actress could come into Sisirkumar's room unless he had sent for anyone. Jhinge had no role in *Sita*, but she came to the rehearsals every day and sat in a corner of the room. There was a minor role in the play, that of Tungabhadra, being played by Niradasundari. She suffered from whooping cough that got really bad at times and then was unable to speak her lines. Sisirkumar had decided that whenever that happened he would get Jhinge to play the role instead. But luck had not favoured her so far, although she dressed for the part and sat it out every single night.

Jhinge stood silently, gazing at him.

'What's up?' asked Sisirkumar. 'Did you lose your way? Did you think this was the ladies' room?'

'Baro Babu, may I press your legs?' she asked, her voice quivering.

'Press my legs? What on earth for?' asked Sisirkumar. 'Am I suffering from gout or arthritis?'

'I want to serve you. That's why I would love to press your legs.'

It would have not been unnatural for Sisirkumar to lose his temper at this moment. But he asked her quite gently, 'Has anyone told you that you are likely to get a good role by pressing my legs?'

The girl looked visibly nervous. 'No, no, oh no! No one has told me that.'

'Listen to me, Jhinge,' said Sisirkumar. He uttered three difficult words often used in theatre. 'Try pronouncing these three words correctly – "dushprobritti", "jagajjanani" and "proloyjhanjhha",' he told her. 'You make a mess of the words every time you utter them.' Then he demonstrated just how she pronounced them. 'I'll give you a role only when you are able to pronounce each of these three words correctly. And get this straight. Don't ever dare to cross this threshold again unless I send for you.'

Jhinge instantly stepped away from his line of vision.

Sisirkumar could hear her muffled sobs. He had to get up at last. He came to the door and found Jhinge crying, her face covered with her hands. There was no one nearby.

Sisirkumar took a few puffs of his cheroot while he watched her intently. Then he burst out laughing and said, 'Silly girl! An actress never covers her face while crying! The face has to be emotive even when one is shedding tears. How will the audience see your expressions if you keep your face covered?'

The girl quickly removed her hands from her face. There were tears in her eyes.

'Baro Babu, please have mercy on me!' she whispered in a muffled voice.

'How on earth does mercy come into the picture?' asked Sisirkumar. 'Listen girl, one cannot get a good role by coming into my room on the sly or pressing my feet or by crying like this. This is what is known as folly – one of the words I asked you to pronounce properly. Stand in front of the mirror and practice the words I told you. You can come and reel them off to me tomorrow.'

This trivial incident changed Sisirkumar's mood. He lay down yet again without pouring himself a drink.

When Hemendrakumar walked into the room a little while

later he found Sisirkumar staring blankly at the white wall, the bottle resting on the table.

'What's this? Have you been drinking already?' asked Hemendrakumar.

Sisirkumar was startled. 'Is that you, Hemen? Come in. No, I haven't been drinking although I wanted to, quite badly.'

'If you want it that badly, you'd better have a little,' said Hemendrakumar.

'The great poet will be coming this evening,' said Sisirkumar.

'Are you afraid of his discovering liquor on your breath? Well, we shall be there to welcome him when he arrives. You'll be busy putting on make-up in the green room at that time since you appear in the very first scene. By the time you come to meet him at the end of the play there will be nothing to smell.'

'I would rather not,' said Sisirkumar. 'If I have a sip now I'll immediately long to have more and it could well be too much.'

'If you feel that way it's better you don't,' said Hemendrakumar. 'I saw a long queue in front of the ticket counter while coming in. I couldn't help noticing that the people in the queue all appear to be gentlemen from the way they are dressed. Not our usual rowdy crowd. When we were young, theatres used to be chockfull of drug addicts and drunkards who mainly flocked to see the actresses dance. They were not bothered with either the acting or the play.'

'Let's go and take a look then,' said Sisirkumar eagerly. 'The ticket counter holds our fortune. A long queue is a welcome sight!'

The two of them crossed the empty hall and peeped outside the door. The queue had reached the street outside. But there was no pushing or chaos of any kind.

'Most of them look like college students,' said Hemendrakumar, 'or perhaps postgraduate students from the university.'

'I must tell you a funny incident,' said Sisirkumar. 'As you know, I have been addicted to the theatre from a very young age. I would often save up my lunch money to see plays without informing anyone at home. Once I had gone to buy a ticket for a show when Amritalal Bose, the famous actor, saw me. He often sat near the ticket counter, smoking the hookah and speaking to people. He lost his temper at the sight of me and shouted, "You there, young lad! How dare you come to the theatre at your age, neglecting your studies? Get lost immediately and never let me see you here again!"'

Hemendrakumar burst out laughing. 'How would he have known what a wave the same boy was destined to create in the world of theatre!'

'He was a very good man,' said Sisirkumar.

Soon Manilal arrived. Hemendrakumar had written the songs for *Sita* while Manilal had choreographed the dances. Nepa Bose, the old dance master, had initially been appointed but was dismissed soon after. His style was outdated and all of them felt that this play had to be fresh in every aspect.

Both Hemendrakumar and Manilal were busy people, but they made it a point to attend the shows every evening. The show was scheduled for 7.30 p.m. The actors and actresses would be in the theatre by afternoon. Everyone was ready. But even then Sisirkumar made Prabha practice her lines a few more times. Then he called everyone and said, 'All of you must do your very best tonight. There should be no mistakes.'

All the tickets had been sold out that night. The hall was packed to capacity with the 'House Full' board stuck outside, but it was written in Bengali, not English. Once again, Sisirkumar had changed the usual practice of writing everything in English – in the new set-up they would only use Bengali.

Saratchandra had seen the play the previous night but was there once again. 'I couldn't help myself,' he said. 'The play has been drawing me like a magnet.'

Rabindranath Tagore arrived in time for the play, accompanied by two others. As a rule, he would never visit ordinary theatres to watch plays written by others. But he had heard a great deal about Sisir Bhaduri and was curious to see him perform. Tagore was a world-famous personality and his visits would find mention in the day's newspapers. Many people had been surprised that he was actually visiting a professional theatre. Rabindranath and Saratchandra were given seats side by side in the upper balcony.

The performance was flawless. During Sisirkumar's heartbroken lamentation in the last scene, one could hear the audience sobbing as the hero cried out Sita's name, his voice steeped in tragedy. Even the most practical of men were moved by his grief. After a few moments of hushed silence there was a storm of applause. It went on and on. Sisirkumar had to appear before the audience three times for his final bow.

People who wanted to congratulate him personally came to the green room after the show. But Rabindranath Tagore would obviously not be among them. If Sisirkumar wanted to find out what he had thought of the play he would have to go to Rabindranath himself. Sisirkumar changed his costume hastily and dashed upstairs, making his way through the eager crowd, only to discover that Rabindranath had left already!

'He left quietly soon after your last dialogue,' Saratchandra informed Sisirkumar.

Sisirkumar turned pale at his words. It could mean just one thing. The poet had not liked his performance. Had he left so that he wouldn't have to spell it out in words?

Manilal looked at Sisir's face and said, 'I am sure Gurudev liked the play or he wouldn't have waited until the very end. It is so late already. I'm sure that's why he couldn't wait any longer.'

'Perhaps he has to leave for Shantiniketan early tomorrow morning,' added Narendra Deb. 'That is why he had to rush.'

But Sisirkumar was not convinced. Didn't the great poet have even a word to say to him? Could he not have waited just a few minutes longer? That meant he had been a failure. All his efforts had been in vain.

There were many others waiting to congratulate him. But Sisirkumar ignored all of them and dashed into his room. He slammed the door shut.

His friends thought it wise to not disturb him that night.

5

Sita's Ordeal by Fire, and Usha

It was common practice for actors and actresses to celebrate together following the prolonged vigour and excitement of staging a show. In fact, it was a tradition practised by all theatre groups right from the time of Girishchandra Ghosh. It seemed the natural thing to do after nearly five hours of concentrated effort and tension. Sometimes the celebration took place in the house of an actress where no one minded if one of the party had had a drop too many. Amritalal, the famous actor, had even composed a verse about it:

> Me and Gurudev – two pals, clear,
> Go to Binny's to down some beer –
> But I've caught a cold from the drink so dandy
> So fetch me, quick, some Beehive brandy!

Sisirkumar only drank with a few of his close friends. He never visited any actress' house. He spent a lot of time teaching them the basics of acting but was not on intimate terms with any of them. Rather, he was quite apathetic towards them.

He had kept himself in check all day. Now he poured himself a generous glassful of whisky and drank it in a single gulp without adding a drop of water to it. He lit himself a cheroot and began pacing about the room restlessly like a caged lion.

His heart was brimming over as he told himself again and again, 'Rabindranath did not like it. That means I am a failure as an actor. Why did I ever give up everything to join this world? To be happy with applause from a pack of Tom, Dick and Harrys? My friends have praised me because they cannot bring themselves to be impartial. All this time I've never had a touchstone to test my real worth. I realize that now.'

Sisirkumar's pride and aggression had ebbed away by the time the bottle was empty. He was now a defeated and dejected man. Tears filled his eyes.

'Usha, is this your way of punishing me?' he whispered in a muffled voice. 'Usha!'

This was the name he whispered in his heart of hearts every time he cried out 'Sita, Sita!' at the climax of the play, the scene that was considered to be his best and the epitome of brilliant acting. The image of a woman ablaze, enveloped in flames, would flash through his mind. No one else knew about it. No one, except Sunitikumar.

Eight years had passed. But the image of Usha's flaming body haunted him even now.

Sisirkumar's father and mother had been people with strong convictions. They had forced their son to get married to the daughter of a doctor from Agra. She was pretty, but a simple, ordinary girl. She had no knowledge of poetry or art. Sisirkumar had decided to educate her and mould her according to his taste. But his family was extremely traditional, steeped in meaningless superstitions. His guardians insisted on their daughter-in-law remaining home, confined indoors with the other women. Her only duty was to look after the needs of her in-laws all day long. There was no scope for anything else. Child marriage was common enough in those days and took place even in Jorasanko's Tagore family. But there the young brides who came from villages were educated and taught to appreciate art, culture and music so that they could keep pace with the modern world. The same women who came as ignorant brides had later blossomed into remarkable women like Gyanadanandini Debi and Kadambari Debi.

But such modernism was unknown in the Bhaduri family. Tagore's *Ghare Baire* had had no influence on their outdated beliefs. Sisirkumar was not permitted to take his wife along when he visited his friends, nor was he allowed to introduce them to her when they came over to visit. Even close friends like Sunitikumar and Srikumar had never seen Usha. Sisirkumar's parents refused to acknowledge that their son was highly educated and had a world of his own and that his wife should be allowed to groom herself to be a worthy companion. In their opinion a wife was meant to be no more than a partner in bed at night.

Such an unequal marriage led to a superficial attraction between couples on a purely physical level during the first one or two years of their wedded life. But neither love nor understanding could grow under such conditions.

A son was born to Sisirkumar and Usha. Sisirkumar tried his best to educate his wife to the extent that they might have something in common, something to talk about, apart from mundane family matters. But it was beyond her to match his intellect. Finally, Sisirkumar gave up trying and turned his attention outside his home. He had always enjoyed discussing literature, especially drama, with his friends. Since it was not possible to call his friends over to his place, he spent most of his time in their homes instead. Sisirkumar was nocturnal in his habits and did not mind spending his nights discussing and debating about his favourite subjects. Sometimes he stayed over in their homes and did not return home even at night.

Usha, young and naive, did not know what to make of it all. She felt utterly lonely and helpless around her in-laws. Her father-in-law had passed away and her formidable mother-in-law was now at the helm. She criticized Usha and found fault with her at every step. Quite often she shouted at Usha without any rhyme or reason and tortured her with her barbs and nasty comments. Usha wept in secret but there was no one to comfort her or take her side. Her parents were far away. The only person close to her was her husband, but she hardly ever got to see him. When he was home, she tried to tell him about his mother's unkindness but Sisirkumar refused to listen.

Gradually Usha began to believe that her husband was attracted to another woman. So seldom did he return home at night that she became convinced that he was spending his time with someone else. If she tried to question him about it, he got angry and refused to speak to her. Usha felt stifled by his silence and would be finally driven to beg forgiveness. Things would go back to normal for a while and then the same thing would happen again, leading to acute acrimony. Sisirkumar often ranted in English, which Usha could not follow. She would fall at his feet, begging his forgiveness, saying, 'I have no one but you!'

Sisirkumar hollered at her, saying, 'I do *not* spend my nights with another woman. I'm telling you this once and for all. Don't ever badger me about it again.'

But poor Usha because desolate and miserable. Moreover, the suspicion once ingrained refused to be driven out. Bruised by her mother-in-law's relentless torture, she sought escape in her husband's arms. But when her husband appeared to be indifferent she vented her wrath on him. Sheer pain and disappointment made her bring up the same subject over and over again – 'I know you're in love with another . . .'

An enraged Sisirkumar stopped talking to her altogether.

After a few days of silence, Usha asked to be forgiven once again. But Sisirkumar refused to be moved by her pleas. Finally he said, 'Do what you please but don't try to talk to me again.'

'I'm sorry, really sorry,' cried Usha in a feeble voice. 'I'll never say it again. Please forgive me for the last time.'

But Sisirkumar was livid now. 'I asked you to study but you are not interested,' he shouted. 'The only thing you *can* do is complain against my mother. Go away!'

Then he looked at her and said, 'What are you waiting for? Get out for heaven's sake! I hate the very sight of you.'

Usha stared at him in stunned silence for a few seconds and quietly went away.

A little later, as Sisirkumar sat talking to his mother, he heard the sound of glass breaking inside a room.

Kamalekamini pricked up her ears. 'What was that? Sounded like someone dropping a bottle.'

'It's nothing. Your talented daughter-in-law must have broken a bottle again,' said Sisirkumar sarcastically.

Soon afterwards they got a strong whiff of kerosene oil followed by the sound of someone running up the staircase.

Sisirkumar felt uneasy. Something was clearly wrong. He rushed inside, really worried, and noticed drops of kerosene on the staircase. Then he heard the sound of screaming from the terrace. Sisirkumar rushed up the stairs to find Usha entirely enveloped in flames. Only her face was untouched. The scene was similar to Sita's ordeal by fire. But this time the fire showed no mercy.

'Save me!' Usha cried. 'I don't want to die. I made a mistake. Save me, please!'

Sisirkumar ran to her and tried to beat out the flames with his bare hands as he shouted, 'Ma, Ma! Please come here quickly! Tara, Bishu, please come here! There's been a terrible accident.' Sisirkumar's hands were severely burnt but he could not put out the fire. There was a torn mat in a corner of the terrace. Bishwanath picked it up and wrapped it around his sister-in-law's burning body.

Sisirkumar's house was in Jugipara Lane near Maniktola. His close friend Sunitikumar Chatterjee lived in Sukia Street nearby. A young boy came running to Sunitikumar's place that afternoon and asked him if he was acquainted with any honorary magistrate. 'I must take him home at once,' said the boy. 'Dada sent me to your place. There has been a terrible accident in our house.'

Sunitikumar contacted a magistrate in their locality and went to Sisirkumar's place. There was a crowd in front of the house by then. Usha had been brought downstairs from the terrace and a doctor, who was a relative, was examining her burns. Parts of her sari stuck to her burnt skin and it was impossible to detach it from her. Her face was scalded too. Sunitikumar saw his friend's wife's face for the first time. She was panting loudly and screaming in pain. Sisirkumar sat in a corner of the room like a statue made of stone. His hands were bandaged. He looked up as Sunitikumar went up and stood by him. In a strange, hollow voice he said, 'So you've come? Listen, never be indifferent where a woman is concerned.'

The honorary magistrate came up to Usha and asked her, 'Why did you do such a thing, my girl?'

'I made a mistake,' said Usha in a halting voice. 'It was because of a false, childish suspicion. Please save me. I've committed a sin, haven't I? No one else is responsible. It was all my doing . . . Oh, oh! How it hurts! It's unbearable.'

The magistrate was writing a report when Usha stopped screaming and asked in a quiet voice, 'Where is he?'

Sisirkumar got up at once and came to her bedside. Usha looked up at his face and asked, 'Am I going be punished for what I have done?'

'No, of course not,' said Sisirkumar. 'No one will say anything.'

'Am I going to live?' asked Usha once again. 'Really?'

'Of course you will live,' said Sisirkumar. 'The doctor says so too.'

Usha turned her face the other way and said to herself, 'If I live, I shall have to do so with dreadful scars all over my body, including my face. Everyone will feel scared to look at me. And you won't even look at me then! No, I couldn't bear that. It's much better that I die.'

Those were her last words. She never recovered consciousness. Within five minutes her heart stopped beating.

Usha had not succeeded in making her husband care for her during her lifetime. But death enhanced her value in his life as never before. Sometimes death can transform an ordinary person into someone special. Despite all her resentment and pain Usha had been able to forgive her husband. She did not hold him responsible for her accident and made that clear to the magistrate.

In the past, for days on end, Sisirkumar would not speak even a word to Usha. But now he thought of her every single day and shed tears of remorse.

The bottle was nearly empty now. He would not be able to sleep at night. It was painful to remain alone at a time like this. He walked out of the room, tottering slightly. Bhikha, faithful as ever, sat outside his door as usual.

'Shut the door, Bhikha,' said Sisirkumar. 'And go to sleep.'

The road was totally deserted now. There were no vehicles. The gaslights were on but their light was inadequate. Even the familiar roads and houses looked mysterious in this curious half-light.

Sisirkumar walked along the middle of the road. Suddenly there were a couple of police constables in front of him. It was nearly three in the morning. No one was allowed to walk on the road alone at this time of the night in Calcutta. If it was an emergency he had to provide proof that it was indeed so, or else he was taken into custody as a thief.

Before the police could ask him anything Sisirkumar gave a careless look and waved them aside saying, 'Make way. Let me pass.'

It was obvious from his manner of speaking that despite being drunk he was no riff-raff and was from a good family. He could not possibly be a thief.

They let him pass without a word. Sisirkumar walked on until he reached a double-storeyed house. He came to a sudden halt and looked up. It was pitch dark and all the doors and windows were shut.

'Suniti! Suniti!' Sisirkumar shouted loudly.

After he had called out a few times, one of the windows of a house nearby opened. A loud, hoarse voice said, 'Who is shouting at this time of the night? Shut up!'

'You shut up,' said Sisirkumar, 'it's Suniti I'm calling.'

Almost immediately the door opened and Sunitikumar walked out, bare-bodied, wearing just a lungi. He was neither surprised nor shocked.

'What's up?' he asked Sisirkumar with a laugh. 'Aren't you going to let anyone sleep?'

Sisirkumar shook his head and said, 'I don't feel sleepy. Why should anyone else sleep when I'm not sleeping?'

'You know, I sleep very soundly and it's really difficult to wake me up,' said Sunitikumar. 'It was my wife who shook me awake and said, "Your crazy friend is here – the great genius."'

'Are you joking?' asked Sisirkumar.

'Of course not,' said Sunitikumar. 'Don't you remember I had introduced my wife to you and had told her that you were both crazy and a genius? Come inside.'

'I'm feeling really upset tonight,' said Sisirkumar.

'Why?' asked Sunitikumar. 'Is there any special reason? I couldn't make it to your show tonight. Was there any problem?'

'Rabindranath did not like the play,' said Sisirkumar in a hoarse voice. 'He didn't speak a single word to me.'

Sunitikumar watched him closely for some time and then said, 'Is that why you rushed to see me so late at night? It's quite possible that Gurudev did not wish to wait amidst such a huge crowd. I'll find out what he thought of your performance later on. Tell me, how much did you drink tonight?'

'A lot! I finished the entire bottle,' admitted Sisirkumar in a voice like a child's when caught doing something naughty.

'You become restless whenever you drink too much,' said Sunitikumar. 'Sisir, you must marry again. You are a true artist. A great artist cannot do without a woman in his life. Otherwise life loses its charm and tends to get lopsided.'

'But . . .' began Sisirkumar.

'There are no buts about it,' said Sunitikumar firmly. 'Usha forgave you before she died.'

'I know she did,' said Sisirkumar in a broken voice. 'But I can't forgive myself!'

6

Shantiniketan, the First Visit

As they came out of Bolepur station and looked around there seemed to be no other vehicle in sight. Would they have to travel by a bullock-cart? Sisirkumar had brought his brother Bishwanath, and Jogesh Choudhury, with him. They had spent the night on the train and now dawn was breaking. Just a few passengers alighted here. Some of them climbed on to the waiting bullock carts. The rest began to walk.

Sisirkumar lit his cheroot without even washing his face. He turned to his younger brother and said impatiently, 'Bishe, quickly go and see if any other vehicle is available. I refuse to go on a bullock-cart.'

Jogesh turned to one of the men on the street. 'Could you please tell me how far the Shantiniketan ashram is?' he asked.

'It is around three or four miles away,' he replied.

'That's where Gurudev lives,' said Jogesh again. 'How does he go home when he has to travel from the station?'

'Oh you mean Thakur Babu?' the man asked. 'There were no motor cars in his father's time so they always went by bullock-cart. But a foreigner has presented him with a motor car now and he travels in it. He sends the car over when important guests come to see him from Calcutta.'

Jogesh felt amused at his words. Sisir Bhaduri was no less important than other celebrities. Then again, they had not announced their visit in advance. Bishwanath spoke to the cart drivers and addressed his brother, 'There's a thick padding of straw and a mattress laid out in the bullock cart. You won't find it too uncomfortable,' he said.

Sisirkumar shook his head vigorously.

Jogesh turned to him now. 'Baro Babu, the man said it's just three or four miles away. Let's walk. There's a soft breeze blowing.'

Sisirkumar agreed at once.

Once they left the station behind they came across a few brick houses, a few thatched shops and open fields on both sides of the road. The unpaved road was made of red, muddy soil. One could see a row of palm trees in the distance. Before long they noticed piping hot jalebis being fried in one of the shops and Bishwanath immediately bought a dozen. But Sisirkumar refused to touch any. He did not like to eat anything in the morning. Moreover, he disliked sweets. But Jogesh was fond of eating.

As they walked on, the edge of their dhotis turned a dusty red. A little further on they found a well where a few santhal women stood drawing water. Sisirkumar came to a sudden halt. The effect of the previous night's drinking session still lingered and his eyes felt sticky. He asked them for some water. One of the women poured him some from her pot. Sisirkumar spread his palms and took the water, splashing his face and drinking the rest.

'How deliciously cool the water is!' he said in a voice full of satisfaction.

Jogesh followed his example and said, 'I've heard that the water here is good for one's appetite.'

'The Tagores are famous for their hospitality,' said Sisirkumar. 'I'm sure they'll feed us well.'

'The poet will see us, I hope?' asked Jogesh.

Sisirkumar lifted his eyebrows. 'Why won't he?' he asked.

'No, I mean, we hadn't written to him earlier, informing him of our visit,' said Jogesh. 'After all, he is a renowned poet and people keep visiting him from all parts of the globe. Suppose he doesn't have the time to meet ordinary people like us from Bengal?'

'He couldn't have forgotten that he is a Bengali himself,' remarked Bishwanath. 'I haven't seen him wearing Western attire at any function.'

'Although he travels all over the world he writes mainly about his own country,' said Sisirkumar, looking serious. 'His heart belongs to our Bengal. If he is too busy to see us today, we'll wait until he is free. A couple of days, if need be.'

Jogesh's remark left Sisirkumar with a gnawing feeling. The Tagores were an old and well-known family. They were not given to spelling out their dislikes bluntly. If he had really disapproved of Sisirkumar's performance in *Sita* he would avoid meeting them under some pretext or the other. Sisirkumar continued to walk, telling himself, *We shall cross the bridge when we come to it.*

Charuchandra Bhattacharya lived in Shantiniketan, and Sisirkumar knew him well. They sought him out first. Charuchandra immediately made arrangements for their stay in Atithi Bhavan. 'You'd better rest now,' he told them. 'A literary meet has been scheduled for this evening, where Gurudev will read out his new play. I'll take you there.'

Atithi Bhavan was a small double-storeyed building. There were four or five rooms in all. The upper floor was occupied by two foreigners. There was no question of the famous Tagore hospitality here as everyone was supposed to go to the canteen for their meals. It served simple vegetarian fare. Jogesh and Bishwanath were highly disappointed. Jogesh asked on their way back, 'Are the people of the Brahmo Samaj vegetarians? I'd never heard it before. How do they manage to live day after day on just rice, dal and potato mash?'

'The school at Shantiniketan is known as the Brahmacharya Ashram. That's why only vegetarian food is served here,' said Sisirkumar. 'I'll tell you a funny story that my friend Sukumar Ray once told me. Sukumar, as you know, has a great sense of humour. He is also a good singer and comes to meet the poet quite often. During his first visit he too had come to the canteen for his meal, where they had served their usual meal of plain rice, dal and some fried stuff without any fish or meat. Suddenly Sukumar caught sight of something round being served and thought it was egg curry and then realized, after a closer look, that they were just big, round potatoes! He immediately parodied one of the poet's own songs, 'Ei to bhalo legechhilo alor nachon patay patay (I loved it so, the dance of light on the leaves)', singing it as 'Ei to bhalo legechhilo alur nachan hatay hatay (I loved it so, the dance of potatoes on the ladle).'

Charuchandra came to call them exactly at half past four. By now Sisirkumar felt quite refreshed after a short nap. The literary meet was on the terrace of the same building.

Rabindranath was seated in a velvet-covered chair. Some of the professors and students sat on a rug on the floor while the rest stood around due to lack of space. The vast, open sky, with the sun playing hide-and-seek among the clouds, served as a gorgeous backdrop.

Charuchandra must have already informed the poet about his visitors.

'Come, Sisir, come here,' said Rabindranath without any preamble. 'I know some newspaper has wrongly reported that I did not like your play but that's not true.'

'You didn't say anything that night. That is why my opponents took it for granted that you didn't like it,' said Sisirkumar in a soft voice, 'and the thought pleased them very much, I'm sure.'

'They were wrong,' said Rabindranath. 'I was in a tearing hurry that night. But I had told Manilal that I really enjoyed your acting before leaving. Didn't he tell you that I'd said so?'

'Manilal is a friend,' said Sisirkumar, 'so when he told me about it I was convinced that he was merely trying to comfort me. I was keen to hear your opinion from your own lips. That is why I have come all this way.'

'Come and sit near me,' said Rabindranath. Sisirkumar and his friends went up to the poet and touched his feet. There was no place to sit. Some of the people who were seated got up and made place for them. 'I was really charmed by your acting that night and your interpretation of the character was fantastic,' said Rabindranath. 'But the play itself was very weak. Quite insipid, in fact.'

Sisirkumar gave Jogesh Choudhury a sidelong glance. No one had introduced him to the poet. And now there was no question of rectifying that error without embarrassing the poet. Poor Jogesh wore a glum look. Rabindranath spoke again and said, 'But you managed to establish an extraordinary example by making a weak creation an outstanding success. Do you know what I was thinking as I watched you play the role of Ram? I must write a play on Arjun! You would make a wonderful Arjun on stage.'

'I would consider it the best possible gift if you really write a play for us,' said Sisirkumar. 'I've been feeling the absence of good plays in Bengali at every step. I find only your plays worth reading. I'd have loved to present your *Chirakumar Sabha* but couldn't think of a suitable Akshay. I couldn't do it myself as I can't sing to save my life! I had thought of *Bisarjan* too.'

'You could do *Bisarjan*, of course. You would make a wonderful Raghupati and you wouldn't need to sing. Or even the role of Jay Singh.'

'But you produced *Bisarjan* yourself,' said Sisirkumar. 'Many among the audience will remember your fantastic portrayal of the character. They are going to boo me if I try to do it too.'

Rabindranath burst out laughing. 'Of course not! Why should they boo you? Your interpretation of the character will be quite different from mine. Besides, am I not getting old? I know I still put on make-up and appear on the stage to collect funds for Vishwabharati but I can't do it indefinitely. You are a young man and youth always carries its own glamour. Do you know, Sisir, I feel a real craving to write a new play after a long time? In fact, I am supposed to read a new play tonight. Would you like to hear it too?'

'Of course,' said Sisirkumar. 'We never expected to be so lucky and hear you read your own play during our short stay.'

Rabindranath began sorting the loose sheets of his manuscript while everyone waited eagerly.

Before starting to read the poet looked up at Sisirkumar and said, 'Whatever you may have to say, I don't like your custom of having a painted background in stage plays. It is a European tradition that has managed to creep into ours. But it is quite unsuitable for our plays. To me it seems a childish attempt to please the audience and an unnecessary and forced addition that stands between literature and art.'

'I absolutely agree, sir,' said Sisirkumar. 'The painted background stands still while the characters move on. When the actors leave the stage, the background is reduced to a picture frame, totally unnecessary.'

'Why do you use it, then?' asked the poet. '*Meghdoot* (The Cloud Messenger) as composed by Kalidas is in itself a series of pictures in verse. If someone were to add illustrations to explain it, it would be unfair not only to the poet but to the readers as well. A poet is content with his own poetical depictions. He does not need the help of visual imagery. In fact, he is likely to think of it as a hindrance. In fact, in some cases, blatant audacity. To take an example, one can imagine the hermitage from the descriptions in *Shakuntala*. One does not need to have a painted backdrop of the hermitage when enacting it on stage. We never had this custom earlier.'

'We've been copying the stage traditions of the Europeans in toto,' said Sisirkumar, 'they don't believe in giving the audience the opportunity for imagination. Or perhaps they don't have enough faith in their ability to do so. They always have a painting of a palace as the backdrop when enacting *Hamlet*. In fact, our own jatra's tradition of having all sides open is far superior. There are no backdrops to cause any kind of constraint, leaving the audience free to imagine the situation as they choose. But we have not been able to hold on to . . .'

'You chose to have a painted scene as the backdrop of your stage,' said the poet, stopping Sisirkumar mid-sentence. 'This trend of using a backdrop robs the viewers of their imagination. It has almost become a mechanical rule now. You see, the crowd is quite overwhelming in the jatra shows too, but the audience's imagination is not curtailed by imposing backdrops. When I produce a play I refuse to have sets. Sometimes I don't even permit the childish practice of lifting and lowering the curtains. I feel you too should give it a thought.'

The poet started reading the play. It was called *Goray Galad* (The Initial Error).

Dark clouds hastened the onset of evening. A couple of lanterns were lit to provide additional light. Rabindranath read the play, bringing to life each character using a distinct style of speech for each of them, as though directing his cast. He completed his reading without a single pause.

'Sadhu, sadhu!' the audience broke out in a chorus. Jogesh and Bishwanath were about to clap but stopped themselves in time. Many had special words of praise for the play. But Sisirkumar said nothing.

After some time Rabindranath said, 'What about you, Sisir? You haven't said anything. The others are mere listeners while you are a director. Your opinion carries far more weight.'

'As a listener, I am charmed and fascinated. Your language is incomparable,' said Sisirkumar. 'But the director in me feels differently. Shall I tell you frankly what I feel, with your permission?'

'Of course,' said the poet, 'speak nothing but the truth.'

Sisirkumar hesitated a little before asking, 'Supposing I were to produce this play, which role would you suggest for me?'

'Why, Chandra, of course! Didn't you like Chandra's character?' he asked.

'Yes, of course I did. But you have made him disappear before half the play is over. That will make it difficult for me to retain the tempo of the play,' said Sisirkumar.

'Indeed! What other flaws did you detect?' asked the poet.

'I can't exactly call them flaws but the play did feel a bit slow in places,' replied Sisirkumar.

Jogeshchandra took this opportunity to add his bit as the poet had earlier criticized his play, and remarked, 'The dialogues are too long in places. The actors might stumble while saying them.'

'A bit more speed . . .' began Sisirkumar.

The poet stopped him and said, 'Please give me your frank opinion. Do you feel that this play is not worthy of a stage performance?'

'You would succeed in making it suitable if *you* produced it because nothing is impossible where you are concerned,' said Sisirkumar, 'but I wouldn't dare to try it because I know how the audience responds. It would be safer for me to stick to *Bisarjan*.'

Rabindranath's face reddened and he said in a somewhat harsh voice, 'So you feel that the play is quite worthless!'

Then he did something very strange. He tore the manuscript to shreds. Most of the people watching were astounded. Rabindranath stood up and threw the torn papers on the floor and said, 'Charu, see to it that our honoured guests are taken care of. Ask them to stay for another day.'

Then he briskly walked down the stairs.

The rest of the people began whispering among themselves. Some shot sharp glances at Sisirkumar.

Sisirkumar nearly passed out with remorse. He had never meant for things to take this turn. He had never heard of the poet displaying his anger publicly. They knew him to be the living image of courtesy. Sisirkumar called Charuchandra aside and said, 'Charu Babu, what was my mistake? The poet himself asked me to tell him how I truly felt.'

'You acted immaturely. It's not wise to be brutally frank on all occasions. Besides, the poet is not used to verbal criticism although he realizes his own mistakes later. Haven't you seen how often he makes changes and alterations to his own plays? But he doesn't like to have his mistakes pointed out by others. I find something else more puzzling. As a rule he is quite possessive about his work and I've never seen him destroy even a single page of his writing before. But he tore up the entire manuscript this evening!'

'He left in such a rage,' said Sisirkumar. 'Shall I go and beg his pardon by touching his feet? He has no idea how much I revere and admire him.'

'No, my dear, don't try to ask his forgiveness right now,' warned Charuchandra. 'His anger will wear itself out after some time. He asked you to stay on another day. Do that and take a look around our village. You won't find such a vast expanse of khoai anywhere else. The red laterite soil is unique to this area.'

Sisirkumar came back to his room and sat quietly, smoking one cheroot after another. Neither Jogeshchandra nor Bishwanath dared to speak a word. They were well aware of his temper. Any attempt at conversation would bring on an outburst and he would vent his suppressed anger on the two of them.

Sisirkumar had been determined not to drink here, even secretly, and had not brought a single bottle with him. But his throat felt parched now. After some time he turned his face from the window and said, 'Bishe, find out if there's any coffee to be had in this place.'

'It was not your fault,' mumbled Jogeshchandra. 'Although the poet's language is extraordinary, it is not suitable for professional theatre. You just had to tell him that.'

'Yes, I know. Besides, I had no idea that the poet was so

touchy about criticism. It's a weakness shared by many great artists. I've read that even Bernard Shaw bursts out if anyone dares to criticize him. But the poet did give us permission to put up *Bisarjan*. I shall get his formal permission before we leave.'

'Right you are! We can really make something of *Bisarjan*. Which role do you intend to play?' asked Jogeshchandra.

'I think I'd like to try Raghupati first. It's a very powerful role,' said Sisirkumar.

'But the hero of the tragedy is Jay Singh. The audience's sympathy will be with him. That is why the poet himself keeps playing Jay Singh even at this age.'

'That's true. Let me give it another thought. Which role would you like?'

'Whichever you choose to give me,' said Jogesh.

After Bishwanath arrived with the coffee Sisirkumar took a sip and said, 'I think the poet was absolutely right about one thing. Our own jatra is just the right art form for our plays. Perhaps we were wrong to desert it in favour of the stage with its backdrop.'

'But, Dada, the jatra of yore was patronized by the zamindars. They provided the money and hired them to entertain the masses,' said Bishwanath. 'The viewers did not have to buy tickets to watch it. But now the people have to buy tickets to watch a play in theatre halls. They are the ones who provide us with funds. How could you keep all the sides open as they do in the jatra when that's the case?'

Sisirkumar nodded, saying, 'You are right too. Nevertheless we must explore how we can possibly blend the jatra technique with European stagecraft. How will we be able to retain our identity if we copy these European traditions blindly?'

Charuchandra came to wake them up the next morning.

'You had better get ready fast,' he whispered mysteriously. 'Gurudev wants to meet you exactly at nine this morning. I heard from Rathi that he was awake the whole night.'

'Who is Rathi?'

'The poet's son, Rathindranath.'

'Good heavens! How terrible of me to have robbed the poet of his sleep,' said Sisirkumar.

'Well, see if you can make amends today.'

They got ready quickly and the three of them sat waiting, their tension palpable. Who knew what the poet's mood would be like this morning? Keeping awake the whole night could not be easy at his age.

'I better not go,' said Jogeshchandra nervously. 'I'll stay put here.'

Sisirkumar frowned and thought for a while. Then he said, 'Why won't you go? No need to feel so scared. After all, we haven't done anything wrong.'

Charuchandra came to call them exactly five minutes before nine. It was a short walk to the poet's residence. The students had settled beneath the trees in their classes. Instead of carrying canes in their hands, the teachers wore scarves over their shoulders.

The drawing room was full of paintings. Low stools dotted the room instead of chairs. There was no sign of opulence but everything about the room spoke of impeccable taste and elegance. There was an enormous centre-table laden with delicacies – plates full of fruits, luchi, mohan-bhog and a variety of sweets. This was typical Tagore hospitality.

Sisirkumar looked at Jogeshchandra and raised his eyebrows in amusement.

The poet had not come into the room as yet. A young girl in a red-bordered sari, the end of her sari wrapped around her shoulder instead of covering her head, was arranging dishes of silver. Charuchandra whispered softly that she was Pratima, the poet's daughter-in-law. He introduced her to the guests.

'Why don't you start eating? Babamoshai will be here soon,' she told them sweetly.

'No, no! We shall wait until Gurudev arrives,' said Charuchandra.

The guests couldn't but be impressed by the fact that the lady, despite being a member of the famous Tagore family and the poet's own daughter-in-law, had come personally to welcome them. They were equally impressed, by her simple clothes and easy, cordial manners. This was not common practice among the people they knew in Calcutta. Sisirkumar remembered for a moment that Usha had never been exposed to an environment such as this. Why couldn't everyone else be as natural as this in their behaviour, whether they were Brahmo, Hindu or Muslim? Why were womenfolk confined to their chores within the household? In that way the actresses were better off. They could come out into the open to laugh, cry, dance and sing on the stage amidst people.

The poet arrived soon after. He wore a loose robe this morning. He had just had his bath. The room seemed to light up as he walked in, reminding everyone of what Achintyakumar had described as an 'appearance'. He looked ethereal and there was a glow of satisfaction on his face.

'Sit down, all of you,' he said. 'Sisir, you haven't introduced me to your companions.'

'This is my brother Bishwanath and this is Jogesh, who is like a brother to me,' said Sisirkumar, not disclosing the latter's identity. 'Both belong to my team and help me in various ways.'

The poet did not realize that Jogesh was the playwright of *Sita* whose work he had criticized. 'I hope you didn't face any inconvenience here?' he asked affectionately. 'Eat to your heart's content. Food is not something to be left aside.'

'I heard you didn't catch a wink of sleep last night,' said Sisirkumar penitently. 'If it is because of . . . .'

'There is nothing unnatural about losing a night's sleep,' said the poet, interrupting him. 'It happens to many. Tell me, can you name a particular category of people who feel happy despite losing a night's sleep? I don't mean thieves, of course, so don't mention them.'

Sisirkumar did not reply but looked at him eagerly.

The poet smiled and said, 'It's a strange breed called "writers". If they succeed in writing something satisfactory at night they are not bothered about losing sleep. You had not approved of my play so I wrote it afresh last night.' Then he turned back and said, 'Rathi, where are you? Are you done with the manuscript? Please bring it here.'

Rathindranath arrived there and said, 'It's an entirely new play!'

The poet handed the manuscript to Sisirkumar. 'Here you are,' he said. 'There was an "initial error" (*Goray Galad*), but now "all's well, finally" (*Shesh Raksha*).'

7

The First Jolt

Rehearsals ran simultaneously for three plays from noon to six in the evening, sometimes until six-thirty. The Improvement Trust was constructing a new road called Central Avenue. Rumours were afloat that several slums and buildings would have to be demolished to make room for it, Manomohan Theatre being one of them. If that happened, Natya Mandir would have to pack up once again and find a new venue. It was a disturbing thought.

At the end of the rehearsals, Sisirkumar would sit around with a few of his cronies discussing various topics, ranging from literature, art, theatre and politics to the theory of languages. Quite often the 'liquor goddess', as Nabinchandra Sen called it, also appeared to keep them company. The way Sisirkumar drank was different from the way others did. Alcoholics usually make it a point to drink after sundown. Some drink within limit, while some are not satisfied until their steps start faltering. The days when Sisirkumar chose to drink, he would continue nonstop. He would carry on in the same vein for a few days, not stopping until he was totally knocked out. This would be followed by a period when he would not touch a drop and that would continue for some days. At such times, no amount of coaxing could tempt him to pick up a glass. One of his friends called this pattern his 'new moon phase' and 'full moon phase'.

Sisirkumar had been in his new moon phase for a week.

Saratchandra had lately become a regular visitor and expensive liquor would be arranged for him. Sisirkumar's childhood friend Aleek would often bring in these expensive bottles. Sisirkumar would keep away a few of these bottles to entertain Saratchandra and, on those evenings, Sisirkumar would keep him company.

In Rabindranath's presence an awkwardness prevailed over Sisirkumar, a sense of deep reverence, for the great poet robbed him of words. But it was easy to be perfectly free with Saratchandra. One could laugh and joke with him as with an equal. He even permitted impertinence to a certain limit.

Saratchandra had visited him the previous night. The bottle and glass had been set before him but Sisirkumar refused to keep him company this time.

'What's up, Sisir?' Saratchandra had asked him, amazed. 'Are you observing a fast or ritual?'

'No, Sarat-da, I have other thoughts occupying my mind,' replied Sisirkumar. Addressing Saratchandra as 'dada', elder brother, came quite naturally. But it was quite impossible to address Rabindranath as 'elder brother' or 'uncle'! He was just Rabindranath or 'Kabiguru', and 'Gurudev' to the Shantiniketan crowd.

Sisirkumar was worried about presenting *Bisarjan* differently. Added to this was the worry of finding a new hall for his theatre. He couldn't put it up just anywhere. The audience preferred familiar venues and only four theatres were up and running at the time. Even then, Alfred Theatre on Harrison Road attracted a very small audience.

Aleek had informed Sisirkumar about a place that was not a theatre but a private residential. Aleek was an elderly zamindar whose family income had begun to dwindle. He was on a selling spree, selling off properties, farmhouses, rare pieces of furniture and expensive gems to fund his hedonistic lifestyle. He was a widower and childless too, and was therefore determined to squander all his possessions before he died. He was very generous with his friends, spending lavishly on them. And he was equally lavish when it came to spending on his inamoratas, usually a new one every night. He had often asked Sisirkumar to accompany him during his nocturnal excursions, but in vain. He had dragged Sisirkumar along with him several times, saying, 'Oh come on! How will you ever get to know about the colourful side of life unless you visit such places? Stop confining your life within these four walls!'

The house discovered by Aleek was in Rajballav Para. It belonged to his uncle who was in urgent need of money and was willing to sell it off for a song. It was a huge house with a ballroom that was almost as large as an auditorium. But there were several problems.

'To start with, I don't have the kind of money to buy such a place now,' said Sisirkumar. 'Secondly, it's not practical to have a theatre right in the middle of a residential area. We've tried it before and it failed because the residents raised objections. Besides, a theatre requires a wide road with markets and shops nearby and ample parking space for the phaetons.'

He paused for a while and said, 'But I would like to see the house in any case. Perhaps it might do for something else I have in mind.'

'You mean a national theatre?' asked Aleek.

Sisirkumar nodded.

'Well, that has been your dream for a long time now. But who is going to fund it? Can you think of a possible donor?'

'Deshbandhu told me that he would find me someone.'

'But he is busy with a hundred other things. Is he likely to remember his words? I too remember that he had mentioned it.'

'He spoke of it just the other day,' said Sisirkumar. 'He held my hand and said, "Sisir, surely we can provide you with a national theatre, which will promote the cause of good theatre and its general improvement. It would be a real shame if we can't! You would teach the youngsters and concentrate wholly on producing good plays without having to worry about money. I shall be back from my tour soon and arrange everything within a month. I have also spoken to Subhas about it." Can't we depend on his word?'

'Yes, we can, if he has said so. But I doubt if this house will remain in the market until then. However, I suppose we can always find another.'

Aleek suddenly changed the subject and remarked, 'I am absolutely bowled over by the performance of that actress Prabha in every play of yours. Is she someone's mistress?'

'You be happy with your girls on Free School Street,' said Sisirkumar, 'and don't keep eyeing my theatre girls.'

'It's common for the depraved well-to-do to have actresses in their keep,' said Aleek, 'there's nothing unusual about it. After all, how much do you manage to pay them? Of course I shall leave her alone if she is already with someone else. But I do fancy that girl.'

'I've not seen Prabha trying to attract the attention of any well-heeled brat as yet,' said Sisirkumar. 'Her heart belongs to the stage.'

'Is she keen on you, then? And determined to offer herself to you?'

'Of course not!' protested Sisirkumar vehemently. 'But don't you lay an eye on her. Of late, I've noticed her growing closeness to my younger brother Tarakumar. Perhaps they are in love. There is no question of my objecting to the liaison. Besides, it is reassuring because Prabha won't leave my group in a hurry. It's not an easy task to find a girl this raw, teach her from scratch and then, as soon as she learns the ropes, see her break away and join another theatre group the moment someone dangles a carrot before her eyes. I really hope Prabha remains faithful to Natya Mandir.'

'Very well, I take back whatever I said,' said Aleek. 'Henceforth I shall look at Prabha Rani with brotherly eyes alone! Aren't you going home tonight?'

'I think I'd better,' said Sisirkumar. 'I haven't been home for the last few nights. There's no liquor on my breath tonight. I can have a chat with my mother too.'

'How many times has your mother watched *Sita*?'

'It has become quite a hobby with her,' replied Sisirkumar, sounding amused. 'She drops in every now and then and doesn't even tell me about it. The boys open the box upstairs for her whenever she comes. She must have seen it twelve or fourteen times by now.'

'Does she come to see the play or her son?'

'Both, I guess.'

'Do you think she is likely to accept Tarakumar's involvement with Prabha?'

'That's none of my business. Let them sort it out themselves,' said Sisirkumar. 'Aleek, do you intend to drink any more?'

'Perhaps a few drops more. I'm still sober, you know. How can one enjoy drinking alone? I wonder what happens to you sometimes! Sit for a while, let me finish my drink.'

Someone called out from outside.

'Bhikha, the light is on in the room,' said a voice. 'Is your master in?'

'Is that, Hemen?' exclaimed Sisirkumar. 'So late at night . . .?'

Hemendrakumar Roy stood at the door and called, 'Sisir,' in a heavy voice.

Sisirkumar looked at him as Hemendrakumar stood in silence.

Then he pulled a chair and sat down, saying, 'Pour me a drink, Aleek. My throat is parched.'

'What's up, Hemen? Anything wrong? Some problem with Naachghar?

'I've come to give you a piece of news. I don't know how to break it to you,' said Hemendrakumar. 'Sisir, you've been dreaming of a national theatre, haven't you? I just saw the theatre crumble and turn to dust.'

'Don't talk in riddles,' said Sisirkumar. 'The national theatre isn't built yet. So how could you possibly see it crumble? This is not funny!'

Hemendrakumar looked straight into Sisirkumar's eyes and said, 'Deshbandhu is no more! He had not been keeping well of late. You must have heard that he had gone to Darjeeling to recuperate. He has a house there called Step Aside. That's where he breathed his last. Heart failure.'

Sisirkumar's fair face turned dark with shock. Aleek said, 'It's like the fall of a Titan! Which Bengali stalwart remains now in Indian politics?

'We have been orphaned,' said Hemendrakumar. 'I was in the *Amrita Bazar Patrika* office. That's where I heard the news. And I thought of Sisir instantly. They will be bringing in his body tomorrow. We shall all be going. I heard that Subhas Babu is very upset too.'

Sisirkumar stood in stunned silence as tears streamed down his cheeks.

Aleek poured out an extra-large peg and handed the glass to Sisirkumar.

He shot a glance at the glass and downed it in a single gulp like a thirsty traveller in a desert. He did not even care to add water to it. Then he put down his glass and said, 'Give me some more.'

'It's a massive shock and an irreparable loss,' said Hemendrakumar, 'really difficult to accept. Yes, you will need some more, Sisir.'

They spoke of Deshbandhu and recalled memories of him for quite some time. Then Hemendrakumar said, 'I'd better make a move. Won't you go home too?'

'No, not yet,' said Sisirkumar. 'You'd better go ahead.'

The bottle Aleek had brought was exhausted now. 'There's another one in that almirah,' said Sisirkumar. 'Take it out.'

'I too must leave in half an hour,' said Aleek. 'I've an appointment.'

'Where?'

'Free School Street.'

'Who do you go to? Do you have a steady paramour?'

'Yes. I've been seeing her for about a month now. A French girl, as attractive as she is seductive. French girls really know the art of lovemaking.'

'Indeed? Is anyone allowed to accompany you?'

'Do you mean *you* would like to come? Please do! You are most welcome.'

'No, some other time, perhaps.'

'Why not come right now? You'll enjoy chatting with her. You'll be surprised to know that although she is a prostitute by profession she happens to be an educated one. She was speaking of a play by a French writer one night whose name I have never heard before. I think it was Victor Hugo.'

'How shall I communicate with her? I don't know French. *Je ne parle pas Français.*

'At least you know that much. It's more than I do! But the girl knows English quite well. After all, she has travelled all these miles to find herself customers. She can't afford not to know English. Come on, get up. You shouldn't be alone tonight.'

Sisirkumar was already tipsy after consuming so much undiluted whisky in such a short time. His head was reeling. Yet he picked up the second unfinished bottle before stepping out. Aleek had his own phaeton waiting. They didn't need to direct the coachman. Most neighbourhoods in north Calcutta grew quiet at this late hour. But Chitpur was alive with its usual hustle and bustle. The vendors were busy selling flower garlands and ice cream. Lights glittered in several buildings from where strains of women's laughter and the screams of drunkards could be heard.

Chowringhee, a predominantly European locality, was still gleaming with lights. Here, motor cars rubbed shoulders with horse-driven carts and the people walking the streets were mainly British and Anglo-Indian. Free School Street was the busiest locality in this area.

Businessmen from various parts of the country had flocked to the city as the Nawabi era ended and the British began to rule Calcutta. People from other countries were here too – businessmen, scholars, researchers, seekers of wealth and even flesh-traders. The French girls initially went to Chandannagar but eventually made a beeline for Calcutta since it promised a larger market.

Sisirkumar kept sipping from the bottle during the ride. Cold breeze wafted in through the windows. 'How much further is it, Aleek?' he kept asking every now and then.

'We're almost there now,' said Aleek.

'Is Deshbandhu really no more?' asked Sisirkumar once again.

By the time they reached the French girl's room Aleek was more or less steady. But Sisirkumar was totally sozzled. Neither his eyes nor his speech were normal and his steps faltered. The girl's name was Helen. As the French pronounce 'h' very softly, she called herself 'Ellen'. She had golden hair, an exquisitely trim figure, a come-hither look in her eyes and a sweet smile on her lips. She welcomed both of them in a charming voice that was so sweet it felt as though she had known them for years. Needless to say, none of it was genuine. But her performance – which Sisirkumar's experienced eyes observed despite his drunken state – was just superb.

Aleek introduced him. 'This is my friend, a famous actor, known to every Bengali. He is also a very erudite person.'

'Young lady, have you ever acted on stage?' was Sisirkumar's first question.

Ellen gave a tinkling laugh. 'I tried but didn't get an offer,' she said. 'It's not an easy task at all in my country. You need luck on your side.'

'If only you could speak Bengali and I could get someone like you in my troupe!' said Sisirkumar. 'I haven't come across a single educated actress so far. To begin with, please give us two glasses.' He pointed to the bottle and said, 'Would you like to join us?'

'No,' said Aleek, 'she doesn't drink.'

'I refuse to touch the crude liquor of the English people,' said Ellen. 'I only drink red wine.'

As she poured the drink in two glasses Aleek said, 'I won't have any more, Sisir.'

Sisirkumar took a long draught and asked, 'What did you tell my friend about Victor Hugo? I'm not familiar with French literature. I should have learnt the language to read the plays of Molière in the original. I know that Victor Hugo had written a novel named *Les Misérables*. Did he write plays as well?'

'Of course he did,' said Ellen. 'He wrote poems and plays too. In fact, he is better known for his plays in France. This friend of yours often speaks of the Bengali theatre so I told him about an incident in Hugo's life.'

'What was the incident?' asked Sisirkumar. Then he turned to his friend said, 'Aleek, you rascal, why won't you drink any more?'

'Have you heard of the famous French actress Mademoiselle Mars?' asked Ellen.

'No, I haven't. Is it a French name?'

'That's the name she used when she shot to fame. She could really sway the French audience. Even the playwrights and directors had to give in to her. Victor Hugo was a young playwright at the time, shuttling between one theatre and another with his play, in a desperate attempt to have it accepted. But no one so much as glanced at him. He faced dire poverty and starvation. He didn't even have a roof over his head. Can you believe that someone who was destined to become the emperor of our literature in the days to come just had 50 francs in his pocket at the time, enough to last him about a week?'

Suddenly Sisirkumar muttered, 'Deshbandhu, Deshbandhu!'.

Ellen did not understand what he was saying and asked, 'What?'

'Don't mind him,' said Aleek. 'Please continue.'

'Finally Comédie-Française accepted one of his plays,' said Ellen. 'It was called *Hernani*. I suppose you people would pronounce it with an "h"! Unfortunately, some problem with the actress playing the lead role cropped up during the rehearsals. Somewhere in the script was the expression *mon leon*, which means, "my lion", which would be fine if she were addressing a king. But the hero of the play was a bandit, and Mlle Mars refused to call him that. There was a heated argument during the rehearsal one day when Alexander Dumas was also present. I'm sure you've heard his name?'

'Of course,' said Aleek. 'We've read his *Three Musketeers*.'

'Duma! Dum duma dum dum duma,' drawled Sisirkumar as the glass fell from his hands and his shoulder drooped. He was totally knocked out.

Ellen's tinkling laughter at the sight sounded like the shattering glass.

'Your friend heard nothing of what I said,' she said, lightly smacking Aleek. 'Just look at him, he is fast asleep! Come, let's go to another room.'

Sisirkumar could not recall how or when he had returned. He woke up late in his own room at the theatre the next morning. He had no idea where he was when he opened his eyes. And then he wondered if it was daytime or night.

Sunlight coming in through the window made him realize it was late afternoon. What had happened to him last night? He remembered going somewhere with Aleek in his phaeton. But what had happened after that? There was an unknown girl, her skin the colour of sandalwood-paste. She was saying something and laughing a lot. What was there to laugh at, eh? Didn't she know the great Sisir Bhaduri? And that it wasn't a done thing to laugh like that in his presence? Who was the girl, anyway? A harlot! A strumpet! What was she saying? Victor Hugo, a pal of hers? Rubbish!

Sisirkumar sat up rubbing his eyes. Where had he met the girl? He was in his own room now. Had it been a dream then? Where was that rascal Aleek?

'Bhikha! Bhikha!' he called out. Immediately Bhikha appeared outside his door.

'What time is it?' Sisirkumar asked him.

'It's past one,' said Bhikha.

'Hasn't anyone come for the rehearsal?' asked Sisirkumar.

'There's no rehearsal today,' said Bhikha.

Sisirkumar frowned. 'Why? What do we have this evening?'

'There's no show tonight. Some important person has died.'

Sisirkumar sat in grim silence.

The theatre seemed unusually quiet; quieter even than someone's residence. The sounds of the city could not be heard here. But whispers of actors and actresses of days gone by seemed to reach his ears.

'Bhikha, get me a coffee,' said Sisirkumar. 'What are you serving me for lunch?'

After his bath, Sisirkumar had a hearty lunch of paratha and a thick mutton curry. He drank several glasses of water. One tends to feel thirsty the day after one has had too many drinks. After lunch he lay down with a collection of Ibsen's plays.

He could remember vaguely that he had been to see a European girl with Aleek the previous night. What was it she had said about plays? He couldn't remember very well.

A little while later, two of the actors came to see him. They wanted him to join them for the procession accompanying Deshbandhu's remains. Sisirkumar refused. He was not in favour of a display of grief.

No one else visited him that afternoon. Sisirkumar slept for some time. It was now well past evening but there was no trace of anyone. Would no one come to see him today? What had happened to Aleek? Had he decided against everything he normally enjoyed in honour of Deshbandhu's memory?

Not that it mattered if no one came to visit him. He was quite capable of spending time on his own. He sent for some whisky and recited poetry as he drank. But in between he kept thinking about Aleek's non-appearance. Where was he? Why had he not come?

As the night progressed, so did his inebriation. He was convinced Aleek had gone to see that same girl. He wanted to see Aleek urgently. He asked Bhikha to hire a horse-driven carriage and set off, remembering to carry the bottle of whisky with him. It was not difficult to locate the girl on Free School Street but Aleek was not there.

'It's not his day for visiting me,' said Ellen. 'Our next appointment is for Saturday.'

'Isn't it possible to see you without an appointment?' asked Sisirkumar hesitantly.

'That's the way I like things to be,' she said, 'but you can come in for a while if you want to.'

Sisirkumar entered and sat on the sofa. 'May I have a glass?' he asked.

'You clearly have had a lot to drink already,' said Ellen. 'Can you handle any more? You fell asleep last night.'

'No, no, I shall not fall asleep tonight,' said Sisirkumar. 'You were saying something about Molière last night. I'd like to hear the rest of the story.'

'Molière?' asked Ellen in surprise. 'I never said anything about him!'

'Wasn't there a playwright and actor named Molière in your country?' asked Sisirkumar.

'Yes, indeed,' said Ellen, 'but I was recounting an incident that occurred during a play by Victor Hugo.'

'Hugo?' asked Sisirkumar in surprise. 'Did he write plays too?'

'My dear great actor, it looks like you remember nothing of what I said last night,' said Ellen.

'No, I remember some of it now,' said Sisirkumar. 'There was some problem with his plays. Was it at the press or somewhere else?'

'Dear me, looks like I'll have to tell you the story from the beginning,' said Ellen. 'But my darling, before I begin, tell me, have you come to me just to hear my stories?'

Sisirkumar quickly intejected. 'No, no, of course not! I haven't come here to waste your time. I'd like to have some fun with you as well, and I have the money for it.'

Ellen, dressed in a yellow-and-black striped gown, reminded Sisirkumar of a cheetah on the prowl.

The colours dazzled as she walked. She had a glass of red wine in her hand and walked to a corner of the room. Then she said, 'Imagine that I am the famous Mlle Mars and you, Victor Hugo, a poor and young playwright. You are in the midst of a heated argument about a dialogue in the play.'

'Argument with a heroine?' asked Sisirkumar, amused. 'A joke indeed! Our heroines don't even understand the meaning of all their dialogues! They're all nondescript nobodies from the red light area. They are not educated like you. Tell me, will you consider joining the Bengali stage?'

'Don't be silly,' said Ellen, 'and listen to the rest of the story. Hugo's play had been selected with great difficulty. It was likely to be rejected instantaneously if Mlle Mars raised any objection.'

'No heroine dares reject anything selected by me or raise her voice against mine!' cried Sisirkumar. 'I am the one who selects a play and if any changes are called for in the dialogue I am the one to do it.'

'I don't know about your stage,' said Ellen. 'I'm talking of Paris and Comédie-Française, a famous theatre there. One day Alexander Dumas was present during the rehearsal and he too advised Victor Hugo to give in and accept the slight change in dialogue made by Mlle Mars.'

Sisirkumar was already tottering by this time. He hiccupped once and said, 'Why did Alexander Dumas ever tell him that? What right had he? I don't allow anyone else to make comments during my rehearsals.'

Ellen did not look vexed or irritated. Her profession had taught her to take everything in her stride. She smiled sweetly and said, 'Let's talk of something else. Tell me about yourself.'

'No, no I want to know what happened,' insisted Sisirkumar. 'Was the play staged finally? Who did you say the playwright was? Hugo or Molière?'

'Oh, forget it!' said Ellen.

Sisirkumar took a large gulp of his drink and said, 'No, I won't forget it. I have a very sharp memory.'

Sisirkumar tried to stand upright but his legs tottered and he crashed to the floor, passing out instantly. Ellen came up to him and tapped his cheek gently with her dainty fingers, 'Wake up, my lover, wake up! Didn't you say you wanted to have some fun with me?'

When she realized he was dead drunk she kicked him on his back gently with her tender legs.

Sisirkumar never returned to her again despite Aleek's numerous efforts.

'Drink less one evening and go see her again,' Aleek had suggested. 'You will find her stimulating both physically and intellectually.'

'Therein lies the problem, my dear friend,' Sisirkumar had replied. 'I don't feel like visiting such a place when I am sober. I can go only when I am sozzled. But I lose out on the fun if I'm knocked out.'

Despite his words, a few weeks later, while returning from a dinner at a zamindar's place Sisirkumar wondered if he could drop in at Free School Street once more. He had drunk quite a bit, but not excessively.

His eyes were bloodshot but he was still speaking without a slur and his steps did not falter.

He had taken to visiting a couple of streetwalkers of late to drive away Usha's memories. But he found it impossible to share his thoughts with any of them. They were quite incapable of understanding anything of a higher level and were merely adept at offering their bodies to their bidders.

Sisirkumar wanted to see Ellen not merely because of the physical attraction he had for her but because he remembered quite a bit of the incident she had been recounting that night – a playwright's difference of opinion with an actress because of a single dialogue! He couldn't imagine a similar situation in Calcutta. Heroines with such fine sensibilities were simply nonexistent here. Driven by a feeling of dissatisfaction, he was eager to hear the rest of the story. The zamindar had sent him off in a phaeton. Sisirkumar asked the driver to take him to Free School Street. It was not difficult to locate the house. It was not too late, just half past ten, and the road was bustling with people.

Sisirkumar walked up to the first floor and rang the bell. He had thought he was quite sober but his steps faltered a little. Ellen opened the door. Tonight she was dressed in a black velvet gown and the two strands of pearls around her neck complemented her golden hair. She opened only a part of the door, smiled and said, 'Hello, *mon ami*. What brings you here? You don't have an appointment with me tonight. Besides, I am expecting a guest shortly.'

'I won't take much of your time,' said Sisirkumar. 'I just want to speak to you. Of course I shall compensate you for your time.' But Ellen shook her head. Sisirkumar came forward and tried to hold her hand as he implored, 'Please, listen to me.'

'Sorry, *no*,' said Ellen firmly. 'Darling, you always come here drunk. You are a waster, a real waster. Now please get lost.'

She slammed the door on Sisirkumar's face.

Her message was clear enough: *Never come here again. This door will never again open for you. It is not a place for drunkards.*

Was the story of the playwright and the actress destined to remain unfinished forever?

No one in his group knew French well except Sunitikumar, but Sisirkumar hadn't met him in ages. When they finally met after a few days Sisirkumar asked him immediately about Victor Hugo, the French author – whether he was a playwright as well and had ever had a problem with a famous actress about a dialogue in a play. If so, how did it turn out eventually?

'I don't know much about French plays or the history of French theatre,' said Sunitikumar, 'but Nitish would know. He is an ardent follower of Pramatha Choudhury and has a thorough grounding in French literature. I'll call him over sometime. Don't you remember Nitish? He was a year our junior in college. He teaches philosophy in a college now.'

Before long Nitish Dasgupta came over.

When he heard about the episode, he immediately said, 'It is a famous incident – the tussle between Hugo and Mlle Mars about a dialogue. The line was, *Tu es mon leon,* You are my lion. Alexander Dumas was present during the incident and he wrote about it. Mlle Mars repeatedly asked Hugo to change the words but he just refused to. Finally, after a lot of persuasion, Mlle Mars agreed to say the original words. Many were worried she would skip the dialogue when the play was performed. Or else act so lifelessly that the audience would not be impressed, which would spell doom for the future of the playwright.'

'But why?' asked Sisirkumar in surprise. 'Doesn't the hero have any say there?'

'Our Bengali theatre has been centred around the hero from the very beginning,' said Nitishkumar. 'Take the examples of Girishchandra, Ardhendushekhar, Amritalal, Dani Babu and yourself. It's *you* the audience goes crazy about. Can you name a single actress who has been able to rise to that stature, except for Binodini? But in France it is the actresses who reign over the audience. That is why the playwrights do not dare to offend them. Several celebrities and critics had been present on the opening night of *Hernani*. Monsieur Hugo, the playwright, sat in a corner of the wings, his heart beating fast. Surprisingly, the play appeared to be an instant hit from the word go. The dialogues were so different from the traditional kind that the audience broke into applause every now and then. The heroine herself was no less surprised. But being extremely intelligent she soon realized that the role of Donna Sol was likely to be one of the most memorable performances of her career. So she put her heart and soul into her role and did not leave out the dialogue she had once objected to so vehemently. The audience accepted it as a matter of course, finding nothing out of place.'

'So it was a triumph for the playwright!' said Sisirkumar.

'There is more to the story,' said Nitishkumar. 'You know, the play comprises five acts. The fourth act was just over when a publisher named Meme called Victor Hugo outside for a cup of coffee.'

'A *man* named Meme?' asked Sisirkumar in surprise.

'Oh well, in Bengali we say "mem" for "madam" but the French don't know that!' said Nitishkumar. 'The publisher's name *was* Meme. He said, "Victor, we want to publish this play of yours. Here is the contract form. Please sign it. And here are 5,000 francs.'"

'Hugo was astounded. He had traversed from door to door with the manuscript of the very same play and everyone had shooed him out like a dog! A number of theatre companies had been downright insulting. And here was someone actually offering him 5,000 francs even before the play was over! "But the play hasn't ended yet," Hugo had told him, "what's the hurry? We could discuss it tomorrow morning." And the publisher had said, "No, I can't wait until morning. I can well foresee that there is going to be a sureshot stampede the moment the play ends and publishers will fall over themselves to catch you and offer more money. Very well, I shall give you 6,000 francs. Come, sign it right now." And that's how the episode ended.'

'It's a good story.' said Sisirkumar. 'Do publishers really pay so much for a good play there? No wonder they come out with such fine scripts. Our novelists don't write plays because they just don't sell in our country. With the exception of Rabindranath, of course. He is not bothered about whether they sell or not.'

'It is not just a matter of sales,' said Nitishkumar. 'It is about culture, too. We don't have that culture of theatre in our country. There is yet more to the story. *Hernani* turned out to be a very successful play. It was temporarily shelved after a hundred nights of nonstop performance. But it was performed several times thereafter.

After eight long years, it was being staged once again in the very same theatre. Two people in the audience who had seen the play eight years ago went to see it once again. One of them remarked after the show, "I liked it far more now than I did the first time. And the audience's response was great too. The writer must have changed the play quite a bit." The second one answered, "No, the playwright did not change the play at all. But he succeeded in changing the taste of the audience in the last ten years." Dada, therein lies the success of a good play!'

8

The Stage and Beyond

Muzaffar Ahmed lived in a small room on the first floor of 32 College Street. He was down with fever and coughing every now and then. Nazrul Islam, his roommate, was playing the harmonium as he hummed the tune of a song. He had been at it since evening. Of late, he seemed keener on composing music rather than writing poetry. He had now settled in Krishnanagar with his wife. However, he stayed here whenever he visited Calcutta.

He made up the words as he composed the music: 'Amra shakti, amra bal, amra chhatradal (We're the power, we're the strength, we, the student band)'. It sounded like a marching song. He had become a member of the Krishnanagar Regional Congress Committee of Bengal. It was part of his duty to build a team of volunteers. This included training them to march and keep fit. He called himself the havaldar poet.

Kallol magazine's office was at Patuatola, quite close by. The young writers there often called him over. Sometimes,

Nazrul went by himself and would stand at their door, playfully shouting, 'De gorur ga dhuiye (Come and give the cow a wash).' The tiny room full of lively youngsters buzzed with laughter. The place resounded with songs and poetry whenever he was there.

Nazrul had almost finished composing the song when someone called out to him from the road, 'Kazi-da! Kazi-da!'

Nazrul pushed his harmonium aside and peeped out of the window. It was Achintyakumar who had called him. Premendra stood by his side.

Nazrul waved to them, asking them to wait. Then he bit his tongue, saying, 'Oh dear!'

'What's up?' asked Muzaffar. 'Who was that calling?'

'Two members of the *Kallol* group. I was supposed to go to the theatre with them today. But how can I?'

'Why not?'

'You are ill. I can't leave you all alone and go.'

'Pooh, some illness! It's just a little fever. A lot of people get it.'

'But you refused to see a doctor.'

'Seeing a doctor at the onset of a sneeze is a pastime of the rich. A simple cold and fever gets cured by itself.'

'But I don't feel like leaving you alone.'

'Am I a child? No, no, you must go. Which play is it?'

'A new play produced by Sisir Bhaduri. It is called *Shesh Raksha* (All's Well, Finally) and has been authored by Kabiguru.'

Muzaffar Ahmed sat up in excitement. 'A play by Gurudev produced by Sisir Bhaduri? You can't possibly miss such a golden opportunity! I'd have gone myself if I wasn't feeling so ill. If I go there in this condition now my awful cough will disturb everybody. Are all the poets from *Kallol* going?

'Yes, they are,' said Nazrul. 'Sisir Babu came personally to invite them. He especially asked me, too. Kabiguru himself will be coming this evening.'

'What an opportunity I'll be missing!' said Muzaffar regretfully. 'An opportunity to see the great poet face to face! I've carefully preserved the wire he sent you once.'

'Is it with you, then? I had been looking for it everywhere,' said Nazrul. 'Please give it back to me. I feel like looking at it sometimes.'

'You will lose it as soon as I return it to you,' said Muzaffar. 'You're very careless. Now don't delay any further, make a move.'

Nazrul was fond of dressing up before going out anywhere. He had a special case for the cosmetics he used. He applied 'snow' on his face, followed by face powder, and combed his locks carefully.

Muzaffar opened a tin trunk and showed him the precious telegram.

When Nazrul started a magazine named *Dhumketu*, the poet had sent his blessings. In the magazine Nazrul had made a demand for complete independence of the country in unambiguous terms. As a result he had been accused of being a traitor and was sent to prison for a whole year in the Hooghly Jail. He was refused the status of a political prisoner and shoved in with ordinary convicts. Nazrul and the other political prisoners had fasted in protest, the fast lasting for thirty-nine days. It had nearly killed him. The poet had sent him the wire at the time. It said, 'Give up the hunger strike, our literature claims you.' The poet had also dedicated his play *Basanta* (Spring) to Nazrul while he was still in prison. It was rare for a renowned poet to acknowledge the talent of a rising one.

Nazrul reached downstairs to find another young man with Achintya and Premendra. He was thin and short, and held a tiny cigarette known as Maypole in his hand. This youngster from Dhaka had joined the *Kallol* team recently. His name was Buddhadeb Bose.

All of them boarded a tram to Hathibagan. Natya Mandir, previously known as Cornwallis Theatre, was close by. A lot had happened since Sisirkumar had performed in *Sita* on that stage. In between he had staged other popular plays like *Alamgir, Prafulla* and *Sadhabar Ekadashi*, taking on the roles once played by famous stars like Girishchandra, Ardhendushekhar and Dani Babu. But Sisirkumar seemed to have surpassed them all, not just in acting but also in interpreting the roles afresh. Senior members of the audience who had witnessed the famous stars of yesteryears also admitted that Sisirkumar had given a fresh lease of life to theatre. His fame was now sky-high.

In this time Sisirkumar had grown closer to Saratchandra. A few of Saratchandra's novels had been dramatized and put up at other theatres but they had not been particularly successful. One day Saratchandra landed up at Natya Mandir, a manuscript and an umbrella under his arm, and said, 'Sisir, these people are merely good at making bonde, a popular fried sweet made from gram flour. They've no idea how to go about making sandesh, the delicate dessert made from fresh cottage cheese. You alone can do that.'

The manuscript he had was the dramatized version of Saratchandra's novel *Dena Paona*. It had been renamed *Shoroshi*. A young writer named Sibram Chakrabarty had first thought of converting the novel into a play. He had written the script and had it published in a magazine but Saratchandra had not particularly liked it. He had made a few additions and deletions of his own to the script and brought it to Sisirkumar. Realizing the potential of the script, Sisirkumar had further edited it before it was launched and staged.

Shoroshi was a hit from the very first night of its performance. Jibananda, the protagonist of the play, was a lecherous, cruel and drunken zamindar. It was difficult to imagine the audience accepting such a negative character as the central one. But Sisirkumar interpreted the role with such finesse – projecting him as a split personality, who had in equal measure a sensitive heart, a strong conscience and a sensibility as pure as fire – left his audience spellbound. Charushila, who played Shoroshi, the heroine, was excellent too. Coached by Sisirkumar himself, she proved to be the master creation of an artist extraordinaire.

Shoroshi brought Sisirkumar not just fame but also a great deal of money. Although the play did not surpass the popularity of *Sita*, it was considered to be a brilliant performance. The cream of Bengali society, who had carefully avoided the stage until now because of its association with women of easy virtue, began to flock to Natya Mandir. It became widely accepted that Sisirkumar had succeeded in enriching Bengali culture.

But, despite the grand success of a spate of plays, Sisirkumar was convinced that it was not natural for Bengali theatre to imitate English traditions blindly – of having a painted backdrop that enclosed the stage like a photo frame, and so on. The traditional stage of the jatra – an open stage without a backdrop – was both natural and desirable. A poor country like ours didn't require theatre halls like those of the British. As he had already formed a professional group it was not possible for him to reject the theatre hall altogether and opt for a jatra-style stage in an open field. But he felt a strong desire to blend some of the jatra traditions with his professional stagecraft. *Shesh Raksha* would be his first attempt at that.

The opening night for any play always had a large share of invited guests. The promotional handbill for the play had been designed to look like a letter of invitation, as though everyone was being invited to a wedding. Stalwarts of Bengali culture as well as new and upcoming stars took their seats one by one. Rabindranath was seated in a special sofa at the centre of the front row, looking regal, like the king of some unknown realm. People came by and respectfully touched his feet.

Before the play began everyone noticed that a wooden staircase had been placed at the centre of the stage, coming down to the auditorium. The steps were covered with a red cloth. A pathway, also covered in red, led to the middle of the hall.

A number of new songs had been added to the play. These had been taught to the actors by Dinendranath Tagore, who was considered to be the treasurer of all of Rabindranath's songs.

The first scene comprised an entirely female cast – Khantomoni, Indumati and Kamalmukhi. Their jovial conversations interspersed with songs appeared to be quite a hit. Sisirkumar, playing Chandrakanta, entered in the second scene. It was soon clear that he was equally adept at making the audience laugh.

The play proceeded amidst frequent bouts of clapping.

The young poets of the *Kallol* group sat in the second row, right behind Rabindranath. They weren't just watching the play; they were also keeping a close watch on the poet's face. Was he laughing at the comic situations?

They had reached the last of the scenes where Gadai's wedding chamber was being arranged. Suddenly, to everyone's surprise, Sisirkumar walked down the wooden steps to the auditorium, a sheaf of papers in his hand, the kind that is distributed at weddings. He greeted the audience like the host of a wedding and started distributing the papers among them. The papers contained a printed song: 'Jar adrishte jemni jutechhe shei amader bhalo . . . (Whatever fate has sent our way, we're quite content with, I'm glad to say . . .)'

The actors and actresses on the stage started singing the song. After they had sung the first line twice, many among the audience joined in from various corners of the auditorium. Rabindranath turned around in bemused curiosity.

The incident was not exactly as spontaneous as it seemed. Nolinikanta Sarkar and a few other well-known singers had been taught the song beforehand and they deliberately sat scattered among the audience. But soon many more from the audience joined in so that the actors and the audience became one.

Sisirkumar invited some of them to come up on stage and join them. The play ended on a note of joyous celebration.

After the last bow Sisirkumar came down and stood before the poet with folded hands. He smiled at Sisirkumar and said, 'I enjoyed it. Come and see me at Jorasanko tomorrow morning. We'll talk then.' He looked at the *Kallol* writers and said, 'You must come too.'

Then he walked out of the hall, in conversation with Nazrul.

The *Kallol* group came out and stood by a stall for some tea and snacks, and a chat. Everyone was captivated by the show. What's more, everyone had done well, not just Sisirkumar. Even the actresses had been superb. The audience was all praise for their performance. Only Buddhadeb stood silently, busy smoking.

'Why are you so silent?' asked Achintyakumar. 'Didn't you like it?'

'No, not in the least,' said Buddhadeb.

Everyone stared at him in surprise. Buddhadeb appeared to have a sense of humour at other times! Then why . . .?

'It was simply not Rabindranath's play!' said Buddhadeb. 'I admit that Sisirkumar acted marvellously as Nimchand in

Sadhabar Ekadashi. In fact, he was fantastic. He was also stellar as Jibananda in *Shoroshi* – the way he portrayed the character, it seemed to be the story of his own life. But *this*? This was meant to be a comedy! He seemed like he could hardly give up being Sisirkumar Bhaduri! Where was the poet's Chandrakanta? He was nonexistent! Besides, some actors seemed to rattle off the dialogues without understanding what they implied. One can't have this sort of thing in a play by Rabindranath Tagore. It's quite disgraceful.'

'Why are you getting so worked up about it?' said Premendra after a brief, stunned pause. He put an arm around Buddhadeb's shoulder and said, 'Smile a little, p-l-e-a-s-e!'

9

Enter the Heroine

Natya Mandir had finally managed to arrange for a car for Sisirkumar: a black Buick with a driver in a white uniform and turban. Sisirkumar often drove down to the Brigade Parade Ground in the evening accompanied by one of his friends.

Sisirkumar had been behaving rather recklessly following Deshbandhu's death. He drank beyond measure, at the risk of causing himself injury. His unique way of expressing grief was to torture himself.

Manilal Gangopadhyay, his close friend, had also met with an untimely death a few days ago. It is uncertain if Sisirkumar could have risen to such heights in the world of theatre had it not been for Manilal's selfless cooperation, inspiration and advice. Sisirkumar was the much-adored emperor of theatre. But Manilal, the friend who would have been the happiest at his success, was no more.

This time, too, a dispirited Sisirkumar had been through a phase of self-torture, but fortunately his other friends had come to his rescue. Sisirkumar's fame had brought on new responsibilities. Every single newspaper, including those run by Britishers, followed him closely. They were generous in their praise when he performed well but did not hesitate to condemn him in unambiguous terms if he happened to err in any way. One evening he had actually been drunk while performing the role of the drunken Jibananda in *Shoroshi* and his dialogues sounded slurred, for which at least two newspapers had criticized him sharply. Besides, he had to keep in mind his rivalry with Star at all times. Star presented a number of plays of different genres in quick succession, often attracting a bigger audience. Ahindra Choudhury, their brightest star, was a fine actor though quite melodramatic, and had not succeeded in attracting men of letters, artists and the educated section of the society quite the way Sisirkumar had done. Sisirkumar was not just a star. He was special because he was a personality to reckon with and a scholar even when he did not don the actor's garb.

Star continued its unabated efforts to cause damage to both Sisirkumar and Natya Mandir since *Sita* had been abducted. Some people, appointed by Star Theatre, bought tickets and came to watch Sisirkumar's successful plays and broke into guffaws during the performance just to create a disturbance. Or they kept shouting, 'Louder please,' so that Sisirkumar might lose his cue. Irritated, people from the audience would force them to shut up. Sometimes they would even get beaten up.

Moreover, there was a looming cloud of suspicion that a few people were being sent by Star to visit Sisirkumar in the guise of friendship. They brought with them an endless supply of alcohol and would persuade him to drink excessively, especially when he was feeling low. Realizing their actual intention, Sisirkumar's close friends were wary of them and did not allow them to visit him freely. One or the other of his friends always made it a point to be around him, especially since Manilal's death.

That evening Narendra Deb was with Sisirkumar in the car. He was a tall man, cheerful and with a ready smile on his lips. His bushy moustache was particularly showy. He had recently married Radharani, a young widow from a well-known family. Both husband and wife were poets. People called them the 'poet duo'.

Narendra was contemplating composing an opera-like musical and had been discussing the idea with Sisirkumar.

At one point he said, 'You know, Sisir, whenever I think that the success of a play ultimately depends on whether the audience turns up to see it and whether a sufficient number of tickets are sold, my inspiration tends to dry up and I can't write from my heart any more. How can anyone create anything worthwhile if he is always forced to think of the box-office? Rather, the playwright should try to create something new that his audience will gradually learn to accept.'

'What do you mean by "gradually"? How gradual should it be?' asked Sisirkumar. 'I have tried to introduce some new features in my plays but the audience is wary of accepting anything different. They simply refuse to accept any change. The response of the audience to *Shesh Raksha* was pretty lukewarm. And if the audience isn't there, it means an empty wallet. How does one make ends meet and clear dues at the end of the month? That is why I have to keep repeating my old plays from time to time. People want to see me either as an emperor or as a superhero like Ram.'

'It's unfortunate that Deshbandhu passed away at a time like this,' said Narendra. 'Had he been here he'd surely have made things work somehow. Can we not create a national theatre of our own? Then we wouldn't have to think of money all the time.'

'How are we to do it?' Sisirkumar asked casually.

'We must make an appeal to the government,' said Narendra. 'After all, the government has been opening schools, hospitals and parks and setting up offices to get people vaccinated. Similarly, shouldn't it also open a national theatre for the entertainment of the people?'

'Narendra, aren't you forgetting that we are not an independent nation?' remarked Sisirkumar snidely. 'Who is going to tell a foreign government what it should or shouldn't do? Are we to go begging?'

'Then let us ask the corporation,' said Narendra. 'Let them give us land and we shall raise funds to build a hall. Even if they pay us around twenty thousand rupees a month we shall be able to manage. Besides, there will be some money from the sale of tickets. We can use it to produce new plays.'

'Naru, you are building castles in the air!' said Sisirkumar. 'We should make *you* the mayor. But the question is, will you agree to give us twenty thousand rupees a month once you are actually in that post?'

'I don't see why you should call it building castles in the air,' protested Narendra. 'Twenty thousand a month means two lakh and forty thousand a year. We pay taxes to the corporation once every three months. Even if say ten lakh people pay just four paisa in three months, can you calculate how much it will add up to? Once we have a national theatre we shall be able to invite famous singers, musicians, dancers and actors from all over the world to come and perform here. Just think how wonderful it would be for our city! Calcutta is such a big city; it is second only to London, among the commonwealth countries. And yet we have just four theatre halls here. Even among those, Alfred Theatre is shaky and Minerva is no better.'

'But then Calcutta at least has a few theatres where plays are performed regularly, all year round. Does any other city in our country have permanent theatre halls? None!'

'That's not particularly surprising,' said Narendra. 'Everyone knows that Bengalis are far ahead of the others where art and culture are concerned.'

'You are a Bengali chauvinist, Naru,' said Sisirkumar. 'Don't say it anywhere else or you'll be bashed up!'

'But Sisir, I've been to Europe,' said Narendra. 'Prague is a tiny city with just seven and a half lakh people. Do you know how many theatres they have? Fourteen! The Bohemian government has built a national theatre there. The corporation also has its own theatre.'

'How many among those seven and a half lakh are educated? And what about our Calcutta? The Bengalis you are so proud of . . .'

Sisirkumar sat up, ending the conversation abruptly. 'Stop, stop!' he told the driver.

Their car had made it around Dalhousie Square, crossed Lalbazar and was now on Bowbazar Street. Sisirkumar had suddenly caught sight of a huge poster stuck on the wall of a house. It said:

Great news! Great news!
An educated heroine is appearing on stage
For the first time in Bengali theatre

Srimati Kankabati Sahu, B.A.

Will appear regularly on the stage
Of your favourite theatre
STAR
(Art Theatre)

Sisirkumar stepped out of the car and read the poster several times. Then he frowned and asked, 'What's up, Naru? Is this a new stunt by Star Theatre?'

'Whoever thought this up deserves some credit. It's quite a startling piece of news,' said Narendra. 'A girl who's a graduate ... on the professional stage! Absolutely unheard of anywhere in the world.'

'And she has a surname, too,' said Sisirkumar.

'Surname?' asked Narendra in surprise. 'Oh, I see what you mean. None of our actresses – right from Binodini to Angurbala, Indubala, Prabha or Ascharjamayee – have had surnames.'

'How can they?' said Sisirkumar. 'They come from the red light area and are born of unwed mothers. They don't have surnames. But has Star really managed to find a lady for its stage? Or has it merely picked up an idol from Kumartoli?'

Sisirkumar got into the car once again and told the driver, 'Drive. Drive fast!'

On their way they saw the same poster on the walls of several buildings, including the Medical College, Calcutta University and the municipal market. Some buildings were virtually plastered with the poster. As they reached Cornwallis Theatre, Sisirkumar went in, calling out, 'Bishe, Tara, Jogesh, where are you?'

Many of the men came to the theatre on weekdays for a chat even if there were no shows. They were all present that evening and came out together when they heard Sisirkumar call.

Sisirkumar sat down on a chair right in the middle of the stage and asked, 'Have you seen Star's posters?'

The entire city had been covered with them. There was no chance of missing them.

Sisirkumar lit a cheroot and asked, 'Is it true? Or is Star merely bluffing the people?'

No one answered. A smile lurked on Aleek's lips as he held his glass of drink.

'What do you say, Aleek?' asked Sisirkumar. 'You keep track of every woman in the city. Don't *you* know?'

'Of course I do,' said Aleek. 'I made enquiries as soon as I saw the posters.'

'Is there really such a girl? And is she a graduate?' asked Sisirkumar.

'Which of your questions should I answer?' asked Aleek.

'Both,' said Sisirkumar.

'In that case, both are true. There is a good-looking girl named Kankabati Sahu currently studying for her Masters. She is keen on acting,' said Aleek. 'As soon as the people in Star got wind of the news, they lapped up the golden goose.'

Sisirkumar raised his voice. 'An educated graduate girl wants to act! Why should she turn to Star instead of coming to Sisir Bhaduri? Couldn't any of you do anything about it? Totally useless, the lot of you! Go and bring the girl here somehow, *anyhow*!'

'Hold on, Sisir, don't get all heated up,' said Aleek. 'Do you know why Star Theatre enjoys so much popularity? It's not because of Ahindra Choudhury or Nirmalendu Lahiri. It's because they have a very sharp and shrewd manager who knows the market minutely. And he knows just how to play the game. You need a manager like that for your Natya Mandir too. I've told you several times before.'

'I had asked you to be the manager.'

'Me? I'm a free bird, my friend. I don't intend to get caught up with responsibilities of any kind. Besides, I know how it would be to work under you! I'd have my head bitten off at every step! After all, you are in charge here. Now listen to what Prabodh Guha, the manager of Star, has done. He has already made the girl sign a contract for three years lest you manage to get hold of her.'

'Three years?'

'Yes. She's going to be an apprentice for the first three months. She'll have a salary of three hundred a month the first year, four hundred the second year and five hundred the third year. It has all been stamped and signed. Now all you can do is cry over spilt milk!'

'I don't care about contracts. We must get the girl here somehow.'

'That's being childish!'

'I don't care if it is. I want to see her. Bring her over, by hook or by crook,' said Sisirkumar. 'Aleek, I give *you* this responsibility.'

'Are you crazy? The last thing I want is to be accused of abduction. I refuse to be involved in such a mad scheme,' answered Aleek.

Jogesh Choudhury was the next to speak. 'Why would we need to bring her forcibly? Which girl in Bengal wouldn't jump at the chance of meeting Sisir Bhaduri if he wishes to see her? Unless she is a stay-at-home wife, of course. We simply have to inform her that Sisir wants to see her.'

'Very well then. Try it and see. But it's quite possible that the Star group will keep a close watch on her.'

Jogesh was successful in his attempt in a matter of days. There had been no question of forcing her. Kankabati had agreed to come as soon as she heard that Sisirkumar wanted to meet her. But she did not come alone. She was accompanied by her younger sister, Chandrabati, and her cousin, her uncle's son. Kankabati's father's name was Gangadhar Sahu. Although he was originally from Orissa he had bought a small zamindari in Muzaffarpur, a small town in Bihar. He was also an honorary magistrate there. He led a luxurious life and was a connoisseur of music. What's more, he was a progressive man, free of the shackles of traditions and rituals. He had educated both his daughters from a young age and trained them in music as well, and had sent them to Calcutta for higher education instead of confining them to the small mufassil town. Sisirkumar also learnt that Kankabati had a lovely voice and mostly sang Rabindranath's songs. She had, in fact, sung in Rabindranath's presence.

Kankabati looked like she was twenty-two or twenty-three. She was much taller than most Bengali girls and was generously proportioned, and resembled the image of the goddess Durga, with the same large eyes and hair that cascaded down her back, covering it entirely. Her younger sister, in comparison, was petite but had the same sharp features.

Natya Mandir's hall resembled a courtroom, with Sisirkumar seated in his chair on one side and the three visitors in three chairs facing him. The others flanked the two remaining sides of the room.

The girls had not touched Sisirkumar's feet, as was the custom. They had joined their palms in greeting instead, as girls from the Brahmo Samaj usually did. The younger sister had a streak of vermillion in the parting of her hair, which the elder girl did not.

'Do you want to act on the stage?' Sisirkumar asked

Kankabati without any preamble. 'Why didn't you come to me first?'

'Nobody suggested it,' said Kankabati without hesitation. 'I was singing in someone's house one day when a gentleman came and asked me, "Would you be interested in acting for Star Theatre?" and I replied, "I'd be proud to." I signed the agreement the very next day.' Then she laughed softly and said, 'You belong to a different league so I didn't dare to think about you.'

'Kanka signed on the dotted line without even consulting us,' added the cousin.

Sisirkumar ignored the comment and looked straight at Kankabati. 'Which song did you sing for the great poet? Will you sing the same song for us?'

Kankabati nodded. She hummed the tune to herself, then looked up and said, 'I didn't feel nervous when I sang for the poet. But you make me nervous.'

'Nervous because of me? But why?' asked Sisirkumar, a little surprised.

'I have heard that you have a hot temper,' said Kankabati.

'Indeed! And who is responsible for spreading this rumour?' asked Sisirkumar.

He shot the others a quick glance. They turned their faces away to hide their smiles. No one had dared to say such a thing to Sisirkumar's face before!

'Well, you don't need to feel nervous now,' said Sisirkumar. 'Please sing.'

Kankabati sang in a clear, open voice:

'Ei lobhinu sango tabo sundaro, he sundaro . . .
Ah beautiful, your presence I have desired . . .'

Sisirkumar listened intently to the entire song. Then he sighed and said, 'Well done! A lot of my actresses in Natya

Mandir can sing but they are not able to express the real feeling in Gurudev's songs. I feel as though I have listened to the real thing at last, for the first time ever. You really do sing well. But why did you suddenly decide to act?'

'I enjoy acting,' replied Kankabati, 'I have often taken part in our college socials.'

'College socials are very different from the professional stage,' said Sisirkumar. 'I wonder if you are aware that all the professional actresses come from the red light area. They are rather looked down upon. You come from a good family. Won't your parents have any objections?'

'My mother died a long time ago and my father . . . he too is no more,' said Kankabati, 'but I don't think he'd have objected had he been alive.'

'What about your younger sister? Does she want to join the stage too?' asked Sisirkumar.

'No, no. She is already married and her husband won't allow it,' replied Kankabati.

'But people from the cinema have been after Chandra,' added her cousin. 'Acting in films isn't half as strenuous as acting on stage.'

Sisirkumar then asked Kankabati directly, 'Will you join my group?'

Kankabati shook her head and said, 'No, I can't. The manager of Star has clearly told me that I cannot break my contract. If I do I'll have to face imprisonment.'

'I'll see to your contract . . .' began Sisirkumar.

'No, sir! Please don't insist,' said Kankabati's cousin. 'She came to see you because you had called her. But we don't want to get involved in any mess.'

The subject was dropped, and Hemendrakumar and Saurindramohan too arrived on the scene soon after. After a round of tea and sweets Sisirkumar saw Kankabati and her companions off at the door.

When he returned Hemendrakumar said, 'Sisir, you look as if you are greatly disappointed. But what is so special about the girl? I admit she is educated and has acquired a Bachelor's degree. But is there any guarantee that she will make a good actress just because of that? I would say those who have worked their way up are likely to be far more sincere.'

'You haven't heard her speak,' said Sisirkumar. 'There's a uniqueness about her. I've never heard something quite like it before. You haven't heard her sing either. Do you know why our *Shesh Raksha* wasn't a success? It's because no matter how hard they try, our girls are quite incapable of evoking the emotions in Rabindranath's songs. But this girl's rendering is altogether different. I still hope to produce other plays by the poet. If I do I'll need someone like her.'

'But they are educated girls from good families,' said Saurindramohan. 'Is there any guarantee they won't disappear when they feel like it?'

'Yes, we'd have to take that risk,' agreed Sisirkumar.

The actors and actresses stood in a group. Prabha was among them. She stepped forward and asked politely, 'Baro Babu, if you don't mind, may I say something?'

'Say what you want to,' said Sisirkumar, a little preoccupied. 'There's no need to be nervous.'

'It's about this educated girl who was here a while ago. She isn't very young, must be about twenty-three or twenty-four at least. Why didn't she wear vermilion in the parting of her hair?'

Sisirkumar was astonished at the question.

'No vermilion?' he asked. 'How would I know why? Probably because she isn't married.'

'But she is a Hindu girl, isn't she? Sixteen years is the latest by which Hindu girls are married off. Beyond that the parents of the girl would be treated as social outcasts. Her parents might be dead, but she must have other relatives. How could they possibly allow her to join the theatre? It's unheard of!'

Sisirkumar raised his voice and said, 'Listen, Prabha, I didn't bother with such considerations. She might belong to the Brahmo Samaj or be a Christian, for all I know. Besides, can't a Hindu girl remain unmarried if she chooses to? I don't know much about these matters.'

Prabha looked away glumly and said, 'Baro Babu, you are an educated man while we unfortunate orphans don't even know the names of our fathers. We are not educated, which is why you are always taunting us. Is it our fault that God has sent us to this world with a destiny like ours?'

Sisirkumar spoke in a softer voice now. 'Taunt you? No, I never do. I scold you so that you may speak more clearly and deliver your dialogues better. You have made far greater progress than many of the others. Don't you remember what Karna had said in the Mahabharata? A higher force decides where we are to be born but acquiring qualifications is our responsibility. You have now reached a stage through your own efforts where you can play a queen or a maid with equal finesse. In fact, you are so good that many well-educated girls would do well to take a few tips from you.'

After this exchange, everyone got busy talking of other things. Sisirkumar became preoccupied.

After a couple of days Sisirkumar went on a solitary drive without telling anybody. He had been feeling restless for quite sometime and decided it would do him good to breathe in the fresh air by the Ganga.

They were driving along the wide, newly constructed Central Avenue. As they came around the Kolutola bend, he suddenly asked the driver to stop and turn left.

They were on Mirzapur Street now, where he looked out for a particular pharmacy. He found it after a while and stopped at the door of the yellow house right next to it. His heart was beating fast.

Why had he come here? He was the great Sisir Bhaduri, who never went anywhere without an invitation. He had learned his lesson that night when he was insulted by the French girl. Why was he here then? This was not an area in which he could visit anyone with the might of money. He had no idea what kind of reception awaited him. Despite his pride, his heart fluttered strangely, a feeling he was experiencing for the first time.

He knocked on the door.

It was not opened by a servant but by a young woman. It was Kankabati herself.

'Why, it's you!' said Kankabati, surprised.

'I came to speak to you about something,' said Sisirkumar hesitantly. 'Did I disturb you?'

'I was just about to go out,' said Kankabati. 'Had you come a minute later you would have missed me.'

'Oh were you going out? In that case . . . Then it wouldn't be right to waste your time,' said Sisirkumar. 'I'd better . . . .'

'I am not in a great hurry,' said Kankabati. 'I could go a little later. Actually I was going to the library to get some books. Please take a seat. Would you like a cup of tea or coffee?'

'Neither,' said Sisirkumar. 'I just need five minutes with you.'

'Whatever else you might say, please don't ask me to ditch Star Theatre. The lawyer has specifically forbidden it.'

'No, I haven't come here to ask that of you.'

The drawing room was simply furnished. There were a few sofas, a rectangular centre table and a couple of framed paintings of landscapes on the wall.

Kankabati wore a striped sari, simple and inexpensive. She wore no bangles, just a wristwatch with a white strap. Two diamond studs gleamed in her ears.

They sat on separate sofas, facing each other.

'Tell me,' said Kankabati simply.

Sisirkumar mumbled, 'I'm not sure what I want to say. I didn't really give it a thought. I came without thinking, actually.'

Kankabati burst out laughing. 'Do you really expect me to believe that the great Sisir Bhaduri has come visiting an ordinary girl like me without a reason?'

'I'd better leave today,' said Sisirkumar getting up, 'you are in a hurry now.'

'Very well,' said Kankabati.

As they stood up Sisirkumar asked, 'Which library do you go to?'

'The Imperial Library,' replied Kankabati.

'Do you go there every day?'

'No, maybe twice or three times a week.'

'It's in Dharamtala, not close by. How do you go?'

'I take a tram.'

'Would you object if I offered you a lift in my car?'

Kankabati thought for a while and said, 'No, why should I object? That would be really convenient for me.'

Sisirkumar had never seen a girl from a good family going

out alone. Kankabati didn't inform anyone and simply closed the main door from outside. She was carrying two books. After they sat in the car Kankabati asked, 'Were you really going that way? Or is it just for my sake?'

'I was not going anywhere in particular,' said Sisirkumar, 'so any direction is fine with me.'

'Now, isn't that odd? To not have a specific destination! You came to see me but you had nothing to say,' said Kankabati. 'Wouldn't it be fun to just get lost?'

'If only I could!' said Sisirkumar. 'Get lost, I mean. Not just in my imagination but in reality! Sometimes I wonder ... all this dressing up, putting on make-up and performing roles – what if I were to leave it all and go away?'

'People everywhere are showering praises on you,' protested Kankabati, 'don't you enjoy it? Is it not like an addiction?'

'Yes, I do enjoy it,' said Sisirkumar, 'but sometimes the whole thing gets on my nerves. What are you reading these days? Let me see.'

He stretched out his hand and took the books from her. One was Dostoevsky's *Crime and Punishment*. The other was a bound volume containing three novels by Bankimchandra.

Leafing through the pages of the second book, Sisirkumar asked, 'Don't you read poetry?'

'Are poetry books something to be borrowed from the library? One must have them at hand,' said Kankabati. 'I have all of Rabindranath's books at home.'

Sisirkumar murmured to himself:

'E katha janite tumi Bharat-Ishwar Shah Jahan . . .
You knew it well, god of India's fate, Shah Jahan
Time grabs it all – one's life, youth, wealth and state

And yet it was your goal
To make timeless the anguish of your soul . . .'

Then he paused and asked, 'Do you know this one?'
'Of course I do,' said Kankabati and quoted the next line. Then she said, 'The poem is from *Balaka*. But there is another poem in the same book that I like even better:

'He prio, aji e prate nijo hate ki tomare dibo daan . . .
My love, this morning
What should be
A gift to you from me?
A morning song?

The burning rays of the sun
Exhaust the morning,
And its listless song
Ceases, weary,
Upon its wilting stem.'

As soon as Kankabati paused, Sisirkumar continued:

'Oh friend, what do you crave
When you stop at my door
At the break of day?

What should I bring you
The evening lamp, just lit?
But this light belongs
To a corner of this still abode

Would you carry it on your way
Amidst a crowd
Where the breeze will put it out?'

Kankabati remarked in surprise, 'Do you also know poetry?

Everyone believes that only the roles of kings and emperors suit you!'

'But even a king sometimes feels like a beggar and needs to kneel before someone special,' said Sisirkumar. 'Do you know this one –

> Amare je dak debe e jibane tare barambar,
> Phirechhi dakia . . .
> The one who will proclaim and call my name
> In this life, oh I shall call him too
> Again and again . . .'

'Let me continue,' said Kankabati.

> 'Tabo kanthe mor naam jei shuni gaan geye uthi, "Achhi, ami achhi" . . .
> My heart sings when I hear you call my name –
> "I'm there," it says in joy, "oh I am there . . ."'

All roads reach their journeys' end sooner or later, sometimes far too soon. As directed, the driver stopped the car in front of the Imperial Library. Dusk was setting in but the road was still full of people. Traffic in this locality was regulated by the British.

'Okay then,' said Kankabati.

Sisirkumar nodded but whispered, 'Will the world come to an end if you don't go to the library this evening?'

'I am not worried about the fate of the world,' said Kankabati with a smile. 'Should I not get down here? Then where shall we go?'

'A little further down until it's dark,' said Sisirkumar.

'Very well, let's go,' said Kankabati. 'Take a look at the sky. I think there's going to be a storm, but I am not afraid of storms. I know how to make them my friends.'

Once the car started moving, Sisirkumar said, 'I went to your place without giving you prior notice. When I knocked and you opened the door I was taken by surprise. My heart skipped a beat. I have seen a lot in my life and I'm not young any more. But I had no idea that my heart could beat like that, even at this age! It was like that poem, "Je nari bichitra beshe mridu heshe khuliachhe dwar (The woman, strangely clad, opened the door with a smile)".'

Kankabati laughed once again, saying, 'Was I strangely clad? But I was no less surprised than you were. When I heard the knock on the door I thought it was the milkman or perhaps some salesman. But, heavens above! I opened the door to find the emperor himself!'

'But your face didn't show how you felt.'

'That's because I didn't let you see it,' said Kankabati. 'When I saw you I immediately remembered that I was bound by my contract to Star.'

'If I were to visit you sometimes, just to speak with you, would you mind? Or would you get angry? I haven't spoken so freely to anyone in ages, you see.'

'But you hardly said anything when you were in my house.'

'Yes, that was strange too,' admitted Sisirkumar. 'People know me as a great talker. Quite often I don't let anybody else open his mouth. But I was totally speechless in your presence. One can express far more through poetry. I realized today that there are times when words are not necessary; a lot can be expressed through silence…"Only themselves understand themselves, and the like of themselves, As Souls only understand Souls."'

'Where are these lines from?'

'Walt Whitman, "Leaves of Grass",' said Sisirkumar.

'I haven't read him. I've read a little of Shakespeare,' said

Kankabati. 'I was rather amused by a snippet I read the other day which said he didn't merely write plays but acted in them too.'

'Yes. He was a stable boy at first. Then he started playing minor roles. Finally he became the owner of the theatre and the chief playwright. Do you know which role he played in *Hamlet*?'

'I'm not sure.'

'The role of the ghost; Hamlet's father. Just imagine the great Shakespeare playing the role of a ghost!'

Kankabati broke into peals of laughter.

The car came to a halt near the broad steps leading down to the river.

The Ganga was full of steamboats and ferries. It seemed as though the traffic here was heavier than on the city's main road. This was the time when many people crossed the river. Since there was no bridge, ferries were the only means of crossing it.

The sky was thick with dark clouds. The last crimson rays of the setting sun flashed through the chinks in the clouds. A flock of cranes flew in the sky.

Many Englishmen and women walked along the riverbank every evening. Some of them came here regularly for a walk. The ladies dressed in dainty gowns and the men in their top hats. A few walked hand in hand, as if reliving the promenade along the River Thames back home.

Natives were not permitted to walk on this stretch. Not that there was a rule in black-and-white stating this, but everyone was expected to know that the natives could only approach the river beyond Posta. This part of the riverside was reserved for the ruling class. If a native turned up here by mistake he would not be arrested but the white pedestrians would glare at him fiercely, and if he dared to remain here after sundown drunk white soldiers from the fort nearby would be sure to assault him.

Sisirkumar and Kankabati did not get out of the car.

The clouds had moved a little, making room for a streak of light from the setting sun throwing its reflection on the river like a crimson snake.

Kankabati whispered, 'He birat nadi . . . Oh river wide, Your deep and silent, ever-flowing tide . . .'

'I don't remember this one,' said Sisirkumar, 'please continue.'

Kankabati recited the rest of the poem.

'What a charming, impeccable accent you have,' said Sisirkumar, 'and your voice is so melodious! Kankabati, you have been in this city all this time . . . Yet, how is it that I never noticed you before?'

'I am just an ordinary girl, not the kind one would readily notice,' said Kankabati.

Sisirkumar caught her hand impulsively and said, 'I don't feel like letting you go. Whether we act together or not, couldn't we . . . .'

Kankabati trembled and tears streamed down her cheeks.

Sisirkumar let go of her hand, looking flushed with embarrassment. 'What did I do?' he whispered. 'Was it improper of me to touch you? Have I unknowingly hurt your feelings?'

Kankabati wept silently.

'I didn't mean to insult you, believe me,' said Sisirkumar penitently. 'Please forgive me. I did it without thinking.'

'You have been my hero ever since I was a child,' said Kankabati trying to hold back her tears. 'I remember visiting the fair at the Eden Gardens as a little girl where you had set up a stage and performed *Sita*. I was holding my father's hand. You had enacted the role of Ram. It was such an unforgettable experience! I thought you were an angel straight from the heavens, not an ordinary human being. I have worshipped you in my heart ever since. I have shed tears of longing as I wondered if I would ever be lucky enough to get near my idol, to speak to him just once. And now, the very same angel is actually seated beside me and has held my hand! I can't believe it is for real. Do I really deserve something so wonderful?'

'I am not an angel,' said Sisirkumar in a dry voice. 'I am an ordinary human being with the usual set of virtues and vices. I have cravings and desires. But there is one thing I can say honestly – I could swear it if you like – I have never felt so weak in the presence of a woman before. It is not lust but a strong attraction, and I can't fathom the reason for it. No other woman has been able to give me the kind of pure, simple joy that I have felt in just speaking to you.'

Kankabati wiped away her tears and sat with her head bowed.

'I don't feel like letting you go,' said Sisirkumar once again. 'What if I were to abduct you right now?'

'Where will you take me? What will be my place in your life?'

'I could put it lyrically as, "Your place shall be within my heart,"' said Sisirkumar. 'But it wouldn't ring true because I am, in reality, a prosaic man. You shall always be by my side, as my soul mate.'

'What if they try to snatch me away from you?'

'They will not succeed,' said Sisirkumar. 'No power could take you away from me. I shall guard you with my love as long as I live.'

'And if you get tired of me?' asked Kankabati.

'I shall never get tired of you,' said Sisirkumar, 'but perhaps *you* might, since I am much older than you are. My hair would fall, and my skin would get . . . No, I can't take you away by force at this moment. Please think about it. If you ever feel that . . .'

Kankabati leaned forward and placed her hand on his heart.

A storm broke out soon after. It was wild and turbulent.

10

'Bharatnari'

The entire city was a-buzz with the rumour that Natya Mandir had abducted a new actress from Star Art Theatre. Star had once swiped *Sita* from under Sisir Bhaduri's nose, and now Sisir Bhaduri had had his revenge. Except, this time it was not a play that had been snatched away but a woman, alive and kicking, beautiful, educated *and* a graduate!

The rumour was threatening to become a regular penny dreadful. The damsel was reportedly imprisoned in a dark and gloomy secret chamber where no living creature dared to enter; the police had given up all attempts to find her; she was already reduced to half her size from weeping constantly, and so on and so forth!

But the facts were quite different. The evening by the Ganga when two hearts had come together had heralded more meetings between Sisirkumar and Kankabati. Then one day Kankabati landed up at Cornwallis Theatre by herself and made straight for

Sisirkumar's room. She was carrying a bag containing her clothes in one hand and held a cage with a mynah in the other.

As soon as the news reached the Star group they tried everything in their power to rectify the situation. They tried a police case at first, followed by a charge of abduction. But the police could not be of much help because Kankabati stated quite clearly that she was an adult, twenty-three years old. She was independent, had no guardians, and had come of her own free will without being forced by anybody. The police had no right to intrude on her personal life.

There followed a court case of breach of contract against her. Every day news of the hearing caused a ripple of excitement. The city could not boast of any significant entertainment other than the theatre. News of upcoming plays and gossip about theatre stars constituted a major part of popular discussions. Of course, the bioscope had been introduced a few years ago. But although it portrayed stories, they were silent. The characters felt like puppets and failed to draw an audience like live stage shows.

Both the theatres had employed well-known lawyers but Natya Mandir lost the case.

All said and done, Star Art Theatre had a strong argument. Kankabati was legally bound by her contract for three years. The British judge gave his final verdict, which clearly stated that during the specified period Kankabati could perform in Star Theatre alone and could not join Natya Mandir or any other theatre group. At the same time, Star Theatre could not force her to act because acting, after all, was a form of art. And no art worth its name could be created by force. Under the circumstances, if Kankabati so desired, she could remain quietly indoors during this period, but she would not have the right to act for any other theatre company. Also, being an adult, she had the right to reside wherever she chose.

Both parties had assembled in the courtroom on the final day. The Star group let out yells of triumph once the verdict was announced. The Natya Mandir group hung its head low in disappointment. Frankly speaking, the Star group had not gained anything positive from the decree. They were exultant simply because Sisirkumar's group's pride was dented. Moreover, the judge had also warned Sisirkumar not to go against the law.

Prabodhchandra Guha, the manager of Star Theatre, strutted out of the courtroom proudly, dressed in a pleated Shantipuri dhoti, a silk overshirt, socks and pump shoes, with a cane in his hand. As he walked out, his shoes creaking, he found Sisirkumar standing beneath a tree outside. Their eyes met but Sisirkumar turned his face away.

Prabodhchandra was older than Sisirkumar.

'Look here, Sisir Babu,' he said with a broad grin, 'listen to me. This kind of rivalry is pretty common in our line, isn't it? People are perpetually walking out of one group to join another. Why get annoyed about something that's part of the game? Personally, I consider you a great actor and I admire your talent. By the way, I have some excellent cheroot with me. Would you like to try one?'

'Have you come here to add insult to injury?' asked Sisirkumar.

Prabodhchandra's smile grew broader as he said, 'Oh no, I haven't! I was convinced you would lose the case. What do you plan to do next? If you don't mind telling me, that is.'

'Not at all,' said Sisirkumar, 'I intend to appeal.'

'And if you lose again?'

'I shall go to the High Court. And if I lose there, to the Supreme Court.'

'But all that will take time! How long do you intend to carry on like this?'

'Until that girl is a tottering old dame.'

'But it will cost you a fortune!'

'I don't care. I'm prepared to lose all I have for her sake.'

'I know you are capable of that. A man of your magnanimity can afford to play ducks and drakes with his life. We are ordinary mortals and cannot take such risks. We always have to look out for profit in the long run.'

He took out a leather case from his pocket, extracted a Havana cheroot and shoved it into Sisirkumar's hand. Then he said, 'I am releasing the girl. You can have her.'

Sisirkumar frowned.

'We shall not pursue the case,' said Prabodhchandra. 'Enough money has already gone down the drain. Besides, we're not even sure if the girl can really act. And she is far too tall to suit our heroes. You can try her out and find out if she's any good. But you'd better pay us some money. Not a large amount. Just three thousand will do.'

'Are you transacting at a cattle-fair?' said Sisirkumar. 'Do you really expect me to buy her for hard cash?'

'Oh no, no!' said Prabodhchandra, pretending to look ashamed. 'I meant it as compensation. After all, we've had to shell out a lot of money for this case.'

'When you had stolen the rights of *Sita* in such an underhand manner I had to shell out a lot of money, too, towards the sets and so on,' said Sisirkumar. 'Did you pay me any compensation then?'

'But you did put those sets to good use eventually when you played your version of *Sita*,' said Prabodhchandra. 'Hasn't it been your lucky mascot? You have always performed it to a full house. There's no doubt that I feel envious of your unmitigated success. But, brother, there's no denying the fact that I also feel proud of you for having raised the bar of Bengali theatre.'

'Thanks,' said Sisirkumar, his voice softening.

Prabodhchandra patted him on the back and said, 'I know what the girl means to you besides her possible acting talent. I don't want to play a spoilsport. She is all yours. No hard feelings.'

Everyone was aware of the court verdict, but no one had any inkling about what Prabodhchandra had told Sisirkumar. Sisirkumar was in no mood for discussion. He headed straight home from the court.

Sisirkumar had rented a house close to the theatre, where Kankabati had now set up home.

Sisirkumar walked in to find her feeding grams to her mynah. He feigned a depressed look and glumly said, 'Have you heard the news, Kanka? We've lost, hook, line and sinker.'

Kankabati looked up. 'Bishu was here a little while ago. I've heard everything from him. But we haven't lost at all!'

'What do you mean? Haven't you heard? The judge has given the verdict that you will not be permitted to join Natya Mandir before the three years are up?'

'But he has not ordered me to leave you,' she said with a bright smile. 'As a matter of fact, no one can take me away from you now. You had said it too. Never mind if I cannot perform on stage. I have you and that's more than enough.'

'You shall always be mine,' said Sisirkumar. 'I shall make you the queen of the Bengali theatre.'

'Who's that? Who is it?' said the mynah in a voice that sounded startlingly human.

Sisirkumar burst out laughing. 'Why does it always say

that?' he asked. 'Have you not taught it to utter the names of Lord Krishna?'

'She refuses to learn anything I try to teach,' said Kankabati. 'I can't imagine where the wretched bird picked up these words.'

Sisirkumar knelt before the cage and said, 'Mynah, say, "Bharatnari has arrived."'

Never before had so many write-ups and rumours done the rounds about a girl who had, graduate or not, not yet made an appearance on stage. There was simply no end to people's curiosity about her. Sisirkumar realized that she should be introduced while this interest was uppermost on people's minds.

Natya Mandir was readying itself to present the play *Digbijayee* (Conqueror of the World) on a really large scale. The historical play written by Jogeshchandra Choudhury had a gripping plot and colourful characters. It was quite evident from the rehearsals that the role of Nadir Shah would add yet another feather to Sisirkumar's cap.

But what was Kankabati's role?

Charushila and Harisundari Blackie were playing the two female leads, Siraji Begum and Sultana Begum. There was no question of replacing either of them. Charushila was still riding the crest of popularity following her superb portrayal in *Shoroshi*. She was considered a real asset to Natya Mandir along with Prabha. Prabha fell ill often these days but Harisundari Blackie was a veteran and played every role with ease.

All actresses started off in supporting roles, without any dialogues. Gradually they were assigned a few lines according to their talent. It was unheard of for any actress to play the lead right after joining the group. Besides, why would other actresses put up with it? Kankabati was an educated girl from a good family and the other actresses found it difficult to befriend her. But they dared not treat her with contempt as she was the boss's beloved.

After a great deal of deliberation, Sisirkumar finally managed to solve the problem by introducing her in the new play in an entirely new role. He added a new character without changing any of the existing roles. All plays composed by Jogeshchandra were more or less half-written by Sisirkumar. However, he never took credit for them. In fact, it was Sisirkumar who worked out the scene transitions and also composed many of the dialogues. The new character introduced by Sisirkumar in *Digbijayee* was called 'Bharatnari'. All the other characters in the play were Muslims but this character, without a name, remained secular. She represented the soul of India and roamed from place to place singing songs, all of them composed by Rabindranath and selected carefully by Sisirkumar himself. Eventually, Kankabati's name was also included in the posters.

Digbijayee had a grand ceremonial inauguration. All the tickets were sold out in advance.

Kankabati made her first stage appearance when she walked in, singing, 'Gram chhara oi rangamatir path (The red, muddy path beyond the village . . .)'

The audience broke into applause as soon as the song was over, and Kankabati emerged victorious from her ordeal by fire.

Sisirkumar was outstanding. As Nadir Shah he surpassed all his previous performances. No one could hold a candle to him in the world of theatre. Yet, despite her brief appearance, Kankabati managed to leave a definite impression in the hearts of her viewers.

Just as Sisikumar as a young boy had watched Girishchandra Ghosh perform with great admiration, a young teenager named Shambhu Mitra came more than once to watch Sisirkumar perform. He was spellbound by Sisirkumar's brilliant performance as Nadir Shah, by his bold, royal gait as well as the extraordinary modulation of his rich baritone.

11

Rabindranath Once Again

Natya Mandir managed to earn some profits after presenting a series of hits, which was unusual for them.

In the meantime, Kankabati had succeeded in charming her audience once again by singing in the newly composed musical *Basanta Leela*. She had also acted in *Bisarjan*, *Buddhadeb-charit* and Saratchandra's *Palli Samaj*, performing each role commendably. But Sisirkumar's insistence on giving her an unsuitable role in *Bisarjan* had been considered absurd by critics and they had torn him to shreds for his decision.

Kankabati had played the role of Krishna in *Basanta Leela*, which had many songs but no dialogue and had been able to carry it off well. But in *Bisarjan* Sisirkumar had cast her as Jai Singh, which had turned out to be a real blunder. Although men had conventionally played female roles, the audience was just not prepared to accept the reverse. A woman playing the role of a man was unthinkable.

Kankabati succeeded in living down the blunder with her other performances. It was customary for theatre groups to repeat performances of earlier successful plays alongside that of new ones. Natya Mandir had a string of such plays – *Sita, Alamgir, Prafulla, Sadhabar Ekadashi* – and Kankabati stepped in whenever the actresses who had earlier played the lead roles and earned themselves a name were unavailable. It meant a great deal of hard work under the direct tutelage of Sisirkumar. But by now Kankabati knew all the popular female roles by heart and could perform them with the utmost ease. Often, just to get Kankabati into trouble, Prabha and Charushila would pretend to be ill even though a performance had been announced.

A livid Sisirkumar would then send for Kankabati and ask, 'Can you play the lead in *Sita* tonight?'

Kankabati would nod a determined yes. All this time Prabha's name had been inseparable from that of Sita. But Kankabati proved she was equal to the challenge and succeeded in winning the hearts of her audience with her performance. There was nothing she would not do for Sisirkumar.

With funds now in place, Sisirkumar decided to present yet another play by Rabindranath: *Tapati*.

His friends frowned upon his decision. *Tapati*? It was a very difficult play and would be far beyond the comprehension of the viewers.

'But why?' asked Sisirkumar. 'The poet himself had staged it sometime ago. I have wanted to stage the play ever since, giving it a new interpretation.'

'But the poet had staged it in his own house at Jorasanko,'

said Sourindramohan. 'There was no question of tickets. Only a select few had been invited to watch it. Any play would succeed under the circumstances.'

'A theatre cannot run unless the galleries are full,' added Hemendrakumar, 'and the gallery crowd would not be able to appreciate a play like *Tapati*. The only people to come and see it would be the ones who receive free passes from you.'

'Star's *Mantrashakti* is proving to be an enormous crowd-puller,' said Aleek. 'It has the audience in tears every time. If we are to compete with Star we should present something sentimental too.'

But their comments made Sisirkumar see red.

'I know the stage is meant to be a business like any other but I refuse to play to the gallery just for the heck of it,' he said. 'I joined this profession to present fine plays. I know some of our plays have been commercially successful, bringing in good money, but my heart was not in all of them. Take, for instance, Sarat-da's *Roma*, based on his *Palli Samaj*. Would you call that a good play? I wouldn't! Sometimes I even hate playing the role of Ram, with his loud dialogues, although it is a money-spinner. No, no, say what you will, but I am determined to stage *Tapati* even if it means a loss. Why won't the audience accept it? We have to make an effort to modify their taste and make such plays acceptable. Who else is likely to do it? Star? Huh!'

'Sisir, don't forget that Natya Mandir is a limited company,' warned Hemendrakumar. 'The other partners might object to a gamble like this.'

'But I had made it a precondition that the other partners are to leave the selection of plays entirely to me,' said Sisirkumar. 'so they can't raise any objections now.'

When he reached home he asked Kankabati, 'Have you read *Tapati*?'

'Yes, I have,' she said. 'The first version of the play was called *Raja O Rani*. I saw it being performed in Thakurbari the other day.'

'Couldn't we stage the play too?' asked Sisirkumar.

'Please do,' cried Kankabati, excited. 'I shall play the role of Bipasha.'

'Yes, Bipasha would suit you,' said Sisirkumar. 'The role of queen Sumitra is a much bigger one, of course. It has a lot of drama but no songs. Prabha could do it. Bipasha has to sing several songs in the play.'

'The great poet himself had played King Vikram. His movements had been rather restricted due to his age,' said Kankabati.

'But he succeeded in carrying it through despite his age,' said Sisirkumar. 'I told him the other day, "Please do *Raktakarabi* the next time," and he had replied, "That's a feat beyond me now. I'll find it too tough. But you are welcome to try it if you like. You have my permission to do it." It is my sincere wish that if *Tapati* succeeds I shall stage *Raktakarabi* next.'

'No one has staged his *Muktadhara* either,' said Kankabati.

'You'd better start learning Bipasha's songs,' said Sisirkumar. 'I'll ask Dinu Babu or someone else from Shantiniketan to teach you.'

'I already know two of the songs,' said Kankabati.

'Go on, sing one of them for me now,' said Sisirkumar eagerly. 'It will help create the mood for me.'

'Should I?' said Kankabati. 'But not here. Let's go to the terrace.'

The mynah spoke again from its cage on the veranda. 'Who has come? Who is it?'

'Don't you know who I am even now?' asked Sisirkumar teasingly.

'You stupid bird, say, "Welcome my love, welcome",' shouted Kankabati.

There was a school next door. It was now in complete darkness. On the other side of the road stood the palatial residence and estate of the Mitters. It had a fountain in the centre of the garden with diffused lights all around it. The enormous house had very few residents now.

A full moon shone above. The heady scent of bakul flowers growing in the Mitters's gardens wafted across.

Kankabati leaned against the terrace wall and began to sing:

'Your seat lies vacant today
Oh brave one, take your place . . .'

'Wait,' said Sisirkumar after the song was over. 'Let me send for a glass and the bottle. I shall listen to the other one then.'

'Must you drink again tonight?' asked Kankabati. 'You drank last night too.'

Sisirkumar laughed. 'Do you expect me not to drink just because I drank last night? Last night I'd also eaten rice, drunk water and smoked my cheroot! What about that? Besides, I drink far less now, after *you* came into my life. My friends tease me, say I am bewitched, that you have turned me into a sheep! Otherwise, why would Sisir Bhaduri scuttle back home the moment the clock struck nine?'

'Why don't your friends go home too?' asked Kankabati, annoyed.

Sisirkumar gently held her chin and said, 'Because, they don't have such a beautiful nightingale waiting for them at home.'

He walked up to the staircase and called out to Bhikha, who immediately brought a bottle, glass and water to the terrace.

Sisirkumar poured a peg of whisky into his glass and took a sip. 'You have never even tasted it,' he said. 'Do you know that many of the actresses drink? And every one of them smokes. I hate seeing them smoking, but no amount of scolding will make them give it up. Just think, how will the audience feel if they see the queen puffing away in the wings?'

Kankabati shook her head. Then she said, 'The moonlight bathing me in its glow is enough to make me intoxicated. I don't need anything else.'

'Go on, sing the other song now,' said Sisirkumar.

Kankabati obliged.

'Jago jago alasha-shayana-bilagna . . .
Awake, all ye wrapped in languid slumber'

Sisirkumar listened, mesmerized, losing himself completely in the music. When the song ended he kept quiet for a while and then said to himself, '"Alasha-shayana-bilagna" . . . what exquisite use of language!'

Then he sat up straight and said, 'Listen, Kanka, "alasha-shayana-bilagna" is a single word and you should sing it like that. If you pause for a breath in between, the meaning changes. Similarly, "tamasha-gahana-nimagna" (sunk in darkness deep) is a single word. Please sing these two lines again.'

That was the beginning of her training.

Kankabati took hardly any time to pick up the right style but the other actors and actresses had to be taught afresh, line by line, word by word. Sisirkumar patiently explained the fundamental difference between the language used by Jogeshchandra or Khirodprasad and that used by Rabindranath, and the consequent difference in pronunciation of the words they used. He explained that when it came to a composition by Rabindranath the words should be clearly pronounced and not enunciated with a sing-song drawl. Nor could they be accompanied by too many physical gestures.

Sisirkumar poured his heart and soul into this project, pushing himself as never before. Everything was put on hold; preparing whole-heartedly for *Tapati* took precedence over all else.

No palace or temple was painted on the backdrop. Initially, Sisirkumar's idea was to have a white screen for the backdrop, but when he watched a rehearsal in the auditorium he found that this made the stage look too bare. Eventually he asked an artist to paint the sun god's idol from the Konarak temple as a symbol of royal power. The costumes were changed too. Traditionally actors playing the role of kings, queens or the king's men dressed up in flamboyant and glittering clothes and jewellery. Sisirkumar decided to do away with this and had a completely different set of costumes specially tailored for the cast. Here the queen was a rebel so she would not wear any jewellery at all. The climax of the play was to have a fire and no stone was left unturned to ensure that the fire looked real.

Sisirkumar not only worked with all his might but also spent a lot of money to perfect his presentation. The other partners tried to stop him at every step but failed in their attempts. Sisirkumar's eagerness inspired all the actors and actresses to put in their best effort and to achieve, as far as possible, the required level of perfection.

Large posters were put up announcing the inauguration of the play.

The night of their inaugural show arrived. As usual, more than half the viewers were invited guests consisting of the cream of society. Although Rabindranath was abroad at the time, a big group from the Tagore family attended the show, including Gaganendranath and Abanindranath. A large group from Shantiniketan came too. The boys from *Kallol* and *Bharati* also turned out in full force.

The programme commenced with the blowing of conch shells. When the curtains were drawn aside, revealing the stage, the audience gasped in surprise. They had never seen such tasteful and artistic stage decor in professional theatre before.

People followed the European custom of clapping their hands to express their admiration. Frequent waves of applause indicated that the play was sure to be a hit. Those who had seen Rabindranath play King Vikram admitted that Sisirkumar had given the character a fresh dimension. The audience applauded every song sung by Kankabati, recognizing Rabindrasangeet at its best. This was the real thing! Prabha also received her share of applause for a heartwarming portrayal of her role.

But something remarkable happened at the end of the show. After the concluding scene with the fire, the final curtain was drawn, but many among the audience remained seated, not realizing that the play had ended. They had seen the queen embrace the fire but had not realized that it was meant to symbolize the end. They expected the play to continue, for there to be a scene involving a verbal expression of grief. Eventually, Sisirkumar had to come out and announce that the play was over.

The next morning all the newspapers were full of praise for *Tapati*. The critics had only unstinted praise for the show this time. In fact, both scholars and critics thought highly of the presentation and called it a milestone in Bengali theatre. Sisirkumar's other plays had been successful too, but this one was in a different league altogether. The world of theatre would continue to be proud of such a well-presented production for years to come.

But ordinary viewers reacted differently and their opinion spread like wildfire. The number of viewers declined drastically from the third night. Only ninety-five tickets were sold on the fifth night, dropping down to a mere twenty on the sixth, most of whom walked out after the third scene, leaving just about seven viewers. The auditorium looked almost empty from the top.

Prabha was the first to notice when she peeped out from the wings.

'Nearly all the chairs are empty,' she whispered tearfully. 'For whom shall I act?'

Sisirkumar stood next to her, smoking his cheroot in grim silence. He was well aware of the situation.

'Look at those empty chairs and do your very best,' he said. 'Show me what you can do.'

Kankabati embraced Prabha and whispered, 'Didi, we are supposed to enact a role in the play. We are not meant to think of our audience at that time. But god above will be a witness of our best efforts.'

Sisirkumar once thought of going into the green room and having a drink or two, but ultimately decided against it. He walked on to the stage instead and, facing the empty chairs, gave the best performance of his life.

After the last scene, Hemendrakumar rose from his seat at the back of the hall and came forward clapping his hands.

'Superb!' he cried. 'Bravo, Sisir! I have been here every night since the play opened but I've never seen you perform so exceptionally before. *Tapati* has been so well produced that it can compare with the finest productions in the world. I am sure Rabindranath would have been delighted had he seen it. Abanindranath and the others also praised it highly. But, Sisir, the number of viewers has dwindled to just seven. And all of them are your friends who received free passes. How can you possibly run the play under such circumstances? You had hoped to improve the taste of the viewers but the long years of foreign domination have corrupted it totally and absolutely. The only things they are able to appreciate are loud melodrama and crude buffoonery. Sisir, I feel really sad today. All your toil and efforts have been in vain.'

Sisirkumar took off the crown from his head and held it in his hand. Then he said, 'Why should you feel sad, Hemen? As you just said, I have seven friends to stand by me. There are many who do not have even that much. Come up, Hemen. We shall celebrate tonight.'

Then he turned back and called, 'Where are you, Aleek? Set up the glasses.'

All his friends knew that this apparent calm augured a turbulent storm ahead. And that is exactly what happened. After a long time Sisirkumar began drinking like a man possessed. Neither Kankabati nor any of his friends could stop him. It went on for days on end.

Then, it was almost as if he awakened from slumber amidst a heap of ruins.

There were no plays ready for presentation. The old ones had been done to death. Once a play had flopped it became exceedingly difficult for any theatre to pick up the reins once again. But the running expenses had to be met no matter what. All their capital had been spent and they had to begin borrowing money. Judging the situation, many of the old and experienced actors and actresses left Natya Mandir and joined other theatre groups. Charushila had never been able to accept Kankabati's importance in Natya Mandir. She not only left the group but also filed a case against Natya Mandir for failing to settle her dues.

When Sisirkumar returned to his senses, he saw that those gathered around him were not his friends. Only creditors awaited him. The theatre-owners were growing impatient too. The auditorium was lit up after a long break and Sisirkumar was obliged to perform his old plays one after the other. But again they failed to attract an audience. Then he took to presenting two plays during a show instead of one, but even this bait did not work. Sisirkumar realized that he could not hope to sail this ship for long. It was damaged beyond repair.

Sita and *Shoroshi* had been the two most popular plays presented by Sisirkumar. He decided to stage both on a Saturday. The hall was reasonably packed this time.

After the concluding scene of *Sita,* Sisirkumar, still dressed as Ram, parted the curtains and stood facing the audience.

He folded his hands and said, 'Ladies and gentlemen, I would like to speak a few words before the next play. Please be kind enough to listen to me.

'This is our last presentation in this auditorium. We shall never perform on this stage again. But please don't think that it marks the end of my Natya Mandir. Natya Mandir will live on although we are leaving this theatre. It will not be possible for us to present plays in Calcutta until the right opportunity comes our way. Destiny alone can determine when we shall be able to perform before you once again.

'I feel you deserve to know why we are leaving this place. The phenomenon that goes by the name of "landlordism" is becoming increasingly pronounced in Calcutta. We have to pay a rent of three thousand two hundred and fifty rupees every month for this building. It is now impossible for us to meet our running expenses after paying such a high amount. The price of tickets is already too high for a country like ours and we cannot possibly raise it further.

'Theatre is exotic. This system of sets, scenes, lights and so on is a borrowed Western concept. If we were a free nation we could have developed the jatra, our indigenous form of art, and showcased it before the rest of the world. And the plays written to suit the jatra form would have been ours too, reflecting our culture with all its special nuances, similar to our keertan, baul songs or the patachitra of Kalighat. The Japanese perform plays that are unique to them. We have nothing special to boast of.

'We had started Natya Mandir with many dreams and ideas in our hearts. It was not just created by Sisir Bhaduri alone. Many friends took an active part in its creation. One of them was my close friend, the late Manilal Gangopadhyay, a writer of renown, and many others like him. Not even a fraction of our dreams has been realized yet. If we are to avoid blindly imitating the West, we need to go ahead with different kinds of experiments. But that requires funds, which we have not been able to raise. We made Natya Mandir a limited company but were only able to sell shares amounting to twenty-seven thousand rupees. We now have to face the inevitable consequence of being in debt. We have to shell out the interest on that loan plus the annual rent for this building, which is forty thousand rupees a year. This has made it increasingly difficult for us to continue. And we haven't moved any closer to our goal. Our situation is like that horse in Charles Dickens's novel, "The horse is going to go, but it's not going." I am an actor and know all about the stage but I know nothing about business.

Anyway, I haven't lost all hope as yet. The image of stagecraft that I have set in my heart with blood and tears shall be a reality some day. I have every hope that I shall be able to build something to the satisfaction of all theatre lovers before I breathe my last. My heartfelt thanks to all our patrons; to all the viewers who bought tickets; to all who have been kind to us and loved us.'

Sisirkumar ended his long address, but for the first time a speech he had made did not meet with applause. Deep sighs were heard from many in the audience, followed by an unnatural silence.

He returned to the green room to put on make-up for what was to be his final performance in this theatre. In a short while Prabodhchandra Guha appeared at the door, cane in hand.

'May I have a few words with you, Sisir Babu?' he asked, clearing his throat.

Sisirkumar turned his head and looked at him without a word.

Prabodhchandra entered the room, pulled a stool and sat very close to him.

'We already knew that you were leaving this theatre tonight,' he told Sisirkumar, 'but what do you plan to do next?'

'Well, I'm not likely to become a hermit,' Sisirkumar replied sarcastically.

'I know that too,' said Prabodhchandra. 'You are not cut out to be one. I have a proposal for you. Please join the Star.'

Sisirkumar raised his brows, 'The Star?'

'It's your eternal enemy, isn't it?' asked Prabodhchandra, smiling broadly. 'Listen to me, brother. We are neither friends nor enemies. We are just travellers on the same path. Some of us have forged ahead while some are lagging behind. There is bound to be competition between us. But we cannot accept a great actor like you leaving the stage and walking out of the race altogether. If we allowed that, it would mean that we are not genuine theatre lovers. We have come to invite you, with due respect, to join us at Star instead.'

'But you already have Ahindra Babu who always plays the lead,' said Sisirkumar. 'What shall I do there? You must know that a tiger and a lion cannot co-exist in the same forest.'

'Yes, I do know that,' said Prabodhchandra, 'but we've been having problems with him of late because he has been demanding too much. Besides, he is joining Minerva. Which means you shall be the sole lion in Star.'

'But . . . but . . . Is this your personal opinion?' asked Sisirkumar. 'I know that you have a boss, Aparesh Mukherjee. Does he want me in too?'

'Do you think I have come here without consulting him?' asked Prabodhchandra. 'He is equally keen to have you. He is a playwright himself and a highly successful one. Which playwright wouldn't want to have an actor like you? He has told me several times in the past that although Ahindra is a very good actor, he cannot hold a candle to Sisir Bhaduri. Sisir is in a class by himself. I know we've been your archrivals. But all of us are well aware that you are the greatest actor of this era.'

'Don't say that,' protested Sisirkumar, 'the greatest actor of our time is Rabindranath.'

'Let's leave him out of this. He is unique in every way,' said Prabodhchandra. 'Listen to me. Aparesh Babu wanted to come himself to request you to join us. But I advised him against it since it wouldn't have looked good. Please agree to our proposal, Sisir. I know you don't have funds at the moment. We shall send you an advance tomorrow itself.'

'Do you want me alone?' asked Sisirkumar after a pause. 'I have a group, none of whom will have a job from tomorrow. I can't possibly ditch them like this. It would be sheer treachery.'

'No, no, not at all! Who says you have to join us alone? You are welcome to bring your group as well,' said Prabodhchandra. 'Jogesh, Jiban Ganguly, Rabi Ray, Prabha, Kankabati and anyone else you care to bring along. Kanakabati was supposed to join Star in any case, remember? But you abducted her. Well, she will be one of *our* stars now! A case of sweet revenge, don't you think? Sweet revenge indeed! Ha ha ha!'

12

New York, 27 October 1930

It started snowing quite suddenly at dawn, heralding the advent of an early winter.

New York never seemed to sleep. One could hear cars and vehicles all through the night. The falling snow made patterns on the roofs of cars, which looked like the flower-decked vehicles bridegrooms rode back in Calcutta.

Kankabati stood gazing at the city from the window of an eleventh-floor apartment. Even the sweater and shawl over her sari failed to keep her adequately warm. In fact, none of them had been able to sleep well at night although the fireplace in the room had been raging. Only close proximity to the fire provided some warmth to their limbs, but they began to shiver as soon as they moved away even a little bit.

When the troupe had complained about the cold on the very first night of their arrival, Eric Elliot had frowned and told them, 'Everyone in this city lights a fire in the room and goes to sleep under blankets. You people seem to be extra sensitive to the cold.'

Elliot was not wrong. People coming to America from a tropical country were bound to feel the cold more acutely than the locals. When Sisirkumar's group left Calcutta in September the weather had been hot and sweaty. From Calcutta they had taken a train to Karachi, where it was equally hot. The weather they had faced during their voyage over the Indian Ocean had been hot too, unbearably so at times. They had their first brush with the cold weather and chilly breeze only after they sailed into the Atlantic.

They had been astonished at the sight of the tall skyscrapers here. A building with eleven floors seemed simply incredible. And the building next to it had twenty storeys! The houses seemed like man-made monoliths.

Sisirkumar stepped out of his bath in a striped dressing gown. It was obvious that he didn't feel the cold quite so much.

Kankabati turned her head and asked, 'How could you possibly bathe in this weather? I'm dying of the cold.'

'There's hot water in there. You should take a bath too,' said Sisirkumar. 'You won't feel so cold then.'

'Oh no, I'd rather give it a miss today,' said Kankabati.

'Wear your socks, dear,' ordered Sisirkumar. 'The feet are the most sensitive to cold.'

'Prabha-didi hasn't stirred from her bed,' said Kankabati. 'I went to her room a little while ago. She told me she feels frozen the moment she gets out of bed.'

'That won't do,' said Sisirkumar. 'Everyone has to get up and get dressed. You know, you should dance a few steps as soon as you get up. Dancing warms up your body. This is how you should do it.'

Sisirkumar raised his arms in the air and began jumping

about and dancing. Kankabati burst out laughing at his antics, then ran to him and held him in a tight embrace.

Laying her cheek against his, she whispered, 'You don't feel the cold if you stay like this either.'

'But my darling, I can't spend the rest of the day holding you in my arms,' said Sisirkumar. 'Don't you remember? We have our dress rehearsal today.'

Kankabati let go of him and moved away.

'Oh dear, so soon?' she asked apprehensively. 'We've only just arrived . . .'

'The more we delay the more money we'll have to spend,' said Sisirkumar. 'The hall has already been booked. All the tickets have sold out for the first week. The cheapest ticket costs twelve dollars, which means thirty-six rupees. Just imagine, people here are actually willing to spend that much for a stage show! Why, in our country, the most expensive seat costs five rupees.'

'Do you think we'll be able to perform successfully?' asked Kankabati hesitantly.

Sisirkumar too had his doubts.

The reception that his group had received on arrival had been too wonderful for words.

Their ship had reached the harbour at night. The next morning the mayor was there to receive them along with the Grand Duchess Marie of Russia, Princess Rospigliosi and other distinguished guests. As soon as the Indian group alighted, dressed in dhotis and saris, every one of them was presented with a bouquet. Then they were seated in six Rolls Royce cars and driven through Broadway with police cars escorting them in front and at the rear. Cheering crowds thronged both sides of the street.

Satu Sen, a young man with a plum job in New York had also come to receive them at the dock. He sat beside Sisirkumar in the car and said, 'Dada I've never witnessed such a grand reception being given to any Indian before. You must be aware that Rabindranath is also here now. But even he hasn't enjoyed a grand welcome like yours.'

'In that case, why have we been singled out for such an honour?' asked Sisirkumar. 'We are nothing more than a small theatre group.'

'But you are considered to be a wonder,' replied Satu Sen. 'Ordinary Americans hardly ever come across Indians. Most of them are under the impression that Indian women are either kept under lock and key or burnt as a sati; that young children who enter the river are all devoured by crocodiles; that the roads in India are packed with sadhus and yogis, tigers and snakes. They are clueless about our art, culture, literature or music.'

'Indeed?'

'Yes. Do you know what a newspaper had reported a few days ago? That you are a raja married to a Rajasthani girl,' said Satu Sen. 'Words like "raja" and "Rajasthani" are quite novel to them. They've also said that you are coming here to dance with a troupe of nautch girls!' Sisirkumar had burst out laughing at his words.

Their trip to America had been a lucky coincidence. It was Satu Sen who had initially attempted to bring them over here.

In New York, several theatres in Broadway regularly put up plays. They included theatre groups not just from America but also from other countries, especially Europe. A group from Japan had recently created quite a sensation. It was the impresarios who made arrangements to bring in theatre groups from other countries at their own risk.

Having lived in New York for a while, Satu Sen had wondered why an Indian group too could not come there to perform. India had a rich tradition of theatre and Sisirkumar Bhaduri was no less talented than any other world-famous actor. Satu Sen had initially come to America to learn stage direction from the famous theatre-person Boleslavsky. He was now the technical director of the New York Laboratory Theatre and was well acquainted with many important people in the theatre circle.

He had got in touch with Miss Elizabeth Marberry, a well-known impresario. Initially she had shown some interest but could not make up her mind about Sisirkumar since no one personally known to her had seen him act or evaluated the acting abilities of his group. She hadn't shown much enthusiasm beyond the initial exchange of letters.

A few months later, a travelling theatre group from Australia broke their journey at Calcutta on their way home. Eric Elliot, their main actor, was keen to see a play in Calcutta. In those days, English plays would usually be performed in the European locality. But Eric wanted to see an original Indian play. A reporter from the *Statesman* suggested he watch Sisirkumar Bhaduri perform in Natya Mandir.

Natya Mandir was staging *Raghubir* at the time. Eric Elliot was greatly impressed by the performance though he could not understand the language. He came in to congratulate Sisirkumar at the end of the show and said, 'I realize that I am in the presence of a very great artiste.' He was pleasantly surprised to discover Sisirkumar's deep knowledge of English theatre.

Before the year was out Eric Elliot returned to Calcutta once again. This time he made it a point to watch *Sita, Alamgir, Shoroshi, Digbijayee* and all the other Natya Mandir productions. It became an obsession with him and he picked up quite a bit of Bengali and Hindi in the process.

Elliot and his group headed to New York from Calcutta. Miss Marberry was Elliot's impresario too. One day, during a conversation, Elliot mentioned Indian plays and Sisirkumar's group. Miss Marberry recalled having heard the name before. She realized that the man must be really talented if a white actor was speaking so highly of him.

A letter was sent out to Sisirkumar from Miss Marberry's assistant Karl Reed, inviting him to perform *Sita* at Broadway. The Roosevelt Company would bear all the expenses, provided they agreed to present the show for a few nights running and the play had at least seven or eight dance performances by the actresses.

The letter had left Sisirkumar in a quandary. The prospect of travelling so far with such a big group was by no means an easy task. None of them had travelled abroad before; in fact, many of them had never stepped out of Bengal. More than half his actors and actresses did not know a word of English.

Sisirkumar no longer had his own Natya Mandir and was now a part of Star's Art Theatre. His shows were still a great success but his heart was not in his work. Once, his *Tapati* had flopped miserably against Star's *Mantrashakti*. Now Sisirkumar played the lead in the same *Mantrashakti* and drew double the number of people to watch the shows. But he considered this to be a cruel joke on destiny's part. He realized that he could not remain in Star for long, and accepted Reed's invitation to America, something Kankabati had always wished for.

He found it very challenging to put together a special team for the project. Most of the artists whom he had trained himself refused to go. Even the thought of a handsome remuneration did not tempt them. Everyone knew that America was a rich and glamorous country full of wonderful sights. But none of them felt adventurous enough to travel so far for the sake of seeing the country. Some of them remarked, 'Goodness me, it's such a cold country! It keeps snowing all the time. We have no wish to go there and freeze to death.' Some others said, 'You don't get rice there and I simply cannot live without eating rice twice a day.' Some others commented, 'People there are said to live on beef alone as one can't get any other meat or fish. I've no wish to lose my caste by eating beef there.' Finally, one of them said, 'They are known to throw stones at dark people the moment they see them on the streets. I'm as dark as an umbrella so there can't be any question of my going.' Only a handful were keen to go just for the sake of seeing a new country. They were not even interested in the money being offered. But none of them had ever acted before. Eventually Sisirkumar was compelled to include some of them in his team, hoping to coach them before the actual show.

Actresses had been even more difficult to find. None of the well known women agreed to go except for Kankabati and Prabha. But, according to the contract, it was essential to have at least eight or ten girls in the group. The American audience would find Kankabati beautiful not just because of her features but also because she had a wonderful figure. Prabha was slim, although she did not have Kankabati's hourglass torso, and would pass muster. But where was he to find the others? Eventually, Sisirkumar was compelled to pick up some plain Janes from the red light area of Sonagachhi and give most of them fresh stage names. They were named Uma (Patal, in reality), Sarala (Benki), Parimal (Panchi), Bela Rani, Kalidasi, Kamala (Handu), Hena (Nimki) and Jadu (Chhoto Rakhali). None of them, except for two, knew how to dance.

Sisirkumar had assumed that they would get at least ten days after reaching New York. They would rehearse the play properly during that time. He had no idea that the dates had been fixed already and the tickets sold out. When Karl Reed was told about rehearsals he was surprised and exclaimed, 'What a strange request! I've heard that this play has already run for three hundred nights. Why do you need a rehearsal then?'

Reed did not realize that no matter how many nights it had run in Calcutta, this was a whole new ball game – a new country with new surroundings that they needed to get accustomed to. Many of them had suffered violent seasickness during the journey and were still reeling. Besides, they were yet to get used to the cold weather. The roads here were so full of traffic that no one felt brave enough to venture out alone to even buy a cake of soap.

They were to have a full dress rehearsal within three days of arriving, and the first show was scheduled for the day after that. Eric had already warned Sisirkumar that dress rehearsals here were meant to be exactly like the proper show with no interruptions in between; no talking and no directions. The dress rehearsal was to take place in Broadway's famous Biltmore Theatre. No one in Sisirkumar's team had ever seen such an enormous entrance before. On the outer wall was written in six-inch bold letters:

THE WIZARD OF THE INDIAN STAGE WITH
A BAND OF NAUTCH GIRLS AT BROADWAY

Along with it was a huge poster depicting a king, holding a bow and arrows, and a group of longhaired dancers, bare up to the thighs, none of whom looked the least bit Indian.

There was a huge dome inside the hall decorated with rich paintings. Images of two flying fairies hung from the ceiling, ostensibly made of gold.

Despite the grandeur, the auditorium was not a particularly large one. There were about five or six hundred seats. There were galleries in the rear on the first and second floors and a few boxes on each side.

Sisirkumar's team gaped at everything, just the way villagers do when they come to the city for the first time. They were dumbstruck at the sight of so much grandeur.

In order to make them feel comfortable, Sisirkumar tapped Jogeshchandra's shoulder, saying, 'You know, Jogesh-da, Abraham Lincoln, the first president of America, was murdered by an actor called Booth. Lincoln was watching a play from a similar box when the actor jumped towards him from the stage and shot him at close range.'

'My goodness!' cried Jogeshchandra looking up. 'How did he manage to jump so high?'

'He swung from a rope,' replied Sisirkumar.

Srish Chatterjee, a new recruit, asked from the side, 'Baro Babu, are they likely to have a bathroom in this grand place?'

'Of course there must be one,' said Sisirkumar impatiently. 'Do you think Americans don't urinate?'

'I need to visit the loo. How shall I find it?' asked Srish with a pathetic look.

'Go and look for it yourself,' shouted Sisirkumar. 'You don't expect me to find it for you, do you?'

Bechachandra, another newcomer, asked, 'Baro Babu, do you think there's any drinking water here? Do the people here drink water? Or do they have only beer?'

'Even if that's so, what's your objection? I saw you downing bottle after bottle in the ship,' remarked Sisirkumar.

'But beer cannot be the substitute for water when one is really thirsty,' said Becha. 'I'm dying of thirst.'

'Don't you have eyes?' snapped Sisirkumar. 'Did you not notice the tap on the side wall on our way in? There's a pile of paper cups beside it. Go and get it yourself and don't bother me with such inane matters.'

They had managed to obtain their stage paraphernalia from

Customs that very morning. There had been no time to check if everything had arrived in one piece. The scenes had somehow been put up. But there were no steps, no platforms and no screens at the back. They had decided that these would be made here but now there was no time. How were they to perform on a bare stage that had nothing?

And what about lighting? True, there were plenty of lights and some burly men waiting for instructions to operate them. But who would explain to them what was needed in the different scenes – where to focus, when to dim the lights and when to darken the stage. Marking up the manuscript and explaining the changes in detail would take a few days. And the manuscript was in Bengali, which they wouldn't understand at all.

Would someone need to stand beside the man in charge of the lights during the play and explain? Just a handful in the team could speak English, but the Americans could hardly understand their pronunciation, and vice versa. Sisirkumar was the only one who could have a conversation with them. But he would be on the stage, acting. How could he be giving these instructions at the same time? Finally Sisirkumar gave them some hurried directions.

Everything here worked with clockwork precision. The second bell had already rung. Before entering the stage Sisirkumar called Kankabati and Prabha together and said, 'Listen carefully. This is the first time that an Indian play is being performed on the American stage. We have to uphold the honour of Bengal. We have to do our very best. They may not understand our language but we must be able to cast a spell on them.'

The success of a play cannot depend on the acting talent of two or three actors alone. Each team member has a significant part to play and even a small slip up can ruin everything. It is the result of teamwork, and everyone, including those behind the scenes, whose names the audience never gets to know, plays a key role. Even during an emotional scene the smallest omission can mess things up. For instance, if the heroine says, 'Listen to the bells ringing,' and the bells don't ring, the audience is sure to burst out laughing.

In Calcutta, plays extended for four hours or more in order to please the audience and make them feel they were getting their money's worth. In fact, no one was likely to mind if the play continued through the night. But here in America they were told that the audience could not be expected to watch a play for more than three hours, at most. As a result, Sisirkumar had been compelled to shorten *Sita* quite drastically, cutting out complete scenes, which ruined the tempo of the play.

Miss Marberry was seated among the audience with Eric Elliot, Karl Reed, a few specially invited guests and magazine reporters. In Calcutta it was the norm to play the flute at the beginning of a play, but their flautist had not accompanied them here so they had brought a harmonium instead. However, Miss Marberry put her foot down the moment she heard it, saying the sound was far too shrill and harsh. It simply wouldn't do. If they really needed music someone would play the organ for them. Their professional tabla player had also not come. Sheetal, the make-up man had been asked to do the best he could. All he could do was play the tabla during dance performances.

The very first scene spelled disaster.

Srish was playing the role of Durmukh. He had been very keen on this trip and so had presented himself as an amateur actor used to being cast in neighbourhood plays in lead roles. They had laughed at this introduction but had included him in their team because he appeared to be a simple, straightforward man. Throughout their journey, whenever possible, Sisirkumar had tried to coach his team members for the roles they were to play, making them repeat the lines until they knew them by heart. But Srish had a sudden attack of stage fright and stammered and stuttered right from the beginning, forgetting all that he had learned. As a result, Sisirkumar spoke his own lines and also gave Srish his cue in a low voice. The acoustics here were excellent. The audience could hear everything. They soon realized what was happening and tittered loudly.

'My God, the man does not know his role!' shouted Karl Reed. 'And I hear the play has run there for three hundred nights.'

But Sisirkumar's team had to continue till the end of the scene despite the humiliation as there was no way out. Miss Marberry sent Sisirkumar an urgent message asking him what had happened to the dance sequence and telling him to bring it on immediately.

Sisirkumar had requested Eric Elliot to allow him to cut out the dance sequences because the girls in his group could not perform the kind of dance the audience here expected. Nor did they have the looks to carry off such a performance. Not one among them would have agreed to expose her thighs and even if anyone did it would not be a pretty sight!

But Eric had told him quite clearly that it would not be possible to do away with the dances. According to the newspaper reports, the 'nautch girls' in Sisirkumar's troup were devadasis from India, used to performing before the gods alone, not for others. What's more, all of them were beautiful virgins being brought to America after a great deal of persuasion on Sisirkumar's part. An opportunity to see them was likely to be an experience in itself.

Kankabati had tried her best to teach the girls the rudiments of dance while they were aboard the ship. Most of them were far too stiff to learn the steps. After a lot of effort all they could manage was to sway to the music.

Sisirkumar had wanted Kankabati to be part of the dance group so that the American audience could at least enjoy watching someone who danced beautifully. But Kankabati had refused.

Although he hated the idea, Sisirkumar was forced to send the girls onto the stage at the beginning of the second act. The song was sung from the wings.

It was a disaster from the word go. For one, their steps did not match. While some of the dancers looked flabby and uncouth the rest were reed thin. A few of the dark-complexioned girls had slapped on layers of powder on their faces in an attempt to look fair and merely ended up looking ghastly. Added to that were the loud beats of the tabla. It was grotesque.

For a few moments Miss Marberry could hardly believe her eyes! Were these hideous-looking girls really devadasis, the beautiful virgins who danced before the gods? And this dancing, such crude, stiff and random movements, could it possibly be the main attraction of this programme? She was livid.

'Eric, who are these women?' she cried wrathfully.

'Seems like a bunch of ghosts!' said Karl Reed from her side.

Eric Elliot looked downcast. 'I don't think Mr Bhaduri has been able to arrange for the right girls,' he said at last. 'We just have to replace them. I have an idea. I'll get hold of some Mexican girls this evening. Many of them have oriental looks and some wear their hair long. They might be able to pull it off with a little make-up.'

'Mexican girls?' cried Miss Marberry. 'Do you think you'll succeed in fooling the drama critics and pass them off as Indians?'

The dancing group had left the stage, making way for the second scene, that of the hermitage. Sage Valmiki made an entrance with Lav and Kush. Sisirkumar had been forced to cut out the scene in between, making it virtually impossible for the audience to understand that eighteen years had passed in between. No one could comprehend the dialogues, nor could they follow the actions.

In India even little children were familiar with the story of the *Ramayana*. No matter which scene was being portrayed the audience had a fair idea what was to be expected. But that was not the case here. The Americans had no idea about the story. Soon they started whispering among themselves.

'Who is this old man?'

'Who are the two kids?'

'Whose children are they?'

Amidst all this confusion Bechachandra, who was playing Shatrughna, walked on to the stage. He was so nervous that he walked like a puppet and gaped through glassy eyes.

'Just look at that man!' cried Miss Marberry. 'Has he ever been on the stage?'

She was absolutely correct. Bechachandra had never played any role in his life, let alone an important one like Shatrughna's.

In the meantime Srish walked in and promptly forgot his lines once again. When Sisirkumar shot him an angry glance he quivered and fainted on the spot and had to be dragged into the wings. This led to further confusion. Sisirkumar, who was supposed to faint in this scene, was left with just an emotion-packed dialogue to deliver. Srish's actual fainting had messed up the entire situation.

The stage was supposed to grow dark soon after showing Sisirkumar falling in a swoon. But the lights did not go out. The crew had not been told and so Sisirkumar had to faint under the glaring spotlight.

It proved too much for Miss Marberry who stood up screaming, 'Stop it, stop it! Cancel the show! Cancel the contract! Disgusting!'

The invited guests smiled quietly.

Karl Reed looked at Eric Elliot and said, 'You cheated us!'

Eric Elliot was unable to defend himself, so he slinked out leaving Sisirkumar to face the music. The next morning the *New York Sun* carried a news item that stated, 'A bogus theatre company has arrived from Calcutta.'

Since no one was ready to pay their hotel bills, an apartment was arranged for with Satu Sen's help to house the entire company until something was settled. No one had a clear idea about what was going to happen next. Would Miss Marberry really cancel the contract? And how was the party to return home when their sponsors seemed to have vanished altogether?

Sisirkumar's normal reaction to such a situation would have been to drink himself to utter oblivion. But Kankabati stood by him, firm as a rock, and did not let him drink more than three pegs at a time. She snatched the bottle from his hand and smashed it, or fell crying at his feet, begging him not to drink any more. After all, they were in a foreign land. If Sisirkumar got drunk he'd have no control over his actions. There was no knowing where he might go and what he might say, causing yet more trouble.

Most members of his team were really frightened by now and spoke shakily. The future looked bleak and uncertain. Would they be condemned to die in a foreign land? There was no question of any more shows and no one had any idea about how they were to return home. They had no food besides bread and butter, and heaven alone knew how long they would be able to afford even that.

This was an unknown land. The traffic here was so heavy that they could not even venture outside. Everyone sat in the living room of their rented apartment and spoke of nothing except their desperate plight. This often led to heated arguments, ending in a free-for-all in which, unable to decide on the actual culprit, everyone accused everyone else. Everyone spoke his on her mind without any reservations. Even Bechachandra who could barely mumble on the stage was bubbling with expletives.

Sisirkumar was not the only one among them addicted to alcohol. Plenty of others shared his addiction, including a few actresses. Strangely enough, despite the lack of food there seemed to be no dearth of alcohol. After drinking, some of them wept like babies, their arms around one another, while some attempted to undress others quite openly and wept as they did it. The drunken brawls, the screams and squabbling made the place a virtual hell.

It became imperative for someone to remain sober amidst the mayhem. Kankabati never touched alcohol, always kept a cool head and was in general quite fearless. She took on the mantle of tackling not just Sisirkumar but the entire group. There were two bedrooms upstairs. Sisirkumar and Kankabati shared one and Tarakumar and Prabha shared the other. The rest of the group lived downstairs. Kankabati shuttled between the two floors, snatching away a bottle from Sisirkumar upstairs or making peace among the brawlers downstairs. She seemed to have acquired a new personality and no one dared to disobey her.

The fear and uncertainty about the future inevitably led to bitterness. The only way to tackle it was to turn their thoughts to something else. Kankabati would sit with them every morning and evening, and get them to join her as she sang songs. One by one they would join in, some shedding tears as they sang.

Sisirkumar was left to growl like an injured lion. Had it been his own country no one could have dared to dump him like this and get away with it. But he was helpless here. The people who had been instrumental in his visiting America had vanished into the blue. Had they really washed their hands off the whole affair? How long could the group possibly depend on Satu Sen's aid?

Sisirkumar spoke to Satu Sen about it. 'I have all the papers of the contract with me,' he said. 'Can't we sue them for breach of contract?'

'Of course we can,' replied Satu Sen, 'and we're sure to win if we do, getting a decent compensation in the bargain. But do you know what is likely to happen? They'll merely try to drag the case on for as long as possible. And it could take as long as three years to settle. How are you going to live here for so long? Who will pay your rent? And how will you survive?'

Sisirkumar sighed. 'Does that mean we have to await their mercy, and remain here with an uncertain future staring us in the face? Everyone is desperate to return home. They are unable to subsist on just bread and biscuits day after day.'

'Please wait a little longer,' said Satu Sen. 'I'm sure we'll manage to find a way out. It is hardly the done thing for any well-known impresario to invite a performing group from abroad and then send them back without allowing a performance. Such a thing is bound to affect their reputation. But it will be rather difficult to get fresh dates in any theatre hall since the previous ones have been cancelled. I have been in touch with Karl Reed. I think they are thinking of putting up the show again in November. They'll also be sending you some money for current expenses within a day or two.'

'I had already told them that I'd be able to stage the show properly if I get at least three days for rehearsal,' said Sisirkumar.

Satu Sen burst out laughing at his words. 'But you can't turn the ugly dancing girls into beauties,' he said, 'and they absolutely insist on having the dances. You'd better get hold of some of the ballet girls who perform here and paint them brown.'

Just then Kankabati came down to the ground floor and said, 'Satu Babu, there's no rice and it's driving everyone crazy. Can't you arrange some rice and dal for us? We could cook some khichdi ourselves if we got hold of the ingredients.'

'I have already tried in various places without any success,' said Satu Sen. 'They've never even heard of lentils. They have heard of rice and also know that the darkies eat it but that's as far as it goes. The staple food of the Americans is potatoes. Couldn't you try eating some?'

'How could one possibly live on boiled potatoes day after day?' said Kankabati pouting. 'It is nauseating!'

'Well, I myself never bother about cooking,' said Satu Sen. 'I'm quite content to live on sandwiches and hotdogs.'

'Hotdogs?' asked Kankabati giggling. 'Did you know that Prabha-di thinks that it is actually made from dog meat? She was quite horrified to hear about hot dogs and remarked, "Goodness me! Do these people eat the meat of dogs too"?'

'Oh no, they don't,' said Satu Sen.

'But even if they don't have dog meat, hot dogs do contain beef and ham,' said Sisirkumar. 'Tell the others not to eat anything without first finding out about the ingredients. I've no wish to be accused of making them lose their caste. As it is they are full of complaints.'

'There was a man selling hotdogs in an open cart the other day,' said Kankabati, 'I tried one. It tastes quite good with mustard. I don't have any superstitions about food. But, tell me, isn't there any Indian provision store here?'

'No. At least I haven't come across any,' said Satu Sen. 'Our people wouldn't venture so far for the sake of business. But I've seen some Chinese shops. The Chinese are quite adventurous and don't mind travelling to any part of the world.'

'There's a theory that the Chinese had been the first to reach the Pacific coast, even before Columbus or Amerigo Vespucci did. So, actually, the Chinese should be credited with the discovery of America,' said Sisirkumar.

'But even if it is so, the Chinese did not carry any arms with them,' said Satu Sen, 'nor did they attack the native Red Indians. The Pacific Coast is what is now California. It was totally devoid of human habitation in those days.'

'Could you please take me to a grocery store?' asked Kankabati. 'I could at least check out what is available. We've been cooped up indoors all this time and haven't seen anything here.'

'Very well. Come along then,' said Satu Sen. 'There's a small shopping complex four or five blocks away.'

The three of them were out on the street in a few minutes. It had stopped snowing and the cold felt less intense. The sun shone brightly and the icy winds had stopped. As they walked along, Kankabati remarked, 'Do you know what catches my fancy the most in this country? It's the women walking on the roads unescorted – absolutely unimaginable in our country. Just look at them; I suppose they are going out to work? And there seem to be an equal number of men and women on the road.'

'Yes. This is something special about America. You wouldn't find it even in Europe,' said Satu Sen. 'Women here have managed to obtain equal rights, the same as men. You find them working everywhere except for the army. In fact, some of the wealthy widows here wield a great deal of power.'

'I like this country,' said Kankabati. 'I wish I could stay here forever. There's no respect for women in our country.'

'But in that case, you'd have to live here by yourself,' said Sisirkumar in a serious voice.

'But you are a highly educated man yourself,' said Satu Sen. 'You could find work here very easily if you wanted to. Don't you wish to stay back in this land of plenty?'

'Never!' said Sisirkumar emphatically. 'Not even if they were to offer me a million dollars! I am nobody in this land. But in Calcutta I am *the* Sisir Bhaduri. Had I been walking on the street like this back there many people would have come and greeted me by now.'

'Shall I tell you an amusing incident?' said Satu Sen. 'It happened about three years ago when I was in Calcutta. I was walking towards Maniktala one day when I saw two men arguing loudly. A third passer-by walked past them, remarking, "Does the fellow imagine himself to be Sisir Bhaduri?" So you see, you have become an icon in Calcutta.'

Sisirkumar guffawed loudly. 'Just look at the plight of the same Sisir Bhaduri in this country! As helpless as Sisyphus imprisoned!'

After walking past another block, Kankabati suddenly stopped short. She took a couple of deep breaths and said, 'I smell rice! Yes, I'm sure it's rice.'

Sisirkumar nodded, saying, 'Yes, it really smells like it.'

They were in front of a Chinese restaurant now. Satu Sen looked at it and said, 'I'm sure it is a brand new one. There were no Chinese restaurants in Manhattan before.'

The menu was displayed on the wall next to the door. Satu Sen moved closer and read it.

'Kanka Devi, you have a fantastic sense of smell,' he said.

'Two kinds of rice are available here – plain rice and mixed fried rice.'

Kankabati almost danced for joy. 'Come on, let's go in and sample it,' she said. 'The smell itself is so appetizing!'

Sisirkumar agreed but he stopped short at the entrance. Then he said, 'Look here, everyone in our group is dying for rice. We can't have it on the sly without letting them know. It's neither right nor proper.'

'Quite right,' said Kankabati at once, 'they'd call us greedy if we did.'

'Very well,' said Satu Sen. 'They are supposed to send you some money in a day or two. Even if they delay, I'll get my salary on Monday. I shall invite the whole team here and give them a treat. The owner of the restaurant will also be able to tell us where they buy the rice.'

'Anyway, even if we don't eat anything today I'm going to smell all I can,' said Kankabati. 'Ah! What a wonderful aroma!'

Three more weeks passed. The rice problem had been solved, but their future looked as uncertain as ever. Satu Sen dropped by from time to time, giving them hope. He was negotiating with another impresario, a Jewish man, who had shown some interest. But there was no hope of booking a hall in Broadway in the near future. Christmas was around the corner and every hall was booked already. Perhaps they'd be able to find one in the suburbs.

Sisirkumar didn't dare to show his temper any more. There was no way out but to accept destiny. He spent a considerable amount of time reading newspapers. On most days there was no mention of India. Despite its size, the subcontinent seemed nonexistent as far as Americans were concerned. If they chose to report anything at all, it was the negative apects – famines, epidemics or the exploitation of women.

Most newspapers were dead against Indian hermits. Since Swami Vivekananda's lecture tour in America, when he had conquered the hearts of the people and received generous donations, many so-called sadhus and sanyasis had visited America, primarily for the sake of making a fast buck. They came every year, dressed in various garbs, put up strange magical shows and gave a few shallow and superficial lectures on Indian philosophy. But whenever they gave newspaper interviews they lambasted America for its 'materialism'.

As a result, a magazine named *Variety Fare* had also condemned Rabindranath quite severely, equating him with these sadhus. They stated that most of Sir Tagore's works were tall claims and his so-called mystical poems were meant for half-baked intellectuals alone. The same was true of his paintings. They also commented that he tried to dress like a sanyasi and was, in fact, the kingpin of the brood that came to America every year in the hope of making a fortune.

Sisirkumar was deeply hurt when he read this. He now felt he had been unwise to come here with his troupe, even if they'd made some money. He no longer felt like being dependent on people who could criticize the poet in such terms. But there was no way of returning to his country on his own. He realized that if one really wanted to be an ambassador of Indian culture abroad, one must possess vast reserves of money and power, like the Emperor Ashoka.

Eventually, the stage was set to present *Sita* at Vanderbilt Theatre on the twelfth of January. As soon as Sisirkumar received the news he started rehearsals within their apartment. They also got the chance to rehearse on stage a few times.

Sisirkumar drilled it into their heads that they must perform with their heart and soul whether the audience understood them or not. 'Don't you remember what happened with *Tapati*?' he said. 'All the chairs were empty but we did our very best. We must do the same now, whether anyone claps or not.'

Sisirkumar was ultimately compelled to leave out the 'dancing' girls in his team. A few Mexican girls were hired and were taught the steps. Their idea of oriental dance seemed to be throwing out their hands and feet wildly and jumping about, but that couldn't be helped. The girls were tall and had a wheatish complexion that was further darkened by adding a few layers of brown paint. Many of them had long hair and looked a bit north Indian. But they were totally unable to manage their saris, and they couldn't imagine dancing without revealing their thighs. Kankabati draped their saris carefully but while they were dancing their saris went up just like skirts, revealing far more than necessary.

Sisirkumar was forced to put up with it as there was no way out. He told himself that he had been compelled to add dance sequences to many of his plays in Calcutta because the audience had demanded it, just as the audience here did. It proved that both audiences belonged to the same class and the difference lay only in the extent of their demand. In Calcutta the audience was content to see just a few swaying girls on stage, but here the audience was not satisfied until they saw a great deal of the dancers' torsos.

Sisirkumar stopped drinking from the day before the performance was to be staged. He bathed twice and tried to remain calm and patient. As he stepped on to the stage he tried to imagine that here the audience consisted not of Americans but celebritites like Rabindranath and Saratchandra, and his friends Sunitikumar and Hemendrakumar. And that he was here to entertain them.

This time the rest of his team also performed without any hitches. They had done India, and Bengal, proud. The auditorium rang with applause when the play ended and the newspapers and magazines showered them with praise. Yet, despite its great success, the performance did not bring in any money. All of it was spent on settling their dues.

On their way back, the group was asked to perform before the governor-general in Delhi before they returned home to Calcutta.

13

By the Sea at Konarak, Puri

It was 2.30 in the morning. Sisirkumar was seated in the veranda of the dak bungalow, the government guesthouse.

There was darkness all around, yet one could discern a faint trace of light if one looked towards the sea. The sound of tireless waves filled the air. The wind blew in sudden gusts, wild and without direction, rustling a strewn paperbag here and there.

The bottle lay empty by his side. Sisirkumar took slow sips from his glass from time to time and alternately puffed on his cheroot.

'Kanka,' he called. 'Kanka, you'd better get up now or it will be too late.'

Kankabati lay on her side on the bed, dressed in the same sari she had worn that evening. She had not changed into her nightdress. Although asleep, her face showed signs of distress.

Sisirkumar was used to keeping awake at night. He could do without sleep night after night because he made up for it during the day. But women were not supposed to sleep until late morning because it was considered indecent. If a visitor came to see Sisirkumar and found him asleep at eleven in the morning, he was not likely to be shocked. But the lady of the house fast asleep at that hour? It was absolutely unthinkable!

Kankabati often had to remain awake until the wee hours but was always obliged to get up by 6 or 6.30. Everyone in the house was up and about by then and the maids and servants required directions from the mistress. She had to see to breakfast, supervise the shopping for all major meals and also meet visitors, if any. In fact, she was quite used to this routine by now.

This night, too, she had gone to sleep really late, just about an hour ago. But Sisirkumar had started waking her up at 2.30 in the morning.

Kankabati fluttered her eyes open after a while and said, 'Why are you bothering me? I've already told you that I won't go out today.'

'But why? Everything has been planned and the car will arrive shortly,' said Sisirkumar.

'Let it arrive. I am not going,' said Kankabati once again.

Sisirkumar stood up and walked into the room. He sat on the bed beside her and stroked her gently. 'Please get up, dear,' he said in a soft voice. 'I know you will enjoy it.'

Kankabati pushed his hand away with a jerk, saying, 'Please don't touch me. Not tonight.'

Sisirkumar withdrew, feeling like a culprit.

Kankabati turned over, her face buried in the pillow. Her entire body shook as she wept silently.

Sisirkumar spoke again, his voice persuasive, 'It's no use crying over spilt milk. Please get up and freshen up. You will feel better once you go there.'

'I said "no",' said Kankabati firmly.

Sisirkumar went back to the veranda and stood sipping his remaining drink. He had made a grave mistake that evening. It had hurt Kankabati to the core. He had not realized at the time that things would take such a bitter turn.

Sisirkumar was virtually bankrupt after his return from America. There was no Natya Mandir and he had severed all connections with Star. He was unemployed now and had been forced to sell his car too.

In Calcutta everyone, including newspaper reporters, kept asking him, 'What are you doing these days? What are you planning to do next?' As if it mattered to them! Sisirkumar could not answer them because he did not know the answer himself.

He had been longing to get away from people and out of Calcutta when Aleek arranged a trip for him. One of Aleek's brothers was the friend of the Collector and the dak bungalow at Puri had been booked through him. The Collector's official staff had met them at Cuttack and brought them to Puri by car. The Collector had also paid them a personal visit.

Puri was full of Bengalis. They even had a club of their own called Sangeet Sammilani. The news of Sisirkumar's visit spread like wildfire and many of the Bengalis came to meet him, some of them keen to invite him to their homes home for dinner.

That evening a special reception had been arranged in the club for Sisirkumar. The car was supposed to arrive at 5.30 in the evening. Kankabati had also dressed for the occasion.

The two young men who had come to escort Sisirkumar to the club looked uneasy when they saw Kankabati. When they had met her earlier they had addressed her respectfully as 'Boudi', as they would their elder brother's wife, and had chatted with her quite genially. But now they completely ignored her.

Finally one of them had called Sisirkumar aside and said, 'Sir, there's a problem with taking her to the club this evening. One of the members informed us last night that she isn't actually married to you. A meeting was called soon after and it was decided that the reception would be for you alone. It's primarily because many ladies from reputed families will also be present at the function.'

'But she is a lady too, and an educated one,' Sisirkumar had told them.

'But she isn't your wife,' the young man had mumbled. 'You know how it is, sir. The Bengalis here are rather conservative. Some of us did protest but the club refused to change its decision. There will be children there too. What if they were to ask questions . . . Anyway, it's quite a short programme and you'll be able to return in an hour's time.'

That was when Sisirkumar ought to have protested. Shouldn't he have firmly refused the young men, saying he wouldn't go for the reception either? But he had felt that such a stand would lead to even more gossip and people would whisper all sorts of things about them behind their back. It would be much simpler to explain the situation to Kankabati later on, after he returned from the function.

So he had just said, 'Why don't you read for a while, Kanka? I'll be back very soon.'

Kankabati had gaped at him in astonishment. Then her face grew crimson at the implied insult. Could this actually be happening to her? Hadn't Sisirkumar been urging her to get ready quickly all this while? And now he was actually leaving her behind!

A full two and a half hours had passed before he returned. People there had been very reluctant to let him go. They wanted to hear all about his trip to America. They also requested him to recite a few poems. They had finally let him go after presenting him with prasad from the Jagannath temple, a plaque, several bouquets and a silver platter.

Sisirkumar looked for Kankabati in all the rooms as soon as he returned. But she was nowhere to be seen. Then he shouted for Bhikha.

Although most of the others from Natya Mandir had left him by now, the ever-faithful Bhikha still followed Sisirkumar about like a shadow. As soon as Bhikha appeared, Sisirkumar asked him, 'Where is Kanka? Has she gone out with anyone?'

'No,' said Bhikha. 'Didimuni has been sitting over there since evening. I called her so many times and asked her to come inside since it was getting dark. But she took no notice of me.'

'Over there' meant right outside the periphery wall of the bungalow. Kankabati sat slumped in a corner. She was building a sandcastle that had windows on three sides.

Sisirkumar knelt beside her and said, 'I have got these flowers for you. Please take them.'

But as soon as he tried to place the bouquet in her hands she flung it far away.

'Nothing much happened over there,' said Sisirkumar trying to pacify her, 'and I didn't particularly enjoy the function. I told them that you were not feeling well. That's why you hadn't come.'

'That isn't true!' cried Kankabati. 'I know they said that I am not your wife, that I'm merely your mistress and a woman of easy virtue, so it's not possible to present me in civilized circles.'

'No. Oh no. It's not that,' said Sisirkumar weakly as he held her arm.

Kankabati broke away from his hold and cried, 'Don't touch me. I'm an untouchable, an object of hatred.'

'For shame, Kanka! How can you speak like that? Have I ever thought of you or treated you that way?'

'No, not when you are in the bedroom,' cried Kankabati, 'but you must have felt like that at other times.'

'No, never!' cried Sisirkumar.

'There's no reason for me to live any more,' said Kankabati. 'I had made up my mind to jump into the sea. But perhaps I wouldn't have drowned as I know how to swim. However, I have decided to go away from here and set you free.'

After that Kankabati broke into a storm of tears which she had held back firmly all this time. She kicked the sandcastle to pieces, rushed inside the house and shut herself in the room.

Sisirkumar sat outside on the veranda for over an hour. He didn't know how to make up with her this time. Besides, he was overcome with guilt. He had taken a wrong decision that evening.

But how long could he sit there all by himself? His whole body felt parched with thirst. The bottle of liquor was locked inside the room. He suddenly realized that there had been no sound from the room since Kankabati had entered it. Could the girl have done something crazy in a fit of rage? Supposing she tried to hang herself? She was so temperamental; nothing was impossible where she was concerned.

Sisirkumar called Bhikha. 'Go and see what your Didimoni is doing,' he told him. 'Isn't it almost dinner time? Go and call her.'

Bhikha went to knock on the door. After a long spell of knocking, Kankabati finally opened the door and told Bhikha, 'I don't want any dinner tonight.'

This was followed by a prolonged bout of bickering and weeping. Finally Kankabati fell asleep, exhausted. Sisirkumar skipped his dinner too. Though he had consumed an entire bottle, he didn't feel drunk. You can't get drunk when you are upset. All of this was entirely the fault of the local Bengali community, and he was having to pay the price!

Within ten minutes a car arrived, its headlights shining. A young man alighted and called out, 'Sir?'

Jiten Mukherjee, the man in question, was the son of a reputed family here. He was good-looking and was known to be a good student. Determined not to work under anyone, he had started an automobile business but was now pursuing law.

Jiten was interested in plays and had written a few. He had even produced some of them with the help of local talent. For him the opportunity to meet Sisirkumar Bhaduri in person and chat with him seemed to be a god-sent boon. For the last three days, he had been escorting them everywhere. In fact, he had arranged this trip to Konarak too.

Jiten walked on to the veranda and asked, 'Are you ready, sir? Where is Didi?'

Sisirkumar couldn't help noticing his new form of address. He had addressed her as 'Boudi' even that morning. But he was calling her 'Didi' now. It occurred to him that Bhikha also addressed Kankabati as 'Didimuni' and not 'Boudi'. He had not noticed it before.

'Your boudi is not willing to come, Jiten,' said Sisirkumar. 'She is not feeling well.'

'That won't do,' said Jiten. 'There are no clouds in the sky tonight so we will surely witness a gorgeous sunrise. It's quite a rare opportunity. She'll feel better as soon as we go out. My mother says the dawn breeze makes all sickness disappear.'

Jiten went inside the room, calling out to her, and refused to listen to any excuse. His cordial behaviour cheered both of them and finally Kankabati rose from the bed and agreed to get ready.

Under Sisirkumar's supervision, Bhikha loaded tiffin carriers, water bottles, a stove and some other articles into the car as nothing was likely to be available at their destination. Sisirkumar wished to enjoy his breakfast along with the glorious sunrise on the beach.

Jiten and Bhikha sat in front with the driver, leaving the rear seat to Sisirkumar and Kankabati. During the journey Jiten turned his head curiously and looked at them from time to time. He was not married yet and was recovering from a failed love affair. He had got to know that very morning that the two of them were not married. But since they had chosen to live together they must surely be lovers.

But do lovers sit so silently, looking so glum?

Konarak was nearly 75 miles away so the car was moving at a high speed in order to make it before sunrise.

Jiten was startled at the sudden sound of sobbing. Who was it? He turned his face to find Kankabati wiping her eyes. Sisirkumar was looking away from her and puffing at his cigar.

They came to a halt a little further ahead. The Konarak temple was about half a mile away but they would have to walk the rest of the way. The morning star gleamed overhead. The huge sun temple stood at a distance on the sandy shore, looking shadowy. In the half-light, even from this distance, one could make out that a part of it was in ruins. There was not a soul nearby.

Slowly, the sky turned a pale blue. 'Keep looking that way,' said Jiten, pointing to the sea, 'The sun will rise quite suddenly from the sea.'

'The breeze is lovely,' said Sisirkumar. 'It feels very soothing.'

As they stared at the eastern sky they saw a golden ball rise out of the sea. Almost immediately the blue sky turned to gold.

'Wonderful! Really wonderful,' cried Sisirkumar. 'Did you see it, Kanka?'

Kankabati stood, silent.

Jiten started reciting a mantra invoking the Sun God.

'Jabakusuma sankashan Kashyapeyam mahadyutim . . .
I worship the sun whose crimson beauty rivals that of the
     hibiscus
The son of sage Kashyapa, his brilliance is great . . .'

'Jabakusum!' repeated Sisirkumar. 'How beautifully the sages had envisioned it! We know now that the heat of the sun is more than 13,00,000 degrees Centigrade! A wonderful hibiscus flower indeed!'

Jiten was keen to tell him the history of the sun temple. After a while, Sisirkumar remarked, 'The Indian craftsmen selected the position of the temple by calculating the latitude. Do you know where the science of Indian astronomy originated? From distant Babylon. The Hindus, Greeks, Arabians and Persians all learnt it from them.' As they approached the temple the teacher within Sisirkumar came to life once again. He pointed to each sculpture and explained its intricacies – which part of it showed Semetic influence, which Indo-European and which Nordic or Aryan.

Jiten kept glancing at Kankabati and wondered if the lady was utterly dumb. She was a famous actress and was supposed to be educated too. But she showed no interest in learning about such a famous temple. She hardly listened to Sisirkumar's descriptions and wandered off on her own.

After seeing some more, Sisirkumar asked, 'Jiten, wasn't there a figure of the Sun God on a chariot drawn by seven horses? I read about it in Havell's book.'

'I think it is in the museum,' said Jiten. 'You must have also read about many of the figures being stolen.'

'I must go and check it out in the museum then,' said Sisirkumar. 'I had that image of the Sun God painted on the backdrop for my production, *Tapati*. Aban Tagore had liked it very much. Don't you remember it, Kanka?'

Kankabati was at a distance. She did not hear him.

They decided to go to the seashore now. There was no road leading to it; they would have to walk across the sand. There were no trees nearby; just a few cactus shrubs here and there.

Sisirkumar walked up to the sea and took a few long breaths. Then he touched his forehead and recited, 'He sundori basundhare . . . Ah beautiful Earth . . .'

'Which play is it from?' asked Jiten curiously as soon as Sisirkumar stopped.

'This isn't the stage and the lines are not from a play,' said Sisirkumar curtly. 'It is from a poem called *Basundhara* by Rabindranath. Of course Kanka would remember much more than I do. Where is Kanka, by the way?'

'She had come here with us,' said Jiten.

'Have you read the poems of Rabindranath?' Sisirkumar asked.

'I have read some of them, of course,' said Jiten. 'It sounded wonderful when you recited those lines. Will you please say some more?'

'In that case, let me recite a little from his "Niruddesh Jatra":

Ar kato dure niye jabe more he sundori . . .

How much further will you lead me,
Maiden fair?
Which way is your golden boat bound?
Oh tell me where!

Whene'er I ask, sweet stranger mine,
You answer with your smile divine.
I cannot fathom thoughts that
In your heart do rest –
You point your finger silently
To restless waves that rise and flee
While the sun is out to set along the west . . .
What's out there? Where are we bound?
And what's my quest?'

Sisirkumar paused a little and repeated the last line once more.

'I remember Rabindranath's "Ebar Phirao More . . ." Shall I recite it?' asked Jiten.

'Where has Kanka disappeared?' asked Sisirkumar, frowning.

'I think she is not in the mood for poetry,' answered Jiten.

'Very well. But *where* is she?' asked Sisirkumar once again.

A few fishing boats had begun to sail into the sea. A handful of youngsters in their briefs played on the open sand. No one else could be seen for miles. There was nothing but sand as far as the eyes could see. Even then Jiten ran to speak to the fishermen. No, they had not seen any lady near the water. Had she returned to the car then, and that too without telling anyone?

As they turned back to go Sisirkumar shouted, 'Kanka! Kanka!'

Jiten also joined in, shouting, 'Didi! Didi!' But there was no answer.

They lost their sense of direction amid the vast stretch of sand. Which side was their car? Were they going in the opposite direction by mistake?

Sisirkumar stopped and said, 'There's the temple. When we got down from the car and started walking we had looked straight. In that case . . .'

After some time they were able to locate the car. The driver and Bhikha were sitting inside. They had not seen Kankabati either. They continued to call and look for her as they walked around the temple. Finally they found her under a huge cactus tree. She sat there, kneeling, almost lost in a meditative trance.

Sisirkumar did not speak angrily. 'What are you doing here, Kanka?' he asked gently.

Kankabati did not look at him. 'Nothing. Just sitting quietly.'

Sisirkumar softened his tone further as he said, 'Please get up now.'

'All of you can go,' said Kankabati. 'I intend to stay here.'

'Stay here?' cried Sisirkumar. 'You mean alone?'

'Yes,' said Kankabati firmly.

Sisirkumar lost his temper now. 'What madness is this?' he shouted, his voice harsh. 'There's a limit to everything! Get up at once.'

He turned back and started walking towards the car, shouting, 'Jiten, if your didi does not come on her own you'd better drag her to the car.'

But Jiten did not need to as Kankabati got up hurriedly and ran towards the car. She opened the door and got inside.

Bhikha was just about to light the spirit lamp. He looked at his master and asked, 'Shall I make the tea now? And peel the boiled eggs?'

Sisirkumar shouted at him too. 'No, I don't want anything,' he said. 'We are returning to the bungalow immediately. Pack up everything.'

No one said a word during the return journey.

Poor Jiten sat stiffly all the way.

After they reached the bungalow he said, 'I shall make a move now.'

'As you like,' said Sisirkumar. But he changed his mind as soon as he got out of the car. 'No, no, don't,' he said. 'You did so much for us, how can I let you go without offering you even a cup of tea? It just isn't done. Please come in and sit for a while.'

Sisirkumar went into the room and quickly changed into a lungi before returning.

The water for tea was already on the boil. He asked Bhikha to peel the boiled eggs while he himself buttered the slices of bread. Kankabati was nowhere to be seen. Jiten was somewhat flabbergasted. Were these two really lovers or a strange twosome playing at being a married couple? He believed that if a man was married it was his wife's responsibility to provide the tea and snacks. Were things different here because these two were not really married? Was marriage more important than love? Here was the famous actor, who had once played the lead in *Sita*, actually stirring sugar into his tea! He didn't know what to make of it.

An earnest desire to be near the great actor, and his curiosity about the antics of the strange couple, brought Jiten back to the bungalow that very evening. Sisirkumar was supposed to visit a rich Bengali gentleman that day but he had already conveyed his inability to keep the appointment.

'Why don't you go?' Kankabati had asked Sisirkumar. 'I don't mind staying alone.'

'No, I shall not go,' Sisirkumar had said firmly.

When Jiten arrived he found them sitting in the veranda, away from each other, both busy reading.

'Come, Jiten,' said Sisirkumar.

'You watched the sunrise this morning,' said Jiten. 'Don't you want to see the sunset too? The sunset in Puri is quite spectacular, I can assure you.'

'I'm sure it is,' said Sisirkumar indifferently, 'but we've already seen one and that's quite enough.'

'Please come,' pleaded Jiten, 'it won't take you long.'

'Ask her then,' said Sisirkumar pointing at Kankabati.

When Jiten asked her whether she'd care to go, Kankabati said, 'I wouldn't mind.'

The sea was not far from the dak bungalow but the waterline had receded considerably because the tide was out. It meant a long walk across the sand.

After walking a short distance, Sisirkumar noticed a stone bench and said, 'I'll sit here. You two can go ahead if you want to.'

'Don't you want to touch the water?' asked Kankabati softly.

'It's not my cup of tea,' said Sisirkumar. 'Why don't you go with Jiten?'

Kankabati walked off towards the sea. Jiten, walking next to her, said, 'You saw the sun almost jumping out of the sea this morning. Now you will see it setting steadily in the horizon and disappearing all of a sudden.'

Kankabati felt the first touch of water on her feet.

The western sky was a violent, bloody red, like the random brush strokes of a crazy artist. A ship was etched against the horizon, perfectly still. It looked mysterious, resting solitary, with no sign of life aboard.

Kankabati lifted her sari a little and walked further into the water.

'Don't go any further,' said Jiten. 'You'll get totally wet if a large breaker comes in.'

Kankabati didn't pay any heed to his words and walked on. She let go of her sari, letting it get soaked, and now stood in waist-deep water.

Jiten was shouting something but she did not hear him. The rumble of the sea drowned every other sound. Kankabati saw a huge wave approaching. Other people on the seashore hastily stepped back. The wave broke over Kankabati and seemed to engulf her, making her disappear for a moment. Then she turned and swam back smoothly to the shore. Jiten heaved a sigh of relief. 'What a fright you gave me!' he exclaimed.

'How can one really enjoy the sea if one doesn't swim?' said Kankabati.

She came out of the water looking like a painting by Hemen Majumdar, her dripping clothes clinging to her body. The setting sun, just behind her, provided the perfect backdrop. It was now time for the sun to sink into the dusky blue water.

On the way back Jiten suggested a few more places they could visit and volunteered to drive them. But they refused the offer. As no one had anything more to say, Jiten took his leave early, hoping to come by again the next morning.

Sisirkumar opened yet another bottle that evening.

Kankabati hummed to herself inside the room. She was behaving normally now and had told Bhikha what to cook for dinner.

Sisirkumar preferred to sit in the veranda, the open sky with a few gleaming stars right before him. As a rule he enjoyed drinking with his friends, but he had got quite used to drinking alone by now.

He had not succeded in getting Kankabati to join him, despite all his efforts. She could not stand the smell of alcohol and hated being near him when he was drinking. She came to the veranda after a while and Sisirkumar said, 'Please sit down, I want to tell you something.' Kankabati pulled up a chair and sat a little away.

'We are supposed to go to Bhubaneswar tomorrow morning,' said Sisirkumar. 'There are many things that are worth seeing there. We'll have to start very early in the morning. I hope you won't behave in such a crazy manner again, will you?'

'Is that all you wanted to say?' asked Kankabati. 'I had thought that... No, I've no wish to see anything. I'm not going tomorrow.'

'Listen to me,' said Sisirkumar. 'We may not get the chance to see these places again in the near future. Isn't it foolish to lose such an opportunity because of a petty misunderstanding?'

'You feel it is petty?' cried Kankabati. 'I had hoped we would spend our evenings reading poetry together, and I would sing for you.'

'Well, sing all you want to. What is stopping you?'

'What is stopping me? Nothing! No one! But you have drunk a lot already, you'll be sozzled in a while.'

'No, no, I'm fine,' said Sisirkumar. 'Please sing.'

'May I ask you something?' asked Kankabati. 'Will you give me a truthful answer? Tell me, what is it that stops you from marrying me?'

'In that case, I shall also ask you a question,' said Sisirkumar, 'and please give me a truthful answer. Was your mother married to your father?'

Kankabati sat mutely for a while. Then she said, 'Why shouldn't I tell you the truth? I had said nothing because you had never asked me before. I remember when we were young we had a second mother. We always thought she was our stepmother because it was so common for a man to have two wives. We considered her children our own brothers and sisters. Much later, after my sister and I grew up, we got to know that she was our father's real wife, and the only one. Our mother, a

Bengali, was actually his mistress. But my father took care of my mother as long as she was alive, just as he would have cared for a wife.'

'Very well, then. Why can't you also accept the situation like your mother had done?' asked Sisirkumar.

'Because my father was not an educated professor like you,' said Kankabati, 'nor had he read the literature of different countries. He was a simple, old-fashioned man and was content to remain one. But haven't the times changed since my mother's days?'

Sisirkumar flung his cheroot outside and said, 'I don't believe in marriage. All those empty rituals hold no meaning for me. I'd said that I wanted you to be my soul mate, my life partner and that's what you have been. That's what you are.'

'But I am not,' said Kankabati. 'It's true that I *am* your partner but what is my place in your life? Anyone could have taken my place – Charushila, Ashchorjomayee, Nirada . . . just about *anyone*! Your Natya Mandir is non-existent now. You don't even have a theatre hall where you can perform. You could throw me out unceremoniously anytime you feel like it.'

Her words angered Sisirkumar. 'What! What did you say?' he growled. 'That I'm dead? Finished? I shall hire a hall once again and build a new group. I shall set Bengal alight, like I did once. And you are going to remain by my side.'

Without raising her voice, Kankabati said, 'But you have not answered my question. Why is it that you find it impossible to marry me? Do you have reservations because of my family's history? You know, these days one can get married without performing any rituals if one wants to.'

'Reservations? I don't really know,' said Sisirkumar, 'perhaps I have. You may not know that I was once married to a girl named Usha. She had committed suicide, hurt by my behaviour. I have not forgotten her even now. And I don't feel like giving her place to anyone else. I'm still haunted by guilt.'

'I know all about it,' said Kankabati. 'Bishu told me about her. But all that happened nearly fifteen or sixteen years ago. There are so many people who take a second wife in the absence of the first. Is it not natural to try and forget the painful past?'

'But there's a difference between "many people" and Sisir Bhaduri,' said Sisirkumar theatrically. 'In my case there's yet another constraint and that's my mother. I can't go against the old lady at this age and I'm sure she'll never consent to a marriage of this sort.'

'But don't you go against your mother's wishes when you drink so heavily? You don't do it with her consent, do you?' asked Kankabati, shooting a deft arrow.

Her remark made Sisirkumar livid. 'You are crossing your limits now, Kanka,' he shouted. 'You know I don't like people nagging me about my drinking.'

'Yes, I knew you'd be very angry and it would be even more difficult to speak to you then,' said Kankabati. 'I know that you are an intellectual, guided by logic alone and free from all religious superstitions. But you fail to understand or appreciate my sentiments in this one vital matter.'

'Why do you attach so much importance to such stupid sentiments?' asked Sisirkumar irritably. 'Marriage! My foot!'

Kankabati was determined not to burst into tears. She wanted to speak sensibly and logically. But her eyes smarted and she stood up abruptly.

She turned at the door and asked, 'And if I were to get pregnant with your child?'

Sisirkumar sat up with a jerk and asked, 'Are you?'

'I don't know,' said Kankabati, 'perhaps I am.'

Sisirkumar curbed his temper and said, 'If that's so, the child is most welcome. Whether it's a boy or a girl I shall give it my name, just as your father did. But I do have a son, you know.'

'He is welcome to remain your only son,' cried Kankabati. 'My children don't need to be called Bhaduri. I'll call them Das instead, the children of god.'

Sisirkumar was amused at her words, 'Well, if god wants to be the father of your children, I don't mind. Go ahead.'

He returned to his drink and muttered lines from Shakespeare and Madhusudan Dutt to himself in between sips.

He didn't notice Kankabati going out of the bungalow from right under his nose.

Kankabati ran across the stretch of sand towards the open sea. The sky was bereft of the moon tonight. All was in darkness except for the faint glow of phosphorus on the crest of the waves. It looked like a chain of dim lights.

Kankabati sat down right at the edge of the beach, where the sands was wet. The breakers touched her feet. It was time for the full tide now. Huge breakers were rushing in closer and closer. The sea seemed to devour her body like a lusty man, its tongue dripping, the waves crashing against her thighs. Kankabati sang a madrigal to the ocean: 'Amar sakal niye boshe achhi sarbonasher ashay . . . I am waiting for you with all I have, hoping for destruction . . .'

14

The Heroine Departs

Star's Art Theatre was in the process of being liquidated, so the theatre hall lay vacant. Prabodhchandra Guha had started a new theatre of his own on Rajakrishna Street and named it Natya Niketan. Krishnachandra Dey, the blind singer, had founded a limited company with a few others and also opened another theatre called Rangmahal. Everyone seemed to be following in Sisirkumar's footsteps and selecting Bengali names for their theatres.

Both the new groups had requested Sisirkumar to join them as actor and director, but for him it meant little more than another job. Sisirkumar performed combined nights for a while; he even joined Rangmahal for a short time. But he was just not cut out to play second fiddle to anyone.

It would be great if he could get hold of Star Theatre now, but where would the money come from? The receiver appointed by the high court for Star Theatre was Sisirkumar's classmate. Anxious that someone else might grab it first, Sisirkumar hired the theatre for a week with his friend's help. Then he went on a fund-collecting spree.

Some of his friends – Sunitikumar, Srikumar and Rakhaldas Banerjee – helped him as much as they could. Then he had to turn to the others who had now become successful doctors, lawyers and barristers. There were many in the theatre world who were against him and tried to put a spoke in his wheel.

The wealthy zamindars, popularly known as rajas and maharajas, owned at least one palatial house in Calcutta since they spent the greater part of the year in the city. Rumours of their extravagant lifestyle, fads and indulgences spread far and wide. But Sisirkumar was somewhat reluctant to approach any of them. Although he gave no reason for his unwillingness, perhaps it was the reminder of his own priviledged circumstances that held him back. He often made fun of and ridiculed the zamindar class.

Barristers were the most affluent at the time. Sisirkumar went to meet one Barrister Choudhury with a reference from a friend. The barrister owned a sprawling property in central Calcutta. Every morning he met a large number of his cronies and acquaintances in his living room. He welcomed Sisirkumar cordially and told him how impressed he had been with Sisirkumar's performance in *Sita* and *Digbijayee*, adding, 'It is good to know that you would like to form a fresh group. It was you who ushered in a new era in the world of theatre. So it is our duty to help you all we can. Have you calculated how much the initial cost is likely to be?'

'I could start work with a working capital of one lakh and fifty thousand rupees,' said Sisirkumar. 'I have received substantial support from various benefactors. I was hoping I could expect around twenty thousand from you.'

'Very well,' said Choudhury. 'Who all have you received help from?'

'I have been promised around seventy-five thousand,' replied Sisirkumar.

'I would like to hear the names of the contributors.'

Not comfortable with publicly announcing the names of the donors, Sisirkumar remained silent. Choudhury repeated his question, this time with greater emphasis.

Sisirkumar was compelled to divulge the details, down to the exact amount promised by each contributor. When Choudhury heard the highest contribution so far amounted to twenty thousand rupees he said, 'Very well. I shall give you twenty-five thousand rupees. It's not an empty promise. I shall give you the cheque right away.'

'Actually, I am not asking for a donation,' said Sisirkumar. 'I'd like to take the money as a loan.'

Barrister Choudhury waved the remark aside as he opened his drawer to take out his chequebook and said, 'But, Mr Bhaduri, I have one condition. You must give up drinking. I have been told that you waste a great deal of your time and energy on alcohol.'

'I'm sorry but I cannot accept that condition,' said Sisirkumar firmly.

Choudhury was taken aback. 'What! You can't give up drinking? Don't you know that alcohol not only damages the body but also weakens one's intellect? You're a highly talented man. You are capable of creating something marvellous. I am sure you could give it up if you really tried. Come, promise me that you won't touch it again, here, right now. I'd like to donate the money for the progress of Bengali theatre. Please accept half the amount as a loan and the rest as a gift.'

'I am aware of the harm caused by drinking,' said Sisirkumar. 'I have read up about it too. If I ever feel like giving it up I shall do it on my own. I am not the kind of person who makes a false promise and then gives in to the temptation of drinking and tries to hide the fact from you. It is just not possible for me to accept such a precondition.'

Sisirkumar stood up to go.

'Wait, please wait,' shouted Choudhury.

'Our country is full of poor and needy people. If you really want to donate your money, give it to them,' said Sisirkumar. 'I am here to raise money for a loan. I cannot accept donations. But thank you very much all the same.'

As Sisirkumar walked out, he heard someone calling him from behind, 'Bhaduri Babu! Bhaduri Babu!'

Sisirkumar turned back to see a man in a suit following him. Sisirkumar recognized him as the man who had been sitting beside the barrister, but had no idea who he was. The man walked up to Sisirkumar and greeted him.

'Namaskar, Bhaduri Babu, namaskar,' he said. 'I am Dilwar Hussain. I have met you once before.'

Sisirkumar remembered him after hearing his name. He returned the greeting and said, 'I remember. You've taken Minerva Theatre on lease and you're running it now.'

'Which way are you going?' asked Dilwar. 'May I offer you a lift in my car?'

'I am headed for north Calcutta,' said Sisirkumar, 'but which way were you going?'

'Please be seated first,' said Dilwar. 'We can then decide which way to go. Bhaduri Babu, it really upsets me to see an esteemed person like you having to beg from door to door to raise funds. We should be treating you with far more respect.'

Sisirkumar gave him a wooden smile as he said, 'Making fun of me, are you, Mr Hussain? Well, go ahead. After all, I'm in no position to retaliate.'

'I would never dare to joke about Sisir Bhaduri!' said Dilwar. 'I just caught a glimpse of your mettle. Refusing a gift of twenty-five thousand rupees so calmly is not an easy thing to do. But how are you going to raise a loan with this attitude? One has to bow low and flatter people in order to get money and I know it's not in you to do it. Had it been possible I would have given you the entire amount myself. But my business is down at the moment.'

'How is that?' asked Sisirkumar in surprise. 'I've heard that your *Bishbriksha* (The Poison Tree) is doing very well.'

'I suffered a big loss after Dani Babu left,' said Dilwar. 'Besides, even before he left he was not really able to draw in an audience the way he once did, so I lost a lot of money. But my fortune seems to have taken a turn for the better since I've introduced Indubala on stage. She sings nineteen songs in the play. The audience has been raving about her. Why don't you come to watch *Bishbriksha* some evening?'

'Very well, I will when I'm able to,' said Sisirkumar. 'Is that why you asked me to accompany you?'

'No. It has long been my desire to get to know you,' said Dilwar. 'Since I have now joined the world of theatre, how can I remain a total stranger to someone like Sisir Bhaduri?'

'It's good to find people from your community getting involved with theatre,' said Sisirkumar. 'It's certainly something new. Many of you are reputed to be immensely rich. I heard that Keshto Babu of Rangmahal has recently taken on a new business partner. Is he a Muslim too?'

'Yes, you have heard right. He is my brother,' said Dilwar.

The car stopped in front of a house in Sonagachhi. 'Please come, sir,' said Dilwar alighting from the car.

'What is this place?' asked Sisirkumar.

'Indubala lives here,' said Dilwar. 'Please come in for a while. You could listen to a few songs while we have a couple of drinks together. We could also talk of other things.'

Dilwar was a happy-go-lucky man and Sisirkumar enjoyed the couple of hours he spent in the man's company.

The next day Dilwar took Sisirkumar to meet a Muslim gentleman, a very successful businessman. He was willing to loan Sisirkumar the entire amount he required, in instalments of ten thousand rupees every month. More importantly, he did not demand any interest for the amount because, he said, his religion forbade it. Sisirkumar could start paying him back after a full year. In return, all he wanted was a box reserved in the theatre where he could take his family to watch the plays whenever he wanted.

Natya Mandir was re-established in the Star Theatre as Naba Natya Mandir or New Natya Mandir.

Sisirkumar thought about what he was going to present on the inaugural night of his new theatre.

At the time Saratchandra alone was considered to be a foolproof writer; any story written by him was sure to hit the jackpot. Everyone in the world of theatre held Saratchandra in high esteem, but they also had a grievance against him. Despite every one of his stories being a surefire hit, bringing him pots of money, he refused to write any of the screenplays himself, which meant he was earning money from the theatre without actually doing much. Earlier he would at least write a rough sketch for the dramatized version of a story he had written but now he did absolutely nothing. He had not written a new novel of late and maintained that he didn't feel like writing any more. He had no fresh ideas, so attempting to write was futile.

'What do you mean, Sarat-da?' Sisirkumar had exclaimed upon hearing what he had to say. 'Our Kabiguru continues to write on so many new subjects despite his age. *He* hasn't called it a day!'

'Rabindranath is a class by himself,' Saratchandra had replied. 'You can't compare him to anyone else. I've led a very irregular life and can't carry on much longer. I know my days are numbered.'

But Saratchandra was very keen to see the stage versions of his stories. He often visited Sisirkumar to watch the rehearsals.

Sisirkumar had dramatized the novelist's *Biraj Bou* and the rehearsals had begun. Many of the original actors and actresses had left his group and he was now busy training new recruits. Even Prabha had left to join another theatre. A new actress named Ranibala had joined his group but the heroine of the play was Kankabati. She had given birth to a son some time ago but had regained her fitness very soon and begun rehearsing regularly.

No one was allowed to drink during the rehearsals these days, including Sisirkumar. But, as a token of hospitality, alcohol had to be served to Saratchandra whenever he was present. He often commented while watching the rehearsals and though Sisirkumar listened to him respectfully, he did not always act on such comments.

One day Saratchandra made an unexpected remark to which Sisirkumar couldn't help reacting. He had been editing out some of the original dialogues when Saratchandra suddenly remarked, 'No, Sisir, you can't leave out anything, not even a word. My dialogues are vital to the story. The audience is going to drink in every word, even if it is from a dog's mouth!'

'But Sarat-da, I happen to be Sisir Bhaduri,' replied Sisirkumar. 'I don't need dialogues to be noticed. People would flock to hear me even if I were to recite the alphabet.'

Saratchandra possessed the rare ability to accept rebuffs gracefully. He burst out laughing at Sisirkumar's words and said, 'Well said, Sisir! I guess I deserved it. It's my great failing that I can't seem to control my tongue. But I'll shut my mouth tight and won't let a single comment escape me anymore.'

'But don't shut it too tight,' said Sisirkumar jovially, 'they've just brought in some hot, freshly fried snacks. Have some.'

Biraj Bou was a hit from the very first show.

The critics were full of praise. Some said that Kankabati in her role as Biraj Bou had surpassed even the great Sisir Bhaduri.

Although a few of his close friends were rather annoyed and condemned the critics as crazy, Sisirkumar was happy about the reviews. He laughed and told his friends that here was a case of the pupil outsmarting the teacher.

When he returned home that night he told Kankabati, 'Just see what the critics have said about you. They are so stupid, they know nothing about theatre and keep criticizing you for no rhyme or reason. Just see how badly they've lambasted you this time.'

Kankabati took the paper from him. Her face turned a bright crimson as she read the review. 'They must be off their heads!' she cried. 'How could they write such rubbish? I am not even worthy of being compared to you.'

Sisirkumar touched her chin tenderly and said, 'No, my crazy darling, they are absolutely right. You were really fantastic, wonderful! But they've not been very fair about my role. After all, I was playing a simple villager this time and not a king. And I don't think I played it all that badly.'

'It's you who deserves all the praise because, after all, I am your creation, totally and absolutely,' said Kankabati.

'But one can't create a sword out of iron ore,' said Sisirkumar, 'I succeeded because you are made of pure steel.'

'Steel that was buried under the earth for all these years,' said Kankabati, smiling mischievously.

'No, you've been getting better and better with each passing day,' said Sisirkumar. 'This review merely proves it. No one, to date, has ever compared any actress's ability with mine or stated that she had surpassed me. Critics had given Charushila equal credit in *Shoroshi*, and that's where it ended. But you too have played *Shoroshi* off and on and I don't think you were in any way inferior to Charushila. In fact, we don't really need Charushila or any of the others any more.'

'But what about *Sita*?' asked Kankabati.

'The name has become almost synonymous with Prabha's, perhaps because she played the role so many times,' admitted Sisirkumar.'But after she left it's you who have been playing it because I forced you to. I don't think the audience has liked you any less. I know for certain that Prabha feels jealous of your popularity now.'

Kankabati folded her hands and said, 'But please don't make me appear in a man's role ever again. It ended in disaster when you tried it the last time.'

'Yes, that was my mistake. I should not have given you a man's role in *Bisarjan*,' said Sisirkumar. 'You are a true and complete woman. By the way, Kanka, were either of your parents fat?'

'Ma had put on quite a bit of weight towards the end of her life,' said Kankabati.

'Looks like you too are going her way,' said Sisirkumar.

'Better be careful from now on. You gorged on all those ice creams in America. Not that I can blame you – they were truly out of this world. I am told even Swami Vivekananda couldn't resist them during his visit there.'

'I'm not likely to get that kind of ice cream here,' said Kankabati nostalgically.

Although *Biraj Bou* proved to be a big hit, Sisirkumar was not satisfied. He was eager to try something new. The dramatized version of a novel had its own limitations. One couldn't really improvise on it as, beyond a point, such improvisation tended to lapse into melodrama.

After some time Sisirkumar came across the manuscript of Khirodprasad Vidyabinod's *Pratapaditya* and liked it immensely. But he decided to play the role of Roda, the Portuguese commander-in-chief, instead of Pratapaditya, the hero.

It had so long been customary for playwrights to assign all foreign characters a polyglot of English and Hindi dialogues. Khirodprasad had done precisely this. But, it occurred to Sisirkumar, how could Roda, a Portuguese by birth, possibly know English? It was not a universally spoken language in those days. It was even more unlikely for him to know Hindi. His ship was supposed to have sailed directly to Chittagong port, where Hindi was never spoken. Roda had not ventured anywhere close to Delhi or any other place in north India. In that case how did Roda communicate with the local people of Chittagong? No one would understand Portuguese there! Did he travel around with an interpreter at all times?

Sisirkumar headed for the Imperial Library at once to do his research until he had the facts on his fingertips. Kankabati always accompanied him to the library, which was just as familiar to her. Both of them knew many of the people there.

Together they did a thorough study of the history of that period. It was soon clear from the available records that Roda had managed to pick up the local Bengali dialect of Chittagong, very different from the prevalent Bengali, with a distinct vocabulary of its own.

One evening as Sisirkumar and Kankabati stepped out of the Imperial Library and Sisikumar was hailing a cab, Kankabati said, 'How different this evening is from *that* evening!'

'That evening?' asked Sisirkumar. 'Which evening are you talking about?'

'Don't you remember?' asked Kankabati. 'That first evening we spent together, when you didn't let me get down here and took me to the riverbank instead.'

'Oh, *that* evening! No, why should I forget?' said Sisirkumar. 'But time changes everything, Kanka, and inevitably so.'

'We had recited so much poetry to each other that evening,' said Kankabati. 'We hardly spoke any prose.'

'Poetry? Oh yes, we did. I still recite poetry sometimes,' said Sisirkumar. 'But the real world happens to be full of prose. You were a slim, young romantic girl that evening, but you are a chubby woman now. And look at me; my hair is flecked with grey. I want to pursue art all day long but I'm compelled to crunch numbers instead.'

'Come on, let's go and sit by the river once again,' pleaded Kankabati.

'Believe me, it can't be the same river any more,' said Sisirkumar. 'Just as you and I have changed, so has the river. The water that had been flowing in the river that evening is different from the water that flows right now.' Then he glanced at his wristwatch and said, 'I'm expecting an attorney at seven-thirty this evening. I'm told we have some legal problems in the offing. I'm afraid we can't make it to the riverbank this evening.

If fate wills, we shall sit together and watch the river flow by some other time.'

'If fate wills . . .' said Kankabati.

Sisirkumar was from western Bengal but he managed to pick up the distinct dialect of Chittagong to a large extent and incorporated it in the dialogues of the new play instead of the usual Hindi-Bengali polyglot of the original. Not just that, he also swayed a little when delivering Roda's lines. He knew that people who had stayed aboard a ship for a long time at a stretch had a tendency to do this even when they were on firm land.

But how was the audience to understand all this?

His co-actors had begun whispering among themselves when they had seen Sisirkumar making umpteen trips to the Imperial Library. Was this a play for foreigners? Where was the need for such painstaking research? It was a Bengali play and not likely to run for more than thrity or forty nights at best. It was ridiculous to go to such lengths for it. This was carrying things too far!

Sure enough, when Sisirkumar entered the stage, swaying slightly, and delivered his first speech in the Chittagong dialect, many of the spectators thought he was drunk. A few of them shouted, 'What's this? How on earth did Roda Sahib pick up the Chittagong dialect?'

As soon as the scene ended, Sisirkumar moved aside the curtain and stood facing the audience. Bhikha followed him carrying some books and a big map.

'Who among you had asked how Roda had picked up the Chittagong dialect? Please stand up and I shall answer your question,' said Sisirkumar, addressing them.

No one stood up or said a word.

'Roda had sailed directly to Chittagong,' he continued.

'There was no English government then. Also, Roda's ship had not touched either Delhi or Agra on his way. The Portuguese, you should know, do not know English and there was no chance of him picking up any Hindi. So he was compelled to learn the local tongue at Chittagong to communicate. All this is on record and not my personal assumption. Bhikha, stand here and hold the map open.'

Sisirkumar pointed to the map and read out select portions from the books. It was quite obvious that he was fully sober tonight.

The audience clapped heartily.

Sisirkumar picked up his books and was on his way out, fully satisfied, when one of the viewers shouted, 'Why couldn't you just ignore the comments of the audience? This is not a classroom. And we have not come here to listen to your lectures.'

Sisirkumar was ablaze with anger. He returned to the stage and said, 'I could not ignore you because I can plainly see how ignorant you are. You merely come here to watch women dance. That is why I am compelled to take a class and enlighten you about the background of the play, about which you know nothing. One needs to have the ability to comprehend and appreciate a play, to realize how much work and research goes into the making of a play. But all you care about is either cheap melodrama or crude ribaldry.'

All hell broke loose after Sisirkumar's last remarks, with the audience breaking up into two groups, each trying to outshout the other.

The play continued but it received a lot of adverse publicity. The sale of tickets dropped drastically. There was no option but to turn to Saratchandra once again. His novel *Datta* was dramatized as *Bijoya* and presented next. Kankabati received a lot of appreciation in the lead role but Sisirkumar's critics took opposing stands. Buddhadeb Bose of *Kallol* wrote: 'Sisir Bhaduri, playing Rashbehari, presented the character as a crude joker and was a real disappointment. He completely failed to project the shrewd, cunning and hypocritical character created by Saratchandra.' Old admirers of Sisirkumar, however, called it 'his fresh interpretation of a well-known character.'

Although the dramatized versions of Saratchandra's novels proved to be money rakers, Sisirkumar could not put his heart and soul into the roles because they did not satisfy him aesthetically. During a chat with his close friends, he once blurted out his true feelings.

'Sarat-da's stories are engrossing and sentimental but I find them somewhat artificial and lacking in depth,' he told them. 'He depicts prostitutes as saintly women despite having firsthand knowledge of what they are actually like. Why does he deliberately do this . . .? I had an argument with him about it. After all, I too have been dealing with these women all these years and know that many of them are basically kind-hearted. But they are not as sophisticated as he portrays them to be in his books. Take the case of Rama in *Palli Samaj* – she behaves like a thickheaded policewoman!'

Sisirkumar had great love and admiration for Rabindranath's creations. He often said, 'No other play gives me the kind of satisfaction I get from merely reading the plays of Rabindranath.'

Although he had tried to modify a few of Rabindranath's plays to suit the theatre and presented them with a great deal of effort, none of them had proved to be a commercial success. He was now considering a dramatized version of one of his novels instead. Rabindranath's *Jogajog* (Relationships) was among his favourites.

During this time a play named *Ritimoto* (Absolutely) was staged in Naba Natya Mandir. The playwright, Jaladhar Chattopadhyay, claimed that the credit for revamping the original play lay entirely with Sisirkumar. But Sisirkumar, never too keen on taking credit, maintained he had not really done much. The play was a hit, and Sisirkumar invited Rabindranath to come and see his latest endeavour.

As a rule Rabindranath did not visit public theatres to watch others' plays since his aides advised against it, claiming it would tarnish his image. But the poet was genuinely fond of Sisirkumar and accepted the invitation.

When he met Rabindranath, Sisirkumar spoke to him about his plans for *Jogajog*.

'That's a good idea,' said Rabindranath. 'I'll dramatize it myself. Why don't you come to Shantiniketan, say, after the Basanta Utsav, our spring festival?'

Sisirkumar reached a day before the festival, along with Kankabati. But this time it was neither a walk nor a bullock-cart ride from the station. A car had been sent to receive him and his stay had been arranged for at Atithi Bhavan, the main guesthouse there.

Basanta Utsav in Shantiniketan meant an exceedingly busy day for Rabindranath with no time to spare for even a chat. So he had sent the first draft of the play to Sisirkumar in advance.

Basanta Utsav meant dance and music and celebrating dol, or holi, the festival of colours. Sisirkumar did not budge from Atithi Bhavan, engrossed as he was in reading the dramatized version of the novel done by Rabindranath himself. Kankabati stepped out, saw it all and returned home, completely drenched in colour.

'Why didn't you come?' she asked Sisirkumar. 'So many people came and smeared the poet's feet with colour while he sat there smiling at everyone. I've never seen such a beautiful smile before.'

Sisirkumar said, 'Kanka, the poet has asked me to see him at four tomorrow evening. Will you come with me?'

Kankabati looked at him for a few moments and asked, 'What would you like me to do? Should I go or shouldn't I?'

'Well, you can, if you like,' said Sisirkumar. 'But we'll be talking shop the whole time. You could also visit him later on.'

'Which means you don't want me to come along,' said Kankabati. 'I have told you before, you have never really looked upon me as your life partner. Nor have you given me a wife's honour. I have remained merely your mate, nothing more.'

'No, no, it's not that,' said Sisirkumar looking embarrassed. 'I've just been wondering what the poet will think of our relationship. I've heard that people of the Brahmo Samaj have reservations about certain things. Can't you see how different things are over here?'

'Well, you don't need to worry or feel nervous,' said Kankabati. 'I shall not go with you. I will keep myself confined to this room.'

She went off to have a bath.

Sisirkumar returned to his manuscript.

It began raining heavily the next morning. Kankabati behaved quite normally, not expressing even a flicker of anger or resentment. She hummed a tune as she stood by the open window. She readied the clothes for Sisirkumar's visit in time and gave him his usual after-meal mouth fresheners.

A person arrived at the assigned time to escort Sisirkumar to the poet. It was still raining. Here, rainwater flowed freely, leaving no slush behind. The unseasonal rain bathed the leaves clean, making them almost smile with glee.

Rabindranath was waiting for Sisirkumar in Udayan. A few people had been invited for tea, including a few women.

After exchanging pleasantries Rabindranath asked, 'Sisir, I heard that the lady of your house has accompanied you here. Why didn't you bring her too?'

Was Rabindranath merely being tactful in referring to Kankabati as the 'lady of the house'? Was he then aware of their actual relationship? Sisirkumar hesitated a little before replying, 'She wasn't quite ready . . .'

The poet gave him a long, steady look. Did his look contain a trace of rebuke? Sisirkumar wasn't sure.

They had a long discussion on *Jogajog* and were in agreement about the minor changes that had been made. But a difference of opinion surfaced over the conclusion of the play. What was Kumu going to do in the last scene?

Rabindranath explained Kumu's character at length, saying, 'She is a rebel and a revolutionary. She is going to walk out on Madhusudan.'

'I don't mind portraying her as a rebel or even a revolutionary but it would seem unconvincing if she actually left her home,' said Sisirkumar. 'Let the play end on a note of rebellion.'

'What does that mean?' asked Rabindranath, puzzled. 'What are you planning to do with Kumu finally?'

'I have to think of my audience too,' said Sisirkumar. 'I can't present the play to an empty hall. The audience is not going to accept a married woman walking out on her husband.'

'Well, if you've failed to mould the taste of your audience, it is not my fault,' said Rabindranath. 'Creating art of the highest order is not possible when one is bent on playing to the gallery all the time. Do you intend to depict Kumu as the typical submissive wife of a Hindu household?'

'No, I shall portray her as a rebel all right. But I shall also show her entering her husband's room in the last scene in order to touch his feet.'

'I don't mind that. But she will come out of the room ultimately,' said Rabindranath.

'No, Gurudev, I shall not show her coming out of the room. The final curtain will fall as she touches his feet,' said Sisirkumar.

But Rabindranath was dead against such an ending. They argued about it for a long time, unable to come to a definite conclusion about the final scene.

However, the poet was really keen that the audience should get to encounter a character like Kumu on stage and listen to what she had to say. He finally consented, saying, 'Very well. Do as you please. No matter what changes you make in the play, it's not going to affect my book. And it is the book that future readers will read. In fact, I plan to write a sequel too.'

Sisirkumar returned to Atithi Bhavan in high spirits.

Kankabati was sitting by the window by herself, sipping tea. Sisirkumar rested his hand on her shoulder and said excitedly, 'Guess what, Kanka, the poet has accepted all the changes I suggested. But there is one condition. I have to retain the original title, *Jogajog*. So far we have been changing the names of all of Sarat-da's dramatized novels. People usually tend to read the novels before seeing the play. Kabiguru's *Jogajog* is going to be the next big attraction of Naba Natya Mandir.'

'That's wonderful,' said Kankabati.

'Sarat-da's *Achala* is our ongoing production. We will follow it up with repeat performances of some of our old hits. During that time we can start rehearsing for *Jogajog*. It is likely to take some time if we are to do justice to the poet's exquisite language.'

'But I shall not take part in this play,' said Kankabati.

Sisirkumar was startled. 'What do you mean?' he asked. 'The audience comes to see you in particular. And Kumu's role is a brilliant one – it's going to be the crowning glory of your career.'

'But I shall not do it,' said Kankabati softly but firmly. 'Please get someone else to play the role.'

'My crazy, foolish girl! Is there any other actress who could hold a candle to you?' asked Sisirkumar.

'You are a creator. A lump of clay or a block of stone is all you need to carve out someone new,' said Kankabati. 'Take anyone you like, Ranibala or . . . .'

'I refuse to listen to such nonsense,' said Sisirkumar, 'you have to play the lead.'

'If you insist on me being in the play give me a tiny role – that of a maidservant or someone else,' said Kankabati. 'I have a feeling that my creative spark is drying up.'

'Rubbish!' shouted Sisirkumar. 'Don't be morbid! You are now at the peak of your career. The public will be after my blood if give you the role of a maidservant.'

'But Kumu's role will not suit me,' protested Kankabati. 'Do you remember how the poet describes her first appearance in *Jogajog*? She has been depicted as "tall, slim and beautiful, like a stalk of tuberose". I might be tall but I'm neither slim nor beautiful – not any longer! People are going to laugh if anyone compares me to a tuberose stem!'

'Who says you are not beautiful?' cried Sisirkumar. 'True, you have put on some weight. But your face is as lovely as ever. Besides, talent matters more than looks. A great actress can make the viewer look far beyond her appearance.'

But Kankabati remained firm. She refused to attend the rehearsals.

Sisirkumar was compelled to try out a few other actresses. But, despite all his efforts, none of them was up to the mark. They simply could not speak Rabindranath's exceptional language. No one but Kankabati was good enough to play the role of Kumu.

Sisirkumar's youngest brother, Bhabanikishore, known to everyone as Putu, also lived in Sisirkumar's house. His other brothers – Bishwanath and Tarakumar – had become actors of repute by now, but Putu was still in college. Of late he had been suffering from regular bouts of fever. Then, one day, blood gushed out of his mouth and his illness was diagnosed as tuberculosis, commonly referred to as the 'royal disease'.

Kankabati loved the boy like her own younger brother. She took on the responsibility of nursing him. There was not much treatment available for the disease in those days. The only thing to do was to provide support and hope. Kankabati took to spending most of her time with him, attending to his needs and telling him endless stories to divert his mind. His brothers were unable to spare time for him, but Kankabati gave him all her time, having lost all attraction for theatre.

One afternoon, Putu lay listlessly while Kankabati told him stories of their trip to America. He had a sudden spasm of coughing and quickly sat up, but could not stop the blood from trickling from his lips. A basin was always kept near his bed but the maid had taken it away to clean it. Kankabati stroked his chest gently as she called for the maid to bring in the basin quickly. But Putu could no longer control himself and as blood streamed out of his mouth, Kankabati had to cup her hands to collect it. The maid came in and looked at them both. Then she said, 'The way you've been looking after him . . . I'm sure even Putu's own mother couldn't have nursed him so tenderly.'

'Stop talking rubbish and bring me some hot water. Quick!' cried Kankabati.

By this time Sisirkumar was desperate, though for an entirely different reason. The launch of *Jojajog* had been advertised and Kankabati's involvement was imperative. He forced her to attend the rehearsals and appointed a nurse to look after Putu. But, despite her busy schedule with rehearsals through the day, Kankabati insisted on looking after Putu at night. She slept on the floor beside his bed. Whenever Putu woke up at night Kankabati woke up too and kept him company. Eventually, Putu was sent off to the hospital on the doctor's advice a few days before the opening of *Jogajog*.

The play was received well, but the response from the audience and critics was mixed. Even Hemendrakumar, a close friend of Sisirkumar, wrote in his review, 'It is quite exasperating to keep witnessing dramatized versions of novels in lieu of real plays. When will the playwrights start writing genuine plays? Although we are told that Rabindranath himself wrote the dramatized version of *Jogajog* it is rather difficult to believe it. We are aware of his deep knowledge and insight about drama. If he did indeed help dramatize this novel for the stage, all I can say is that obviously his heart was not in it. One of the main reasons for this assumption is the fact that many of the characters in the stage version have been introduced with the help of verbal descriptions from other characters. This is not the usual approach of a genuine play. And I felt it again and again while watching *Jogajog*. That is what made me feel that it is not the original work of Rabindranath.'

Despite this criticism of the play, Hemendrakumar was all praise for the two main actors, Sisirkumar and Kankabati. He added that they had done justice to Rabindranath's exquisite language and it had been a real pleasure listening to the dialogues.

A few other critics agreed with him and added that Kankabati's acting had been amazing despite the short time she had got to prepare for it. She was Kumu come to life! In fact, Kankabati was unrivalled in Bengali theatre when it came to performing complicated roles.

Even the general public felt that she had got under the skin of the character and performed the role with her heart and soul.

Rabindranath came to see *Jogajog* on the fifth night of its staging. The auditorium was less than half full that night. The poet and the large group that accompanied him sat through the entire play and remained at their seats after the final curtain call. Sisirkumar came out and touched his feet while Kankabati stood diffidently behind him with her sister Chandrabati.

As soon as Rabindranath looked at her she blurted out, 'I am sorry to have ruined the character of Kumu. I know I look nothing like your description of her.'

But Rabindranath, ever chivalrous, stood up and rested his hand on her shoulder and said, 'Your acting was so brilliant that no one gave a thought to that. Your performance touched my heart.' He reassured Sisirkumar too.

Rabindranath was very curious to know what the general public thought of the show. When he made enquiries he was told that the number of viewers was decreasing with each show.

In a missive to the press he wrote, 'I was anxious when I received an invitation from Naba Natya Mandir to see their latest venture, *Jogajog*. I returned from the show with a sense of wonder and delight in my heart. It is not easy to come across such flawless acting. But if, despite this, the audience feels dissatisfied, it is not fair to blame Sisirkumar Bhaduri, the director of the play.'

In that case, who was to blame? The question needed no answer.

Once again Naba Natya Mandir suffered heavy losses after launching a play by Rabindranath. Sisirkumar's artistic sensibilities had to pay for his lack of commercial considerations, but he proudly told his friends, 'I am here to do business but I shall not forgo my principles. I have been bankrupt once. Looks like I'll have to face it a second time.'

Sisirkumar made an attempt to return to his one-time hits, but the strategy did not work this time. His debts mounted, leading to a number of court cases against him. Once again he was unceremoniously thrown out of the Star Theatre along with his entire crew to live life like a refugee. A man who had offered himself completely to theatre was no longer wanted in that world. There was no place for him in any theatre.

During this period, Sisirkumar was asked to direct a film. By then the silent era had given way to talkies. Sisirkumar did not care much about films. He found them artificial, but he agreed because he realized he needed to earn some money.

He selected the story of Chanakya and decided to play the lead himself, with Kankabati acting as Mura.

The studio was located in Tollygunge, where most films were shot. All kinds of sets were built there – artificial palaces, artificial streets and even an artificial bedroom with three walls, with the camera filming from the fourth side. Sisirkumar found it hard to accept this atmosphere of make-belief. He would insist on shooting outdoors from time to time. He preferred vast fields, real thickets of trees and a real full moon in the sky. The moon painted on the studio screen often shook and trembled in the breeze. Since outdoor shooting was much more expensive the producers were quite against it. But sometimes they had to give in to Sisirkumar's insistence.

An outdoor shoot had been arranged on an uninhabited piece of land a little beyond Behala. The film crew's tents had been put up. The shoot was scheduled during the day when there was enough sunlight, which would be their primary source of light. But it was the month of August and the sun was often shrouded by a cloudy sky. Before each shot the cinematographer gazed at the sky expectantly. If a sudden whiff of naughty clouds veiled the sun it would mean a cancelled shoot and no work for anyone.

Kankabati had been suffering from severe headaches for sometime. Initially, she had kept it a secret from Sisirkumar. But one day the sudden, unbearable pain made it difficult for her to perform. When Sisirkumar pulled her up sharply, she was obliged to admit how ill she felt. 'I have a blinding headache,' she whispered, 'I can't bear it any longer.'

The weather had already been playing truant. If shooting was held up for further reasons it would only add to the mounting costs.

'Your role is nearly complete,' pleaded Sisirkumar. 'Be patient with me for just two more days. You can take a break after that and rest all you want.'

The next day Kankabati fell unconscious in the middle of the shoot.

She was carried to a car and taken straight to Calcutta. For the next four days she hovered between consciousness and unconsciousness, her periods of wakefulness becoming few and far between. The doctors were unable to diagnose her ailment. On the fourth day, she regained consciousness but was still in a sort of trance. She was aware of someone sitting at her bedside. She asked, 'Who's there?'

'It is I, Boudi. I'm Putu. I returned from the hospital.'

'Who's your Boudi?' cried Kankabati shrilly. 'I am nobody's Boudi. Why have you come here?'

'How could I have not come when I heard how ill you were?' said Putu.

Kankabati raised her had a little and said, 'Oh, it's you Putu! But why do you keep calling me Boudi? Don't you know that your brother never married me?'

'I don't care. Even then you are my Boudi and my sister as well. You are the only one I have, Boudi,' whispered Putu.

Kankabati stretched out her hand and touched his forehead. 'How are you, Putu? You still seem to have fever.'

'Not much,' said Putu. 'I'm much better now. But how do you feel?'

'Me? Who am I? I don't even know who I am! But *you* have to get well, Putu,' said Kankabati.

'You have to take a medicine now,' said Putu. 'The doctor was here a little while ago.'

Kankabati burst out laughing; a strange laughter. 'Medicine?' she asked. 'Oh no. My days of taking medicines are over, my dear. I'm no longer myself. Whom will you give the medicine to?'

The caged mynah on the veranda muttered, 'Who is it? Who has come?'

Kankabati shouted at the bird. 'Shut up, you wretched bird! No one has come and no one ever will.'

'Borda has been enquiring about you every day,' said Putu. 'Do you know about his problem? It has been raining on and off since yesterday and the shoot is not yet complete. So he is unable to leave the place. I'm sure it will finish by tomorrow.'

'Yes, it will end,' whispered Kankabati. 'Everything will come to an end.'

She lay quietly for a while, grinding her teeth in agony. Then she said, 'My head is aching terribly, Putu. I'm in great pain. Will you please give me a sleeping pill?'

Soon after having the medicine, Kankabati burst into a storm of tears; a bout of wordless, agonized despair.

Unnerved at the sight of her suffering Putu stroke her head gently, calling out, 'Boudi, Boudi!'

Kankabati quietened after a while. Then she said in a normal voice, 'Go to sleep now, Putu. I shall sleep too. I just have two regrets. The first, that your brother refused to marry me. And second, despite all my efforts I could not make him give up drinking.'

Her eyes closed as she uttered these words.

Kankabati fell asleep, never to wake again. She bade adieu to the theatre of life at the tender age of thirty-two.

15

The Lost Empire

Sisirkumar now lived in a reddish two-storeyed house on Barrackpore Trunk Road, not far from Baranagar. He remained in his easy-chair all day long, his eyes glued to the pages of a book, a cheroot in his hand. There were days when no one came to visit him.

Rabindranath and Saratchandra were no more. Nazrul had lost his memory as well as his ability to speak. It had been six years since Sisirkumar had lost his mother. Two of his brothers – Bishwanath and Putu – had also passed away. Sisirkumar had brought Kankabati's pet mynah with him. But, one day, he discovered its stiff and lifeless body covered with ants. What remained were millions of memories, but he didn't feel like stirring them.

Ashok, his eldest son, lived with him. Bhikha, once Sisirkumar's constant shadow, had returned to his native village against his wishes. Sisirkumar had insisted he go, and had given him two of his expensive rings as a parting gift, and Bhikha had left with tears in his eyes. He had a new servant now. Some of his friends had distanced themselves from him and many of the others had passed away.

Sisirkumar had moved about aimlessly like a gypsy for a few years after being turned out of Star Theatre. The world of theatre had been his empire. He felt like an alien outside it. Another opportunity had come his way after the Star incident. When Prabodhchandra Guha's theatre Natya Niketan packed up, Sisirkumar had taken over and renamed it Srirangam.

But, despite all his attempts for over a decade, he was unable to regain his lost empire after Kankabati's death. Wood mites had taken over his throne and rust had settled on his sword. His old plays no longer attracted audiences. Nor were the viewers keen to see his new experimental plays, such as *Dukhir Imaan* or *Takht-e-taus*. Other theatres of the time were staging plays like *Shyamoli* or the highly sentimental and melodramatic *Ulka*, which were hugely popular. Even Saratchandra's stories seemed to have lost their magic.

None of the regular actors in Sisirkumar's group were available anymore, so he had to make do with unwanted extras, torn sets and costumes, old, faded and damaged stage props, broken furniture and lights that had dimmed with excessive use. The money from the sale of tickets failed to reach even a thousand rupees. Yet, many well-known foreigners visiting Calcutta came to Srirangam for a taste of Indian theatre. Cherkasov, the famous Russian stage actor and the renowned director Pudovkin came to see *Shoroshi* and were absolutely charmed. Both of them admitted that they had understood nothing of the play itself, nor had they known who Sisirkumar was playing. But the moment he entered the stage they realized that here was an actor of outstanding talent. Cherkasov had asked Sisirkumar, 'How can an artist of your excellence manage to act in this shabby, moth-eaten theatre?'

'You know how poor our country is,' Sisirkumar had replied. 'You see the same poverty reflected in our theatres. In your country the government helps the theatres in every way possible. But here the government is not bothered about theatre. We don't even have a national theatre to speak of. So we have to manage by ourselves somehow, to the best of our ability.'

But the admiration of foreign visitors did nothing to soften the heart of his landlord. Sisirkumar was planning to dramatize yet another story by Rabindranath, *Ghare Baire*, when calamity struck once again. He had not realized how high his debts had mounted by this time. Now they could no longer be ignored and his irate landlord confronted him, dangled the court order before his eyes and slapped a lock on Srirangam's door. Sisirkumar's personal belongings were thrown out on the street. Passers-by were stunned to see Sisirkumar standing in a corner of the wide road as his clothes, shoes and books fell about him in a shower, some of them landing at his feet. To the common man he was still the emperor Alamgir or the conqueror Nadir Shah. What's more, he still looked as handsome and powerful as the characters he had portrayed.

But Sisirkumar did not lose hope. He still believed that he would once again find a theatre and regain his lost glory. He was oblivious to the fact that Bengal's audience had already written him off. And there were others who lurked around, determined not to let the banished emperor recover his lost empire, as had been the case with Napoleon. It took Sisirkumar another two years to come to terms with this reality. During this time he sought relief in the world of books on College Street, commuting there from his house in Baranagar.

He sat in a little room in Grantha Jagat, a small publishing house owned by Debkumar Basu, surrounded by a group of youngsters. Sisirkumar had founded a club named Nabya Bangla Natya Parishad. He would come here to read out select old and new plays. The young listeners included Gaurkishore Ghosh, Soumitra Chattopadhyay, Karuna Bandopadhyay, Rabi Ghosh, Binaykrishna Datta, Jyotirmoy Roy, Pankaj Datta, Rabi Mitra, Shamik Bandopadhyay, Nibedita Das, among others. Sisirkumar was eager to get to know each of them personally, even the newcomers. He was particularly fond of Soumitra Chattopadhyay and Rabi Ghosh and had planned to cast them in lead roles when he returned to the stage again.

One day he noticed a plain-looking, shy lad of twenty-two sitting at the back of the room. He raised his eyebrows towards Debkumar and asked, 'Who's that new boy?'

Deb replied, 'Oh he is our Sunil. His surname is . . . hmm . . . yes, it's Gangopadhyay. He's a poet and a friend of Shakti Chattopadhyay, another poet. They run a poetry magazine together.' Modern poetry did not appeal to Sisirkumar, not even Rabindranath's later poems, which he felt were somewhat dry and had said as much one day, and so the newcomer too evoked no further interest in him.

He got so involved in his play reading that it almost felt as though he were boldly striding across the stage while a hall full of enraptured spectators sat before him.

Sometimes he would be invited to perform in the outskirts of the city by various amateur groups. He would take along a group of young actors with him on these trips. The little that he earned from these shows comprised his only livelihood. Gradually it dawned on him that there was no hope of his getting a fresh lease of life on Calcutta's stages. He felt an intense craving to share his vast experience and talent with the new actors, the new generation. But there seemed no chance of his dreams coming true. No theatre was going to give him the opportunity anymore. He wondered at times if the invitations from the suburbs were meant to be charity in disguise, because people felt sorry for him. Was he turning into an aid-seeker on hire?

One evening, after a show held at the University Institute, the sponsors offered him six thousand rupees. 'Why are you paying me so much?' Sisirkumar asked.

One of them replied, 'Sir, this is your honorarium from us. We have heard that you are developing cataracts in your eyes. An operation will cost you money.'

Sisirkumar instantly returned the envelope with the money, saying, 'You don't have to worry about my cataracts. Better look after your own eyes so that you don't get cataracts like mine. Enough is enough!'

Then came a time when Sisirkumar stopped going out altogether. He realized that abject poverty stared him in the face. But he refused to accept charity from anyone. He started selling off his personal belongings one after the other – everything except his books.

His room was still full of books and Sisirkumar buried himself deep in them. He no longer felt like reading novels, stories or entertaining articles. His mind and heart now craved for science, philosophy and scholarly writing, although he knew that at the end of the day none of it was going to help him. He continued to read contemporary English plays and articles on the latest techniques of direction and stagecraft despite knowing that he would never direct a play again. Sometimes new, young playwrights came to him with their plays. Without being rude to them, Sisirkumar told them plainly, 'I can merely read it and give you my opinion. I have no hope of directing or staging a play ever again.'

Sometimes, in moments of solitude, he would suddenly exclaim, 'It is the cause, it is the cause, my soul,' and then ask himself, 'What *is* the cause?'

There would be no answer. Not even Shakespeare had provided one.

His drinking companions did not visit him any more because Sisirkumar had given up drinking sometime ago. However, Aleek, his old friend, dropped in one day. He looked gaunt, his cheeks were sunken. He had sold off his property and now lived in a rented house. But he continued to drink as before. He told Sisirkumar in surprise. 'Sisir, I hear you've given up drinking? Why?'

'No idea,' said Sisirkumar sadly. 'I don't even know why I took to it in the first place.'

'Is it because you want to live longer?' asked Aleek. 'Very well, let's have a competition, you and I.'

'Do you remember the song, "Mahasindhur opar hote ki sangeet bheshe ashe? (What is the song that floats across the ocean of eternity?)." Well, I seem to hear the lines every now and then in my universe,' remarked Sisirkumar.

'But I remember another song,' said Aleek. '"Joubon bedana rashe uchhwal . . . (Ah my days of youth, so full of tender pain, have you forgotten them, oh king of Time, in your absent-minded rain?)".'

One day a bearer from Bishwarupa Theatre brought Sisirkumar a telegram. (It was customary to give a theatre a new name when it changed hands. Under the new management, Sisirkumar's Srirangam was now called Bishwarupa). Sisirkumar read the telegram and laughed at first. Then he swore under his breath.

The telegram was from the secretary of home affairs, Government of India. He had congratulated Sisirkumar on winning the Padma Bhushan. Newspapers had already flashed the news at the start of day.

Sisirkumar felt tempted to crumple the message and throw it away. Was this indeed the Padma Bhushan, or a cruel joke? They had not even bothered to ask him whether he wished to accept the honour before sending him the letter of congratulations! Did they expect him to dance with joy?

But no, courtesy demanded that he should send them a reply.

Sisirkumar sat with pen and paper after a long time to compose a letter in English. Just then the telephone rang.

Sisirkumar never attended the telephone himself. Usually Ashok came from the adjoining room when he heard the phone ring and took the calls on his father's behalf. Most of them were answered in the negative, such as, his father was busy and therefore unable to take the call himself. But today, Ashok covered the mouthpiece soon after answering the call and said, 'Baba, the chief reporter of the *Statesman* wants to speak with you. He wants to come over and ask you personally about your reaction to receiving the Padma Bhushan. He is asking me when he should come.'

Sisirkumar looked up. 'Please tell him there is no need to come to my house. I am writing a letter to the Government of India saying I refuse to accept the award. I don't want to give *any* statement to the newspapers about it.'

He directed Ashok to give the same reply to *Anandabazar, Basumati, Amritabazar* and *Jugantar*, in case they called. Sisirkumar had no wish to speak to anyone.

Even after the country had become independent, no initiative had been taken towards setting up a national theatre. Bengal had been split into two. Sisirkumar had already spoken about it a few times to the new chief minister of West Bengal. But Bidhan Roy, having been a busy doctor all his life, was not really a connoisseur of art, literature, music or theatre. Besides, he was snowed under by the manifold complications of administering a state that was brimming over with refugees. He could not spare the time to consider lesser issues such as the development of a national theatre. Nevertheless, he had passed on the message to his aides in the bureaucracy. But the bureaucrats still retained not just the British pace of work but also their point of view in many matters. They believed that anyone receiving government aid in any form ought to feel grateful. Most of them had not seen Sisirkumar perform.

Their assurances held no real promise and sounded hollow. They had no immediate plans of starting a national theatre but said they might hopefully consider it in the next Five-Year Plan. For the time being, they were likely to start a special cell for the development of drama and theatre. Sisirkumar could take charge of it, if he wished to, as a government employee.

But Sisirkumar did not feel enthusiastic about taking on a government job where he would have to confront red-tapism at every step. He rejected the offer with disdain, and Ahindra Choudhury took it on. Soon afterwards the Sangeet Natak Akademi was established on the same lines and Sisirkumar was made an Honorary Fellow of the institution. But he rejected that too. What good was a fellowship to him? All he had asked for was a national theatre where he could teach stagecraft to the new generation – the nitty gritty of acting, experimenting with new forms of drama – without having to worry about money, the kind of organization that existed in any civilized country in the world. He thought wistfully of the famous Swedish film director Ingmar Bergman. Originally from the world of theatre, he had been the director of their National Opera House.

Sisirkumar found it difficult to complete his letter because of continuous interruptions. The phone was ringing once again.

'Please don't disturb me again,' he told his son Ashok without lifting his eyes from the letter he was composing. 'Just say no to everyone and be done with it.'

Ashok opened his eyes wide. 'Baba, he is calling once again. Please speak to him just once.'

'Who is this "him"?' asked Sisirkumar irritably. 'Just tell him that I'm busy.'

He wanted to say out loud that he wouldn't be available even if it were the chief minister or the prime minister calling. He rested no hopes whatsoever on any of them.

'He had called yesterday too,' said Ashok. 'His name is Satyajit Ray.'

Sisirkumar thought for a while and said, 'The name sounds familiar. Who is he? I can't seem to remember anything these days.'

'He is a well-known film director,' replied Ashok.

'A film director?' exclaimed Sisirkumar. 'Well-known or not, what on earth could he want with me? I have already told everyone that I am no longer involved with acting. Why should he come all this way for nothing? Just tell him that clearly.'

'Baba, he just wants to see you once,' said Ashok. 'He says his father was a friend of yours.'

'Didn't he tell you his father's name?' asked Sisirkumar.

'I had asked him,' replied Ashok, 'but he said that he will say it only if you agree to see him. If you don't, then there's no point in his saying it. He doesn't want you to agree to see him just because of his father.'

'The son of a friend?' muttered Sisirkumar to himself. Then he asked Ashok, 'What's the time? Twelve-thirty? I'd like to take a nap in the afternoon, after lunch. A young boy is supposed to meet me this evening . . . the one who had left his play with me. Very well, you'd better tell this Satyajit to see me tomorrow morning at ten o'clock sharp.' He paused a while and added, 'Listen to me carefully. People from the film circle normally move around in large groups. Please tell him that there should be no more than three of them. I no longer enjoy meeting a sea of unknown faces.'

Sisirkumar returned to his letter once again: 'It is unfortunate that I was not informed about it before, for though your appreciation of whatever merit I possess is undoubtedly gratifying, I find it impossble to accept the honour, on principle . . .'

Sisirkumar turned to his books again after the young playwright left that evening. One of his eyes was giving him trouble and he found it difficult to read at night. He liked switching off the lights and sitting in the dark.

The only thing visible in the dark room was the glow of his cheroot as Sisirkumar sat puffing on it in his easy-chair. Both the windows were open but there was nothing to see outside. The sound of voices and the din of lorries filled the air. He got up after a while and closed the windows.

As he sat quietly in the still darkness he suddenly saw the floodlights, the newly decorated stage and hundreds of eager viewers in front of him, all of them clapping madly.

He seemed to be a part of some magic that carried him back to his first days as an actor. He was *Digbijayee* now, the young hero full of life, striding boldly across the stage, almost reaching the centre with a single step, delivering the lines of the conquering hero . . .

Soon his appearance changed and he now became Jibananda of *Shoroshi*. The stage seemed a different one. It was Srirangam, with its broken sets, torn and patched-up curtains and a damaged backdrop. He was getting breathless as he spoke his lines. There was no Prabha, and no Kankabati either. The scene changed once again as soon as he remembered Kankabati. He was now part of *Biraj Bou,* with Kankabati, who matched his talent at every step, even surpassing him. He had not been present when she lay on her deathbed because he was busy wrapping up some inane film at the time. And the girl had left the world with a broken heart.

Kankabati had been his life companion. But what was more important was that she had been a brilliant actress. She had succeeded in pleasing even Rabindranath in her role as Kumu. What seemed most surprising to him was that people were already beginning to forget her. If her name came up in any conversation they had to be reminded, 'Kankabati, the sister of the film star, Chandrabati.'

Sisirkumar remembered the songs Kankabati would sing for him as they sat on the terrace of their house in Shyampukur, her face alight with hopes and dreams of the future. 'I have been unfair to her,' thought Sisirkumar. 'Is that why I have now been condemned to a frayed destiny? But I never meant to hurt her! Was something wanting in my love? Was it my ego that came in the way?'

The scene changed once again. Sisirkumar saw currency notes flying all around him. Not just paper bills, but even silver coins fell around him in a jingling shower. Lots and lots of money! In a particular stage of his life he had earned a great deal but had spent it all recklessly. Had he confined himself to playing historical roles and lead roles in the plays based on Saratchandra's novels he might never have run short of cash or had to leave his own theatre. But his dream had not been to make money; he had wanted to change the taste of the viewers. His one wish had been to rise above the mundane and produce purely tasteful plays, like the ones written by Rabindranath Tagore. And though his aspiration had merely led him to bankruptcy every time, he was able to tell himself honestly and without regret, 'I did the right thing!'

The lights were going out now, one by one. The entire stage was pitch dark. And he could hear a muffled voice proclaim, 'My beautifully arranged garden has become dry . . . My beautifully arranged garden . . .'

He stood up, breaking the spell, and started pacing about, bumping against the table and chairs in the dark as he muttered, 'It is the cause, it is the cause, my soul . . . What is the cause?'

The evenings seemed unbearably long since he had given up drinking. All his life he had preferred the night, enjoying it better than the day. But now sleep seemed to have forsaken him. Once upon a time Hemendrakumar used to ask him, 'Sisir, how do your eyes remain so bright despite getting such little sleep?'

Everything would become quiet once again at that late hour, except for a plane that flew past his window just after midnight. Sisirkumar would gaze at its gradually fading blue and yellow lights. He enjoyed watching the moving silhouette vanish into the depths of the dark night.

Satyajit Ray landed up the next morning at 10 o'clock sharp. The servant brought the visitors upstairs to his room. Sisirkumar did not bother to dress with care to receive his guests. He was in his usual attire, a silk lungi with a loose top over it, and wore his thick, black-framed glasses. His hair had thinned in front, exposing a wide forehead. But there had been no change in his fair complexion or his well-built body.

As the tall Satyajit Ray bent forward and folded his hands in greeting Sisirkumar stood up to welcome him. Satyajit introduced him to his two friends who had accompanied him. One was Subrata Mitra, his cameraman, and the other was a writer friend who wrote under the pen name Nibaran Chakrabarty.

'From *Shesher Kabita*, I presume?' remarked Sisirkumar as the three of them sat down facing him. 'My memory isn't what it used to be. My son just reminded me. I have seen one of your films, *Pather Panchali*. It was wonderful. I wouldn't have believed that anyone in our country could make a film like that. Despite being so realistic, it is truly artistic too. For me realism has no value unless it is artistic at the same time. But I haven't been able to see any other film you've made. I don't really visit cinema halls anymore. I simply don't like stepping into one. But I must congratulate you on *Pather Panchali*.'

'Please don't address me so formally,' said Satyajit.

The short and thin Nibaran Chakrabarty asked, 'May I congratulate you on winning the Padma Bhushan?'

'But today's newspaper says that he has refused it,' said Subrata Mitra quickly.

'Yes, I know,' said Nibaran Chakrabarty. 'Nevertheless, the Government of India had wanted to honour him.'

'How does that matter?' said Sisirkumar. 'Are they thinking of creating a privileged class by giving some people these honours? Something like the title Rai Bahadur in the British era? I find it disgusting.'

Sisirkumar looked at Satyajit and said, 'I shall tell you an amusing anecdote. Do you know where the official telegram was sent? To Srirangam Theatre, because they don't know my current address. Does a theatre by that name exist now? Srirangam used to be mine three years ago. Then the owner took it away and threw me out on the street because of my debts. Isn't the government aware of that? And they have no idea where I live, and in what condition. I no longer own a theatre. In fact, I couldn't even afford a place in Calcutta proper and was obliged to shift to the suburbs. No one is bothered about my desire to start a national theatre. They merely want to pacify me by offering me an award. I have told them clearly that I am not interested in awards. If they are really interested in doing something for me, let them build a national theatre in Calcutta.'

'Very true,' said Nibaran Chakrabarty, 'but even if the central government does not do it why can't our state government build one?'

'When English plays were first introduced in Calcutta, do you know who helped them start? The wealthy people of the city. When a popular theatre burnt down it was Dwarakanath Tagore who donated the money to build a new one. But they did nothing to help Bengali theatre,' said Sisirkumar. 'Why, even today I can't help but wonder, have the zamindars of Burdwan, Cooch Behar and Bhagyakul all become paupers? Have any of them lifted even a finger to help or promote Bengali theatre? Well, let's leave all that aside for now. Tell me, why have you come to see me today?'

'I have come here with a proposal,' said Satyajit Ray humbly. 'My next film is Tarashankar Bandopadhyay's *Jalsaghar*. We want you to play the role of zamindar Bishwambhar Roy. His is the lead role in the film.'

'Bioscope?' said Sisirkumar, laughing out loud. 'I'm afraid you've come to the wrong man. I severed all my connections with films a long time ago.'

'Please read the script at least,' pleaded Satyajit, 'or I could read it out to you if you like.'

'But that will be of no use now. I have already made up my mind to steer clear of acting altogether,' said Sisirkumar. 'It's not that I'm totally ignorant about films. I have directed four or five myself, although they didn't turn out to be very successful.

I was obliged to do them for the sake of money. My heart was not in that medium of expression. I am not cut out for films. My heart and soul have always belonged to theatre. You know, it's not possible to please two gods at the same time.'

'But this role in *Jalsaghar* would have suited you perfectly,' said Nibaran Chakrabarty. 'In the role you will have to sit in an easy-chair as you are doing now. The location will be the terrace of a zamindar's crumbling mansion. As far as acting goes, that will come to you as naturally as breathing.'

'It's no use trying to make me change my mind,' said Sisirkumar waving his hand. 'My decision is final. I had wanted to do something radically new for theatre but all my attempts ended in failure. Let people remember me just that way when I breathe my last. If I change my medium at this age and work in a film, people will say that I'm trying to alter my image. When they snatched away Star Theatre from me, Rabindranath had invited me to be a professor in Vishwa Bharati. But I did not agree. Do you know why? Because I didn't want people to say that I had reverted to my old profession because I was a failure on stage. They would have taken it as my defeat. I don't want it to happen again. I would rather disappear, like a prehistoric creature.'

Sisirkumar paused, a smile lurking about his lips. 'Do you want to hear something more? Do you know when I last played a role in a bioscope? It was in *Poshyaputra*, under the banner of Variety Pictures. But I was not the director of the film. Satish Dasgupta was. I have never worked under another director on stage. I didn't for films either, before this one. While Satish directed the film, I frequently felt that I am simply not cut out to take orders. You will be the director in your *Jalsaghar* and you will have the final say. But it is just not in me to play second fiddle to anyone. Call it my fault if you like. But that's the way I am made and I know I can't change myself now.'

'But I won't really need to direct you,' said Satyajit, 'you yourself . . .'

'No, no, why wouldn't you? Of course you'd need to, since it's *your* film and it's going to be the fulfillment of *your* dreams. But I can't be a part of it,' said Sisirkumar. 'There's no point continuing with this subject. I had agreed to act in films before because I desperately needed the money at that point of time. But I have no need for money any more.'

The other three glanced around the room. Everything in it showed unmistakable signs of poverty, but for the personality of the owner. The cane in the easy-chair was torn in places. The glass frame of the picture on the wall was cracked. The spread on the bed in the corner looked grimy.

Ashok stood by the door, listening to the conversation. He was very keen that his father act in Satyajit Ray's film. But he didn't have the courage to suggest it to Sisirkumar.

Sisirkumar looked at Ashok and said, 'Well? Aren't you going to serve some tea to our guests? Look under my pillow. I think there's some money there.'

'No, no. We won't have tea,' said Satyajit at once, 'since you are determined not to act in my film I don't think we should waste any more of your time.'

'That reminds me, you have not told me your father's name yet,' said Sisirkumar, 'Ashok said that . . .'

'My father's name is Sukumar Ray,' said Satyajit. 'I think you knew him.'

Sisirkumar brightened up at his words and said, sounding delighted, 'So you are Sukumar Ray's son? Do stay a little longer. You don't resemble him. Yes, of course I knew him.

He was among my close friends,' said Sisirkumar. 'Sukumar, Sunitikumar Chatterjee, another very dear friend, and I spent a lot of time together. Sukumar had a sharp wit and a fantastic sense of humour. He was not particularly impressed by his trip to Europe and had told me that Indians know just as much about printing and block-making as the English do. Did you know that your father could also sing beautifully?'

'I don't remember much as I was very young when he passed away. But I've heard my mother say so,' said Satyajit.

'He was so young when he left us . . . perhaps he didn't even get to see his *Abol Tabol* as a printed book, did he? I know he used to enquire about it even when he was very ill,' said Sisirkumar. 'It is such a wonderful book! I knew many of the poems by heart. The book was out of print for a long time. Is it available now?'

'Yes, it is,' said Satyajit, 'and many more of his books have also been published. I shall send you a full set.'

'Yes, please do,' said Sisirkumar, 'the genius son of a genius father! Not easy to come by, I'm sure! And, who knows, perhaps bioscope in the future will become the medium of art. Isn't that so? Perhaps theatre will cease to exist completely.'

'But why should one lose out to the other?' asked Satyajit. 'Both films and theatre can co-exist, as they do in most other countries. Both are totally different forms of art. You can't compare one with the other.'

'I like the way you keep referring to films as "bioscope",' said Subrata. 'My father and uncles called it bioscope too. At least it is another name for cinema. But nowadays many people refer to it as "boi", book, which makes Manik-da (Satyajit) see red!'

'Boi!' Sisirkumar burst out laughing. 'I remember some people used to call stage plays "boi" too! But despite calling it by that name our middle class has at least learnt to appreciate films to some extent. But they know nothing about excellent stage plays, exquisite paintings or great music. Rabindranath often complained to me, "You haven't been able to shape your audience." He was quite right. We haven't. Nor have we created really good plays. I have only played loud, melodramatic characters all my life. When did I ever get the chance to perform a play that really appealed to me?'

'Why didn't you try writing plays yourself?' asked Nibaran Chakrabarty.

'Perhaps I didn't have the talent,' said Sisirkumar. 'Not everyone can do everything. I had to attend to many things, the toughest challenge being the finances. I am no good at the commercial aspects. There was a time when I earned a lot of money. But I was unable to keep any of it. It was Kanka who looked after my household. But she had no head for money matters either.'

'But we have heard that you made many changes in other people's plays, virtually rewriting them sometimes,' said Nibaran Chakrabarty. 'It seems that many famous stage plays were virtually written by you.'

'One can make changes to an existing play with a solid theme,' said Sisirkumar, 'but one needs a constant supply of new plays to run a theatre. That is, in fact, what first prompted Girish Babu to write his plays himself. He would complete a play in four or five days' time. But they had no lasting value. I may not be a playwright but I can understand and appreciate good literature. That is why I turned to Rabindranath again and again and wanted Bengalis to become familiar with his exquisite use of the language. But I failed every time. Their ears are so badly blocked with grime they could never appreciate it.'

'Buddhadeb Bose has complained that you have failed to produce a successful playwright,' said Nibaran Chakrabarty.

'Writers of the *Kallol* group had great admiration for you but you didn't encourage any of them to write plays. And when they did, like Buddhadeb Bose . . .'

'Yes, I remember Buddhadeb giving me a manuscript for a play,' said Sisirkumar. 'I forget the title. Was it *Indrajeet*? No, it was called *Ravan*. Having just arrived from Dhaka he was under the impression that writing plays would fetch a great deal of money. I rather liked the play and had also started rehearsals. But after a while I felt that the central theme was too similar to Michael's *Meghnad Badh Kavya*, so I called it a day. It is fairly common practice that many plays are eventually dropped despite rehearsals.'

'Banaphool had also written a play called *Sri Madhusudan*,' said Nibaran Chakrabarty.

'Yes, it was not bad,' said Sisirkumar, 'but the kind of English dialogues he had given Michael sounded rather like schoolboys' English.'

'Well, you could have changed the language quite easily,' said Nibaran Chakrabarty. 'Buddhadeb Bose wrote that although you rejected both his and Banaphool's plays, Natya Niketan put up two plays, *Swarnalanka* and *Michael*, on exactly the same theme immediately afterwards.'

Sisirkumar felt his temper rising. 'Listen to me,' he said. 'Drama is not the same as theatre. If I were to explain the difference I'd end up giving a lecture on the basics of both. People who do not have firsthand experience of theatre can be dramatists at best but not playwrights. If you have any more complaints against me, go ahead and spell them out. I have already acknowledged defeat a long time ago.'

Nibaran Chakrabarty covered both his ears and, looking ashamed, said, 'I don't have the impertinence to complain about you. Nor do I have any intention of doing so. I was merely quoting what I had read in Buddhadeb Bose's works. I remember seeing you perform in *Digbijayee* as a boy. To us you are still the same all-conquering hero and we're all indebted to you.'

'That's flattery and I've never let it affect me one way or the other,' said Sisirkumar. 'I am capable of assessing my own ability. I know that I have failed to refine the taste of the Bengali audience. Therein lies my defeat. I had wanted to bring our theatre closer to our tradition of jatra. But now I'm told that jatra itself is imitating theatre.'

'It is not correct to say that you have failed to influence the audience,' said Satyajit. 'We are already feeling the impact of your years of effort. Theatre groups are now performing different kinds of plays, many of them with a decidedly subtle touch. They are also performing plays by Rabindranath and other experimental plays. And the current audience has been accepting it all. I have heard people say that in earlier times many of the people who came to the theatres shouted for dances, whistled and made obscene gestures at the women. The audience of today is quite different. It is more cultured, well-mannered and far more receptive. No one can possibly forget what we owe you for this shift in trend. People who start a revolution do not get to cherish the consequences. The benefits are reaped by the next generation.'

'Revolution devours its own children,' said Sisirkumar softly. 'Perhaps you are right. Rabindranath had told me that he wanted to write a play named *Arjun* after he saw me act. But he could not get around to doing it. So I have remained Karna instead, destined to remain among the disappointed and the unsuccessful.'

Satyajit Ray stood up and asked, 'May I touch your feet before I leave?'

'Why?' asked Sisirkumar. 'You folded your hands in greeting when you came into the room. Members of the Brahmo Samaj do not usually touch people's feet. I think that's fine.'

'But we do touch the feet of our elders and those whom we respect,' said Satyajit. 'It would make me immensely happy if I could.'

Sisirkumar stood up too and said, 'You are so talented; you are going to make a name in the world some day and make Bengal proud. And we shall all be proud of you too. You are my friend's son. Your place is in my heart. Come.'

Sisirkumar stretched out his arms and embraced Satyajit.

Author's Note

The Lonely Monarch is a novel and not a biography. Basing it on facts, as far as possible, I've had to fill the available framework with my imagination. Dialogues constitute the most significant part of a novel that cannot be found either in history, biography or records. Hence I've had to create the dialogues myself, depending largely on the period, the temperament and the distinctive traits of the characters described. But in the case of Rabindranath Tagore, I have taken most of his words from his various works.

Some of the incidents described may not be strictly factual where the time frame is concerned. For instance, it is a fact that Satyajit Ray visited Sisirkumar Bhaduri but I am not sure exactly for which film he would have made an offer since I have not found any written records for the incident. I based that episode completely on hearsay. I personally feel the zamindar's role in *Jalsaghar* would have suited Sisirkumar's personality perfectly, had he really been asked to act by Satyajit Ray.

Deb Kumar Basu of *Grantha Jagat* had been asking me for a long time to write a novel on Sisirkumar Bhaduri. It is primarily because of his repeated requests and encouragement that I mustered the courage to accept the tough challenge of writing this book. Both Deb Kumar and Prabal Kumar Basu have helped immensely by providing me with many books and records on the subject. My heartfelt thanks to them both.